The Lost Brother

Book One of The Order

Adam W F Hall

For Claire

Beside him, his sister was afraid. He didn't care.

He looked on as the window smashed and the men pushed forward, snarling, raging, driven on by fury and bloodlust. He looked on as they met the stranger and the first of them died, cut down by a power and speed that could not be human.

He felt something tear at his mind, gnawing into his brain, and for an instant, something rose from the blankness in his head. He felt it reach out for a moment, before it was replaced by a surge of power as the room caught light.

An inferno claimed those around him, leaving just the stranger standing beside him and his sister behind. Men died in agony, their flesh burned away and their bodies reduced to ash in a moment of searing pain.

Hal felt nothing.

* * * * * * * * *

Part One – Castienne

Steph liked to think of herself as a fairly strong minded woman. Even on the more depressing days, she found something to be proud of, and on the good days, that pride nearly overcame the dreary crap that her life had become. Then there were days like these. The odd little days where she noticed something new and curious. Today – tonight – it was the screaming. More particularly she had realised, with a sort of detached curiosity, that that was what she hated most. She paused for a moment, feeling a guilty warmth as it occurred to her that there were far worse things in the world, before rising to her feet and making her way upstairs. Pausing for just a moment to look in on her mother, unlikely as it was that the noise was disturbing her, she made her way down the corridor to Hal's room.

She pushed open the door, wearily resigned to the sight before her. Hal was sitting bolt upright in bed, his eyes screwed tightly shut, his mouth wide open, emitting a piercing shriek that seemed to rise and fall like a badly tuned instrument. She could almost picture it before she walked in, just as she knew what would happen next. Resignedly, she reached forward and gently shook him by the shoulder. The effect would be surprising, almost shocking if she hadn't seen it time and again. As if switched off, Hal went silent, his eyes flicking open and his mouth snapping shut. His face was blank, and she could see nothing in his eyes – not that she ever could. He regarded her for a moment, then lay back down.

"I had the dream again,"

Steph sighed and sat down next to him, resting a hand lightly on his stomach. He wouldn't stand any more than that, she knew from long and at times bitter experience.

"The fire?"

He nodded once, and she lowered her gaze for a second. He didn't need to go on. She had heard the details of the dream enough times to have them engrained in her own mind – recounted to a series of doctors and therapists over the last year. A large room, well furnished with leather and wood, high up in a building over-looking the sea. A fire surged suddenly through the room, setting light to the walls and the furniture, but leaving the rooms occupants – Hal, Steph and a man Hal didn't recognise – miraculously untouched. Most had thought it was just a kid's nightmare at first, but the recurring nature of it – weekly, sometimes daily – had led some to produce theories, of suppressed memories, fear of being trapped, abandonment issues. The stranger had been explained away as the father Hal had never known, a symbol of power, danger, protection...

All that, and still Steph didn't have a blind clue what to say to the little boy who now lay staring at her.

"There was something new this time. I never noticed it before. The man had a gun."

Steph pretended to ponder this for a moment, knowing it was no good. She knew Hal better than anyone – certainly better than their mother did – and though she hated it, the fact was that she couldn't explain it. She couldn't decide what was worse. The fact that she hated not being able to help, or the fact that he didn't care that she couldn't. Despite everything she did, despite the way he was treated outside the house, he showed her no more affection than anyone else.

"Come on," she said breezily, shaking it off with the speed of experience. "We'll have some chocolate milk."

He didn't protest as she pulled him gently out of bed, steering him out of the room, past the darkened space where his mother was lying unconscious, plugged into a series of humming and ticking machines. He didn't even glance into the doorway, and she guided him down the stairs, feeling him shrug her hand away from his shoulder. She barely even registered it anymore.

* * * * * * * * * *

Mike Fortaca was, by any definition, a dangerous man. Gifted with powers well beyond normal comprehension, equipped and trained to a standard that would make any government agency kill to aspire to, and given a more or less free reign in the world, he had the power and potential to achieve a great deal, as he was already beginning to prove. Yet, at this moment, he felt very... ordinary.

That was the point, of course. He was a firm believer in the idea that a man in his position needed grounding in reality, to remind him that there was more to life than what he saw daily, that there was a point to all he did, and perhaps most importantly, that it was good for him to take a break now and then.

That was why he was currently sitting in the departure lounge of Charles De Gaulle airport, sipping cheap coffee from a cardboard cup, breathing in a lifetime's worth of second hand smoke and quietly taking in the people around him. Even close up, he wasn't much to look at. An average height, fairly muscular young man, close cropped blonde hair, dressed in loose, long shorts and a plain T-Shirt. An unremarkable tourist, but for his bright yellow iris' and the silver skull tattoos on his upper arm. And of course, the contents of his hand luggage.

He pulled a mobile phone from his pocket and called up a number, waiting for a moment while it connected through the esoteric encryption system. A moment later, a voice answered.

"Harpen."

"Hello James, it's Mike. I just thought I'd let you know, I'm on my way back, but I thought I'd take the long way round. Kym and Laura just left on our service; they should be dropping in sometime tonight."

"I heard, I've made contact with the pilot. How was Paris?"

Mike smiled. "A success, of sorts. Not as many as we expected, but victory is victory. Laura did well."

"I look forward to hearing it all over drinks. When can we expect you?"

"Not sure. I fancy South Africa, so maybe two, three days? I'll keep you posted."

"Sure thing, let me know if anything turns up. Look after yourself, and don't get too lucky."

Mike grinned to himself as he put the phone away. Lucky in their line of work meant dead bodies and cover ups, and he took these long journeys as a break from exactly that sort of hassle. Still smiling, he rose and headed for the food court. His cheap coffee was cold, and he fancied a biscuit.

* * * * * * * * *

Steph knew they were lucky, after a fashion. As the well-stocked kitchen in the beautifully appointed house in one of the more exclusive estates in Durban clearly attested, they were not exactly wanting. Even when you factored in medical bills and school fees, they were still considerably wealthy, and when in the comfort of their own home, they enjoyed a good life, if you could forget the dying woman upstairs. Steph shuddered a little at that thought, then shuddered again as she realised just how easy it was to blot her mother out of mind. Partly it was the time - Her mother had been slowly dying for years, and had grown increasingly weak over the last two or three, to the point where was she now bed ridden and rarely conscious. Partly of course, it was the direct result of that illness: Steph had become a mother to her adopted brother, and devoted most of her time to looking out for him.

And God knew he needed it. The dreams were the least of it, sometimes. She glanced over at him sitting quietly in the window seat, sipping his milk and regarding the world outside with eyes that were completely black – an all-encompassing pupil that gave him a chilling gaze that no one could hold for any length of time. Added to that the social issues, the maturity that drove him apart from his peers, and the cold, almost condescending air he carried about him, and it was no surprise he was distant, happier to shut himself off from the world – although 'happy' was perhaps pushing it for a boy who had never shown any emotion other than cold indifference.

It could be worse, she knew. He was certainly never badly behaved; his school reports showed a student who was bright and capable, although always seemingly capable of giving more. At home he was helpful and quiet, and she couldn't even find fault in his indifference towards their mother – it had been so long now, even she was beginning to get past any emotional response.

She just wished he had something, anything that showed him to be an ordinary eight year old boy. It was a wish that was long unfulfilled.

"I think I'll go back to bed," he announced suddenly, striding across the room without looking at her. He paused at the door, glancing back at her. She met his gaze and held it, locked on to the deep black of his eyes for a long while.

"I saw mum die," he said, matter of factly.

Steph looked at him aghast, trying to pick any emotion at all from his voice. Her voice was level and patient.

"Hal, she has been dying for a long time. Since before she adopted you. She has a disease, it can't be cured..."

Her voice trailed off as Hal shook his head.

"No. I saw her die."

She sat shock still as he padded his way up the stairs, then leapt for the phone.

* * * * * * * * * *

"I'm in Joburg, just touched down. Got a connection via Durban, Mombasa, New Delhi and Moscow, so should be with you by Thursday night, all being well."

"That's quite a journey."

"You know me, Chief. Seeing the world, one boring day at a time."

"The world looks the same when it's viewed from airport departure lounges. All quiet?"

"Wonderfully so."

"Well, don't get too settled. No one has been to Durban for a year or two, it might be worth you putting a feeler out. I'll see you soon."

Mike pondered this as he put his phone away, picking up his bag and setting off through the airport. Their business wasn't an exact science, and they relied a lot on instincts, intuition, and, to be honest, luck. If Harpen had a feeling, that was usually a good reason to be alert.

He found what he was looking for, and wandered into the empty chapel, seating himself at the end of a row. Instinct and experience told him he was better off prepared. His kit was immaculate of course, but you could never take chances.

A pistol appeared in his hands suddenly, pulled from a holster concealed under his left armpit. Deftly, he unloaded and reloaded the weapon, cocking it and sliding it back into place. His dagger – an eight inch silver blade intricately carved with symbols – he pulled from his thigh, running his finger down the edge and watching the blood well up for a second before the flesh knitted together. Reaching into his bag, he pulled out his tool kit, checking through the items one by one – a silver crucifix, holy water, and half a dozen short wooden stakes.

Satisfied, he bundled them all up again and left the chapel, making his way through to the check in area. His face was impassive as he stepped through the scanner and allowed the operator on the other side to wave a hand-held detector over him. Smiling his thanks, he picked up his bag from the conveyor and walked on towards the departure gate.

It was like magic, he grinned to himself.

* * * * * * * * * * *

Doctor Kwame Sifah had been their doctor for the better part of three years, due mainly to the fact that he was one of the few people who could stand to be around Hal for any length of time. Between his constant visits to Steph's mother, and the rounds of tests and consultations surrounding Hal, he had grown accustomed to the house and the family.

He was not, however, accustomed to calls from them in the middle of the night, and he had rushed round the moment Steph had called him. She was a level headed girl, forced by her situation to mature well beyond her years, and she wasn't given easily to panic. Her barely controlled outburst on the phone had been all he had needed.

Now however, he was forced to concede that he may have misjudged the situation, and he had found himself close to something else he wasn't accustomed to: Anger.

"You said she was getting worse."

"She was. I mean, he said..."

Doctor Sifah looked at Steph patiently, gesturing to the machines clustered around her mother's bed.

"There has been no change. Nothing. Wait, who said what?"

Steph lowered her gaze, suddenly feeling very stupid. She had called the Doctor on instinct, a panic response to Hal's chilling declaration. Then she had had time, waiting for him to arrive, and a more rational thought had crept over her. Doctor Sifah was going to be seriously hacked off, she knew, but she had nothing else to say.

"Hal said he saw her die. I heard him, and I thought... He was just so...you know what he's like," she finished lamely.

Doctor Sifah sighed, some of his frustration bleeding away.

"Hal has a way about him, I know. He's earnest and quiet in a way that makes you want to listen, but..."

"But what? He can't predict death? He's not a trained doctor? I know that, I knew it when I phoned you. It's just...I believed him."

"Well I've checked her over. She's the same as ever, the same as she has been for the last year or so. There's no way to predict anything, she could live for another ten years..."

"Or she could be dead tomorrow, I know. Look, I'm sorry to have called you..."

Kwame sighed, the anger suddenly gone.

"It's fine. How has he been?"

"The usual. Quiet. Cold."

"He's healthy. Many aren't so fortunate."

Steph noticed his pointed glance around the room, but chose to ignore it.

"Thanks for your time."

* * * * * * * * * *

Mike strolled leisurely out of the airport, already enjoying the sunshine. He had an eight hour stopover in Durban, and Harpen's order was a handy excuse to take a wander about town, maybe grab a spot of lunch.

He froze. Something was buzzing at the edge of his consciousness, like an itch inside his skull. The feeling was somehow familiar, yet he couldn't work out why. His hand hovered over his dagger, his eyes and mind scanning the area around him. Twenty seven weapons, seventeen of them well concealed, two of them worn openly on the security guards near the entrance. One hundred and forty two people in his immediate vicinity, twelve of them potential threats to anyone but him. Nothing that even deserved his attention, let alone something that could cause that indefinable feeling...

He shook his head, fumbling for his phone.

"Harpen."

"Hi James, thought you should know, there's something here."

There was a long pause before Harpen spoke again.

"Support's on its way. What have you got?"

"Not sure. It was just...something I knew, but couldn't place. A burst of something. It's gone now, but I'm certain. I think it's worth me sticking around. See if I can trace it."

"Agreed. Keep me posted."

Mike nodded to himself, slow realisation just threatening to creep over him. A moment later, it was gone, and he called over a taxi.

* * * * * * * * * *

Steph felt they had been sitting in silence for a long time. The two of them were sitting on the beach, almost alone. It was gone midmorning, but strangely quiet, only some tourists a few hundred metres away. She hadn't really felt like going out, but at the same time had just wanted to be out of the house. Hal hadn't protested, although he didn't seem to especially be relishing the outdoors.

"So you saw mum die?"

Hal didn't look up from where he was running sand through his fingers. She realised that was the closest thing to a normal action she had seen from him in a long time.

"Yes."

There was another long pause, before she reached across and pulled the sunglasses from his face, turning his head to face her. His eyes were devoid of anything.

"You saw it?"

"As I left the sitting room. I saw her dying."

Steph nodded slowly, not knowing what to do with this information. Hal shrugged, then said something that completely floored her.

"Should I be upset?" his tone was level, but curious, and she found she didn't know what to say as he went on. "I know I probably should, but you aren't anymore, and..."

He trailed off, looking back out to sea. His hand had stopped sifting the sand.

"Hal, I..."

It was her turn to trail off, as she realised he wasn't listening. He turned his head slightly.

"There's a man coming."

She looked up and down the beach, confused. "No there isn't."

"There is. The man from my dream. He'll be coming to the city soon. I just saw it."

"What? Hal, I think..."

She didn't know what to think. His voice was certain, as certain as he had been the night before.

"Saw it how?"

He shrugged, then went back to sifting sand through his fingers. He refused to say another word.

* * * * * * * * *

Mike flicked his eyes open, rising to his feet and pulling on his jacket in one motion. His two companions eyed him warily, but didn't move. They had been here three days now, and Mike had only had that strange feeling one more time, around mid-morning two days before, and it had been too quick to get a fix. This was different. Stronger, clearer, and apparently long lasting.

"I can get follow this. Get the car and bring every bit of kit we have."

It took them just minutes to get out of the hotel, securing their room and its contents behind them, and bundling into their vehicle – a high tech and considerably non-standard 4X4 that had arrived as a gift from Harpen two days before. Laura was driving, her right hand gripping the wheel, her left loading specially made shells into a shotgun. She was dressed for combat, full black trousers and jacket covering segmented form-fitting body armour, her pistol and dagger not even concealed on her thighs. Kym, seated beside her, was more lightly attired, eschewing the jacket and body armour for a long sleeved shirt that showed off his massively muscled form, his pistol replaced with a larger version of his dagger. Both blades were strapped to his forearms, and he was flexing his fingers over the handles.

Mike ignored them both, concentrating on the buzzing in his mind, forcing it to stay centred. He had placed it, realising he knew the feeling all too well.

Sorcery.

* * * * * * * * *

Steph shook her head as she pushed open the door, wincing at the noise. Hal was sitting bolt upright in bed, his eyes screwed tightly shut, his mouth wide open, emitting a piercing shriek that seemed to rise and fall in a way that was all too familiar. He was dreaming again, and she knew exactly what dream. With a sigh, she reached forward and shook him awake.

* * * * * * * * *

Mike shuddered suddenly, the buzz ebbing away despite his efforts to hold onto it, leaving just a barest trace behind. Kym was regarding him with those red-tinged eyes, and Harpen's face was gazing at him from a screen set in the back of the chair.

"It's just this second gone, but I'm certain. Sorcery, but raw, unfocussed."

"Not a Strigoi then?" Harpen asked, his voice seeming to come out of the air all around them. Mike shook his head.

"I've felt them all before. They were nothing like this. Turn left here."

The car swung them around a bend, taking them into what was clearly one of the more affluent parts of Durban. The houses around them were luxurious and sprawling, and protected by state of the art security systems and round the clock armed response. Nothing to them, obviously, but it paid to at least be aware of these things.

"Have you still got it?"

Mike nodded. "A residue. Enough to trace. Left here...there it is."

The car pulled to a stop outside the gates of an impressive looking structure, a large stone walled building with a wide balcony running around two sides. Lights were on in two of the upstairs rooms.

"You sure, Mike? I'm reading the building as clean, an adult and two kids upstairs, no other signs." Laura turned the screen to show him. Mike nodded.

"I'm sure. This is something else. Stand down, we need to think about this."

Kym snorted. "Balls to that. Let's go in, grab them and ask them what the hell they've been dabbling with."

"Not a good idea if they have been dabbling," Harpen's voice cut in. "Mike is right, this is apparently out of our realm of experience. Stand down, back off, and gather every bit of information on that family. I want to know what the hell we're dealing with. Then if you have to, you can bring them in. Mike, call the shots. Don't argue, Kym, this is far more his field than yours. Good luck."

Mike watched him sign off, his eyes narrowed as the car pulled away.

* * * * * * * * * *

It took them the better part of the night, and by next morning, they had gathered every piece of information on the house and the family that was available. Laura had accessed information from the government, school, hospital, and extensive reports from a Dr Sifah. A night time break in by Kym had furnished them with architectural details and history of the property, although the latter had only proven useful as a chance to keep Kym busy. Once compiled, Mike had read it through, cross referencing and analysing every detail.

It painted quite a picture. If he was right, this was a momentous occasion, one that would be remembered and that would make its mark very clearly in the history of his order.

For all that, the situation was delicate. He was potentially messing with real power, and he shuddered at what could have happened if he had unleashed Kym to raid the house the previous night.

He would have to play this very carefully.

* * * * * * * * * *

"Is everything ok?"

Steph stopped short, panic on her face for a second before she could compose herself. There was a man sitting on a bench just a few metres away, his pose casual and his clothes scruffy. His eyes were hidden behind a slim pair of sunglasses, but she could tell he was looking straight at her. He was smiling slightly, like he knew the punchline to a joke he was about to tell, and she couldn't quite bring herself to walk away.

"I'm fine. Why?" she replied, a little too fiercely. He shrugged.

"You seem troubled. I'm Mike, by the way."

"Look, I don't have any money..."

His smile broadened.

"I'm not going to ask for money. I'm not from around here, I was just passing through, stopped for a bit, saw you looked troubled and thought I'd give you a friendly word."

She hesitated, unsure of what to say.

"Thank you. I'm fine," she said flatly.

"Really?"

Even when she looked back later and understood who she was dealing with, she still found it baffling that she hadn't simply walked away at that point.

"Yeah...No," she said quietly, suddenly feeling the weight of her problems and slumping down on the bench next to him, an arm's reach from him. "It's...I don't even know where to start. My mum is dying, and my brother is...odd. Troubled."

"Is he happy?"

She paused, surprised by the question, more surprised that he had ignored the reference to her mother.

"Yes! At least, I think so. He doesn't really show it much. Truth be told, he doesn't show anything much." She was unable to keep an edge of bitterness out of her voice. "Look, I'm sorry, this isn't your..."

"I stopped you," he shrugged. "Maybe I can help?"

She looked at him more closely. He was barely into his twenties, a young man with a constant smile and a curious intensity about him, and she found herself warming to him. She smiled as she replied.

"Why would you do that?"

"Would you believe, I'm a nice guy?"

She eyed him with mock seriousness, then smiled.

"I don't know."

"Let's talk. If you don't like me, I can leave at any time."

"Look, I really don't see what you can do. No offence, and thank you. You've made me smile at least."

He didn't move as she rose to her feet and started to walk away.

"Can I least know your name?"

She turned. "Steph Castienne."

He nodded, his smile broadening.

"Nice to meet you. Will you do me one thing?"

She nodded, and his smile dropped.

"Don't let him scare you. He's just a boy."

Mike paused, watching closely as this sunk in, seeing the emotion in her eyes pass from panic to denial to confusion and back. Finally she just nodded and walked away, and he watched her go, his smile back on his face. A vehicle rounded the corner slowly, and he climbed inside as it pulled to stop next to him. Laura nodded her head in greeting, and he settled into the seat before calling Harpen.

"How's it going?"

"I think it's him. Everything we've pulled up so far points to it, and I just met his sister."

"Sister?"

"Adoptive," Mike corrected himself. "Boss, I think I need to play this my way."

"Mike..."

"I can't just pull him in. The family is...not good, and the sister has nothing else going for her. And if I'm right, we did this.

"That's not all we've done. By the sound of it, she has access to our funds."

Mike ignored this. "I could just make him disappear and drag him in. It's probably the best thing, but I'm not sure it's the right thing. For her or him, but I think for us too. You remember what his father was like, he could fight us every step of the way if we don't play this right. I'm thinking if we have her onside..."

Harpen seemed to consider this. "Maybe. Ok, play it your way, we can always drag him in in the long run. How safe is he from detection?"

Mike shrugged.

"We've turned up nothing here yet, so we should be safe. I've got Kym combing the city, and I'm going to get him to widen his search in the next day or so."

"Probably best to keep him busy. He'll be champing at the bit otherwise. I'm going to trickle a team down to you over the next few days, and I will be there as soon as I can. There aren't many available, but you can have whoever is. There is a safe house down the coast a little way, they'll bed in there. You're in charge. Do it your way, unless it gets tricky."

* * * * * * * * * * *

Something was...wrong. He knew it the instant his eyes opened, even though there was nothing but darkness around him. Outside, far above his head, he could feel the sun, even through the roof of solid rock, and it pained him. His senses were dulled, his mouth dry, and his rage simmering barely below the surface as something – someone – knocked on the door again.

He pushed his hunger down as the door opened and a woman walked in, wasted and ill looking, her eye sockets empty. He shook his head to clear it, fixing his eyes on her, his mouth curling into a slow smile. There was only one reason she would disturb him at this time, only one reason she would dare to stir in the day.

She shuffled forward, her mouth hanging slack, her gaze riveted on him despite her missing eyes.

"Speak, sister. What have you seen?"

Her voice when it came was raspy and weak, little more than a dry rustle. But what she said made his blood sing.

"The hunt is on, sibling. The Order and their minions will gather and there will be fire and blood. A night from now, east of here."

Jasper Strigoi rose from the floor, ignoring the pain under his skin.

"Rest now. As soon as we can, we move. Can you guide us?"

She nodded once, and Jasper took hold of her to help her to the floor, where she curled up, whimpering. He closed the door carefully, then lay back down, a smile on his face as he shut his eyes.

* * * * * * * * * *

Steph had agonised for a while before leaving the house, and had turned back nearly a dozen times, feeling like an idiot. Even now there was a voice in her head chiding her for being stupid. She had just found herself so thrown, and hadn't really been able to think clearly, and even now wasn't really sure what she was doing.

Hal had known. He had known the moment she walked in that she had met a man, but most chilling was his pronouncement that it was the man from his dream. She had agonised, tempted to dismiss him, but she knew too well to do that.

She rounded a corner and stopped, now feeling like more of an idiot than before. The voice in her head was crowing an 'I told you so' as she looked at the empty bench where the day before Mike had been sitting, as if she had really expected him to be there. This was just too weird, and she shook her head in disappointment as she turned to go home.

"Hello again."

She jumped, despite herself. Mike was standing a few metres away, a cup of coffee in his hand. She stuttered for a moment. She could have sworn she had planned out what to say to him, but for the life of her she couldn't think of a thing.

He cocked his head, faintly amused. "Would you like some breakfast?"

She just nodded dumbly, and followed him down the street a little way, not saying a word as he guided her to an outside table and ordered her a bacon roll and a coffee. He seemed to just take her silence in his stride, and she had a creepy suspicion he knew what she was going to say. He seemed content to wait for her, and he didn't even make eye contact until she pulled an envelope from her pocket. He looked at it with interest.

"What's that?"

She finally found her voice, and it was neutral as she spoke.

"It is a description of my brother's dream. The one he has had for years, like clockwork. Always identical. Specifically, it's a written description of the strange man in his dream, one that he doesn't recognise as any one he has met, but who always appears the same."

"Should I assume from your tone that you would like me to read this?"

His own tone was infuriatingly light.

"If you like. I suspect you know what it says."

"Why would you say that?"

"Take off your sunglasses."

She expected him to argue, but he simply reached up and removed them, his eyes locked on hers. The iris was yellow, just as she had expected. Just as Hal had always seen in his dream.

He was still smiling.

"So now what?"

"Why are you here?"

"I like this place," he gestured around them at the cafe.

She regarded him for a long time, feeling the fear inexplicably ebb away. She didn't know what to make of him, but her instinct to run was being over ridden by something else. She stared at the table top for a while, unable to find anything to say.

"How is Hal? How are his visions?"

She shrugged, about to reply, then she froze. His smile had gone.

"Two nights ago, around one thirty?"

"How do you know?"

He nodded, as if satisfied, but ignored her question.

"And his eyes are completely pupil, all black?

She fought down the rising panic. His demeanour hadn't changed, but he seemed somehow more intense.

"Who are you?"

His eyes fixed on her intently.

"Someone who can help him. I work for an organisation that specialises in the esoteric. Your brother is unique. It's in my interest, and the interest of a great many others, that he is cared for. He doesn't belong here, and he doesn't know who he is."

"And do you?"

"I think so. He isn't your brother. You already know that. What else do you know?"

She stared at him for a long while, doubts plaguing her for a long while. Her day – her life – had become decidedly surreal.

"My mum and I...we moved here from Italy, shortly after Hal was born. I remember, she came home one day with this baby, saying our luck had changed. We were moving to South Africa, she told me, and the baby's father had agreed to pay for it. Everything was taken care of in a matter of weeks, and we just upped and moved, our entire life. We were set though, I just never knew just how well until a few years back when I saw what was in our account. Millions."

"You never thought to question any of this?"

"I was ten," she said bluntly. "It was...look, our life wasn't great. I never knew my dad, we were struggling. Overnight I had a baby brother, a full stomach and a good house. Would you question it?"

He shrugged as she went on.

"Plus, mum never knew why. She couldn't lie to me. She was baffled, but just saw it as a lucky break. As I understand it, this guy just gave her a baby and told her he'd pay for her to move. It's odd, but what could I do?"

Mike nodded, seeing the pieces fall into place.

"The man's name was Victor Lemirda. Hal's father."

Steph's eyes widened. "You know him?"

"I knew him. Briefly. He was killed in a gunfight in an Italian hotel, eight years ago. I guess around a day after he handed Hal to your mother."

"Why would he do that?"

Mike shrugged. "I assume it was to keep him safe. More likely she was meant to bring him here to hand him over to someone. Someone she never met."

His tone was even, but still Steph shook her head, anger welling up again. "If you're accusing my mother..."

"I'm not accusing anyone of anything. The fact is, regardless of what was supposed to happen, we never heard of it. Hell, we never even knew Hal existed. That's why we never looked."

He trailed off for a moment.

"I don't think you could grasp what this means. We thought he was dead. We thought the family was finished. That they aren't means a lot to us."

"To who?"

"I belong to group called the Brothers of the Order. We're the leaders and main players in a clandestine organisation that dedicates itself to the destruction of Vampires."

"Piss off."

"I'm deadly serious. Hal has a purpose, a role. A destiny, if you like. That destiny is brutal and cold and will probably kill him, in time, but it is his. And mine. Hal is a Lemirda, a Vampire Hunter and a Brother of the Order, descended from a line that stretches back thousands of years."

She laughed out loud and rose to her feet.

"Thanks for your help, Mike. Whatever the hell you're playing at, I hope it works on the next girl..."

"You've seen him predict the future?"

That stung her, and he smiled as she hesitated before turning back to him.

"I thought so. And it freaked you right out. I have no reason to lie, Steph."

She sat back down.

"He's a Vampire Hunter?"

"Yes."

"And so are you?"

"Yes."

"And he has superpowers?"

"Yes, for want of a better term."

"And so do you?"

"Me, and four other Families. All of them descended from a line going back hundreds of years. Beyond that, we have several thousand other agents. Ordinary people. Sort of."

Her face was blank, and he could tell she couldn't get beyond the idea that this was a colossal windup.

"Would you like me to prove it?"

She shrugged, and he ploughed on, ignoring her scepticism.

"Ok you've got to promise me you won't scream or make a noise."

She shrugged again as he glanced around. There was no one sitting nearby.

"Arms or legs?"

"What?"

"Humour me, Steph. Arms or legs?"

"Arms," she said, her feigned disinterest bleeding away.

"Left or right?"

"Left."

"Left arm. Ok," he nodded. "Remember, don't scream."

He picked up the knife from the table in front of him, held it in his hand for a moment, before unceremoniously punching the blade into his forearm with a wet crunch. She gagged as the tip of the blade emerged from the other side of his arm, and several people glanced their way as she cried out involuntarily. He seemed unconcerned as he just pulled the blade free, blood oozing from the open wound for a moment before he ran his right hand over the gash. When he took his hand away, the skin was clean and whole, not even a bruise remaining.

His eyes met hers again, the smile back on his face.

"Would you like me to show you the leg now?"

She shook her head, feeling sick.

"You have to trust me."

"I do," her reply came instantly, and took them both by surprise. He nodded after a moment.

"I think I should meet him, if that's alright with you."

* * * * * * * * * *

The police had already been and gone, and had apparently found nothing of interest. The truck had been left where it had been abandoned, pulled up on the side of one of the main roads heading into Durban, waiting, he assumed, for a haulage truck to take it away. A pair of trees grew over head, throwing stippled shadows over the vehicle, and Kym Malum raised his hand to shield his eyes as he looked around.

He waved two of his companions round to the cab, while he climbed into the back, his daggers sheathed but worn openly on his sleeves. The truck was empty – he'd known that before he had climbed in, but he could feel a residue, a clammy taste in the air that let him know his instincts had been right. The Malum Brothers had always been unsubtle instruments, and Kym was like all of his line, his powers and abilities focussed squarely on dealing damage. Fortaca, Harpen, even Tyler – they had a different purpose, and he did not begrudge them that.

But he was a Hunter like any other, and though many, including himself, considered him a brute, his instincts were still sharp. Something about a suspiciously abandoned lorry had seemed off to him, and he now took great pleasure in seeing his instincts proved right.

The truck stank of Vampire, which meant only one thing.

The hunt was on.

* * * * * * * * * *

Steph had led Mike to her house in silence, unable to think of anything worthwhile to say. Truth be told, she was terrified – of what she had been told, of what she had seen, of what would happen next – but over all of that was a strange sense of satisfaction: For years she had cared for her brother, but she had never understood him. To learn now that there was an explanation, and others that could help him...

She unlocked the door and pushed it open, opening her mouth to call for Hal, closing it almost immediately as she saw he was sitting at the base of the stairs, as if he had been waiting for them. Steph watched him closely as Mike stepped through the door, a thrill of surprise racing down her spine as she saw Hal's eyes flicker with a moment of recognition. It was weak, and strange to see in his blank gaze.

"Hal, this is..."

"The man from my dream."

Steph went silent as she glanced back at Mike. He shrugged.

"Hello Hal. Do you know who I am?"

Hal studied him for a moment, then nodded.

"The Healer. You're going to take me away to fight."

Steph didn't comment on that, but her face must have given something away as Mike turned to her.

"The boy knows his own future, Steph. More literally, I think, than you realise. We can train him, equip him for that future, but we can't keep him safe."

"But neither can I," she said, resignedly, the full truth of her situation dawning on her. "I don't have a choice."

Mike looked genuinely apologetic. "No. If he stays here, someone else could find him like I did. And he should be with us."

"Someone else? You mean Vampires?"

"Yes."

She sat down heavily on the stairs.

"So what happens now?"

"In simple terms, he disappears. Hal Castienne will have to die so Hal Lemirda can come with us."

"Don't you dare tell me I can't see him again. Don't you dare take him from me."

Mike shook his head.

"It's dangerous..."

Steph's voice stayed level as she replied. "You want to take away my brother to fight Vampires, and then tell me I can't see him because it's too dangerous."

"You didn't believe in Vampires until twenty minutes ago. Hal is one the biggest threats Vampire's face, and they will do everything they can to destroy him. You're a target already."

"And I have been for eight years."

Mike opened his mouth to reply, but paused as Hal took a step forward.

"She'll be fine. And she will come with us."

Steph shuddered a little. Hal hadn't just given an order, or a threat. It was like he had simply stated the way things would be, and the implications chilled her. For the first time, Mike's confidence seemed shaken.

"Hal..."

"She comes with us."

Tears welled in Steph's eyes. His voice was as blank as ever, but that was the closest he had ever come to expressing any emotion. Mike didn't seem to know what to say for a moment, and he seemed to waver between acceptance and wanting to argue. He seemed relieved as his phone rang, and he stepped outside.

Steph turned to Hal, unsure of what to say to him, and he simply stood there, not reacting, as she reached forward to hug him. The brief moment of connection she had felt was lost.

Mike stepped back inside, his confidence apparently reasserted, although the smile was still missing from his face.

"That was a friend of mine. We need to get you out of here."

Steph remained calm. "Are we in danger?"

"Maybe. There are Vampires heading towards the city, and I think it would be too much of a coincidence to assume they weren't attracted by the same thing that drew me here."

"Me?" Hal said, and Steph was astounded to hear a tiny trace of glee in his voice. She didn't know him at all, she realised bitterly.

"Yes Hal. We need to be gone as soon as we can. We can defend you, but not here. I want you in our safe house by sunset. Pack a bag with what you want."

"Don't be ridiculous. This is our home, and our mother is ill. She can't be moved."

A strange look passed over Mike's face, so quickly she couldn't even be sure what she had seen.

"Hal, go pack for you and Steph for a few days away."

To her surprise, Hal nodded and disappeared upstairs, followed by Mike a moment later. He beckoned her to follow, and she followed him into her mother's room, in time to see him run his hands over her forehead.

"Steph, I..."

"Save it. She's dying, no one knows what is killing her or when she will go or how to cure her."

"There isn't a cure. Not anymore, she's too far gone."

"You know what this is?"

That strange look was back for a moment.

"I've seen it before. You being here will make no difference, and you can always come back. If Hal stays here, and they come, she will die. Can Dr Sifah look in on her?"

"Yeah, he has a key, and he usually...How do you know about him?"

He shot her a withering look before walking away. She stared after him, realising she had well and truly lost control of events, and simply kissed her mother goodbye.

* * * * * * * * * *

Mike watched the sun slide below the horizon, tensing as it finally disappeared. He keyed his radio and spoke, his voice carrying to the dozen men and women scattered around the property.

"Be ready."

A series of affirmatives came back to him, and he nodded in satisfaction, content at least that the house was secure. The property was one of many the Vampire Hunters maintained around the world, an unremarkable house in a randomly chosen place. They were meant to serve as safe houses for any Hunters passing through, a place to rest and rearm, and as such it was defended by complex security systems – radio jammers, counter surveillance equipment, infrared sensors, bio scanners tuned to those few who had the privilege to use them, as well as more unnatural devices – nerve shields, sensory deception fields, and others. All of this was designed to keep out anyone but those few who knew of their existence, and shield the house from detection from anyone they didn't want to know of its whereabouts.

Despite all that, it was not designed to be defended in a straight up battle, and Mike had a horrible feeling that was what was coming. The house was far from any other building, perched by itself on a stretch of cliff overlooking the sea, a sprawling three storey property surrounded by high walls. The ground floor was completely open plan, a blank and empty space given over to training, broken only by a single staircase to the first floor, which contained a small but well stocked armoury, and extensive medical facilities that could be operated even by a single wounded Hunter. The top floor was for accommodation, and consisted of half a dozen spartan bedrooms, a washroom, and a large communal room, simply furnished with a dozen large armchairs. At one end was the long window that Mike was gazing out of. Steph and Hal were sitting behind him. Neither of them had spoken since they had arrived, and Mike was secretly glad of that. He couldn't bring himself to face Steph's questions now that he had effectively messed up her life more comprehensively than she had even thought possible. As always, he had ploughed ahead, thinking himself so moral and caring, and things had been made a lot worse by consequences he hadn't seen coming, but should have.

"Are you ok?"

The question took him by surprise, and he could only nod as he met Steph's gaze. There was no accusation, no enmity in her eyes.

"We should be safe here. The house is...protected. Nothing can find us here unless we want it too, and we're...he's hidden."

Hal raised his head.

"This is where my dream happens. The room with wood and leather, overlooking the sea, filled with fire."

Mike's eyes narrowed as Steph suddenly looked around, fear in her eyes.

"What is he...?"

Steph was breathing hard, clearly trying to control herself.

"The dream I mentioned earlier? About a room that fills with fire, with me and him and...you in it. Oh my god, are you telling me..."

"He was seeing his future. And I've just made it come true," Mike said calmly, keying his radio. "All units stand ready. We will be hit, and hit soon."

No one argued, but Kym's voice came through. He was out in the grounds, patrolling the perimeter with the others.

"Inside information?"

"From him. They're going to find us..."

He was cut off by a crash from outside, loud enough to shake the room, and his whole attitude shifted in an instant as his instincts came alive. His pistol was in his hand in a moment, the weight familiar and comforting. He knew battle like few others, and even though this time the stakes were higher, he felt the confidence in his limbs. He was bred for this, after all.

"Kym, talk to me."

The radio was silent, and instead Mike heard Kym's voice directly in his head, a form of communication used by the Brothers of the Order.

They're in. Strigoi, maybe two dozen. They know he's here, and they're coming in for him. I'm at the wall, some have bypassed us. We can't hold them all, and the others are dying.

Mike flipped open a box by his feet, pulling out an assault rifle from inside, locking a large box magazine in place with a click. He was calm, his mind alive as he considered the situation. Steph was in shock, her eyes wide and dilated, while Hal was inscrutable as ever, content to observe the proceedings without a sign of fear.

"Back, both of you. Against the wall, away from the window."

Even as he said it, there was a crash as something hit the window, too fast for human eyes to follow. Steph screamed as a figure jumped into view again, this time perching on the window ledge and battering at the glass with the base of a short curved sword. Mike regarded him in the instant before the glass shattered. A Strigoi Vampire. Tall and lean, with pale skin and curiously deep eye sockets, dressed in an outfit very like Mike's own, he was a blur as he launched himself forward.

Mike reacted, bringing the rifle round and firing before the figure could cover half the distance. The bullets, crafted from pure silver and carved with potent runes, were not enough to kill the creature, but they were enough to hurt it, to put it down long enough for Mike to leap forward, pulling his dagger free and punching it into the creatures chest, driving the blade into its heart with a grunt. Even as he pulled the blade free, he knew it was hopeless. Figures were leaping through the window, and behind him, he could hear a commotion on the stairs as Hunters fought and died to keep the Strigoi from the room he was in.

His mind, enhanced and improved well beyond that of an ordinary person was working even as he moved again, spraying bullets at the open window, launching himself across the room to stand between the Vampires and Steph, who had clutched Hal to herself. Hal had predicted fire, and he knew of only one way he could deliver it.

Kym, I need you to burn this room out.

There was no argument, not that Mike had expected any, and he dropped his rifle as he felt the surge of power course around him, the air vibrating with the energy suddenly running through it. The energy was coursing from Kym's mind, even as he fought like a demon in the grounds below, even as more figures poured through the doorway, intent on murder.

In an instant, the energy was unleashed, and the room ignited around him. He focussed, his arms by his sides and his brow furrowed as he fought to keep the flames at bay. The figures around him screamed and writhed as they were burned to ash, and he felt the heat build up as he fought to maintain the cold air around him and the two figures behind him. He and all the Brothers enjoyed a certain immunity to sorcery, but this was taxing even for him, as he fought to hold back the flames from such a wide area. Only his familiarity with Kym, and, he knew, the presence of Hal, was allowing him to maintain the defence.

Enough.

He sighed as the flames died away, reaching for his rifle even as he heard the roar of flames below him as Kym finished the last of the attackers. He took a moment to glance at Steph, all the blood drained from her face as she stared with unfocussed eyes at the carnage. Outside the small area around her, the room was devastated, the furnishings destroyed and the walls burnt back to bare stone. There was no sign of the figures that had occupied the room a moment before, besides the ash drifting to the floor.

"Hal, look after her."

The boy nodded as Mike left the room, coming across two bodies almost immediately. Two Hunters were sprawled in the corridor, one of them dead, the other close. The first, a man, Mike hadn't met until that evening, but the half dozen skulls tattooed to his arm showed that he would prove to be a great loss in time. The other was Laura, and he dropped to his knees beside her, taking in her injuries at a glance. A long gash in her shoulder had come close to cutting into her neck, and he could feel the pain from her chest, where something – most likely a boot or a bare fist – had cracked her sternum and several ribs. He placed his hands over both injuries and concentrated, a light purple mist emanating from his hands and drifting over her damaged flesh. At its touch, the wound in her neck started to close up, and he ran his hand over the edges of the gash, drawing the muscles and skin together gently, knitting it closed piece by piece. At the same time, the palm of his other hand was resting on her sternum, and he could feel the bones reset themselves under his touch. In a matter of minutes she was healed, as if nothing had happened, and he left her unconscious.

He made his way down the stairs to the front door, passing on the way several more dead Hunters and a single dead Vampire, riddled with bullet holes, stabbed in the heart and with his neck half severed by an axe blade. Mike shook his head at the bodies. The Hunters were trained from childhood and enhanced beyond the level of a normal human, but they were still just a shadow of the Brothers of the Order. He would happily pit them one on one against all but the oldest and most powerful Vampires, but outnumbered in a stand up fight like this, they had been lucky to kill one. Only the Brothers could consistently fight them on their own terms.

Kym appeared in the doorway, holding a bandage over his own stomach. He shook his head as Mike approached, waving him away.

"There are two out here who need you. I'll heal."

Mike ran outside, quickly dismissing most of the bodies as beyond his help. One was only slightly hurt, a stocky man with a pair of machine pistols discarded at his feet. Mike quickly closed the weeping slash in the side of his head, then turned to the other, pulling a broken off blade from his thigh and stemming the blood that poured out.

"They were with me by the wall. I don't think anyone else survived."

Mike shook his head.

"We need to get going. Every Vampire within a hundred miles would have sensed that little display of yours. Nice work, by the way."

Kym nodded his thanks, then turned away, stretching his upper body around gently. "I'll set up to wipe this place from the map."

"Wait," Mike rose to his feet, his gaze fixed on something just appearing in the sky to the north. "Is that..."

"A plane, heading this way," Kym nodded, calmly. "I'll get the kids, leave the rest."

Mike nodded and turned to run for the house, stopping in his tracks as the radio on one of the bodies spat out a blurt of white noise. His own had been ripped off in the fight, he realised.

"Safehouse, this is Harpen, you've got Hunters inbound, is everything ok down there?"

Mike breathed a sigh of relief.

* * * * * * * * * *

At first glance, James Harpen seemed nothing special: He was tall and heavily muscled, certainly, but had nothing that visibly marked him out from his fellow Hunters. There was something intangible though, a presence that marked him out. His eyes were a startling shade of emerald green, and they carried a depth and intensity that betrayed his advanced age even when his body didn't. Thanks to the unnatural energies that had gone into his families' creation, he was to all intents and purposes a fit and healthy mid-forties, although he had been serving the Hunters for decades longer. More than anything else, his talent was nearly unmatched in the Hunter's long history, the long line of silver kill marks tattooed to his arm evidence of a long and successful career.

In all that time, and after all that success, he had never felt this elation, this rush. As he stepped down from the plane door, its VTOL engines barely cooled, he took one look at the boy and knew this was worth his coming. The Lemirda Brother had been thought dead, the family sundered and their talent forever lost. To find him now, alive and well, still young enough to be trained to his full potential…that was a momentous day. Harpen found himself smiling as the boy approached, flanked by Mike and Kym, both drained but up-beat. Harpen took a moment to look into the girl with them, reading a curious mixture of fear and hope in her, and concentrated for a second, dispelling the worst of her negative emotions with a twitch of his mind before returning his attention to the boy.

"Hello Hal, I'm James."

"The Mind-reader," Hal nodded, and Harpen felt the brief touch of the power in him. Hal had not read him in any way. He simply knew.

"We're going to take you somewhere safe. Somewhere you belong." Behind Hal, the girl scowled for a moment, but that quickly melted into resignation as Hal nodded once. Harpen turned away from the two of them issuing a series of orders to those Hunters who had arrived with him. This bolt hole was no good to them anymore, and would be stripped by morning.

* * * * * * * * * *

Steph watched the men and women around her with a detached calm, all her anger and worry having bled away shortly after Harpen's arrival. He carried himself with pride, as they all did, and she was struck as she realised just how well Hal already fit in with them, as if he had always been one of them. At that moment she saw her place in his life, and realised it was over. She had done what she could for Hal, and now he was already gone, his new life begun. She felt out of place, an unwanted guest, until Mike approached her.

"What you do is up to you. If you choose to come with, we can't stop you if he wants you there."

"I don't think he does. Not after he's seen this, seen you. Just promise me you'll look after him."

"We'll do our best."

Steph nodded slowly, watching the last of the Hunters climb into the plane, leaving Mike, Hal and James Harpen on the lawn. She made no attempt to join them, waiting for Hal to make the first move, and to her surprise, he did. Gesturing the others to wait, he walked towards her and stopped a little way away.

"You wouldn't be happy if you came."

Steph smiled, realising there were tears in her eyes.

"Have you seen that?"

"No. I just know."

With that he was gone, running over to the plane and clambering inside. Steph wiped the tears from her eyes as Harpen took a step forward, tossing her a set of keys. She glanced at them, recognising them as the keys to their four by four.

"We'll look after him. Keep the money, and have a good life."

Steph nodded, nothing to say, as the door swung shut, and Hal pressed his face to the window, his face expressionless as he waved. She took one last look at the boy she had raised, and walked away.

* * * * * * * * * *

Hal turned away from the window, his features impassive and his mind blank. He registered little more than a vague difference in his circumstances, and already the loss of Steph was receding from his thoughts. Instead, he focussed on the figures sitting around him. The ordinary Hunters he quickly dismissed from his mind as uninteresting – By any human standards, they were incredible individuals, faster and stronger by far than anyone Hal had ever met, but they still paled into insignificance when they shared a space with the three men across from Hal. They seemed to pulse with barely contained power, their very forms coursing with energy that Hal recognised from within himself. As he concentrated, he felt the distinct form of each. Kym's energy was raging like a fire beneath the surface of the skin, a fire that could be controlled and directed, but that could burn out of control if left unchecked. In contrast, the energy within Mike seemed to flow like water, an all-encompassing stream damned by a fiercely strong intellect, bizarrely at odds with the constant smile and easy going attitude. James Harpen's aura was different again, and seemed to whisper inaudibly, casting around the figures in the room as if alive, flitting between them lazily. As Hal sat there, he felt the energy gather around him, enclosing him in an imperceptible bubble of pure thought. Hal's brow furrowed, his mind reacting instinctively and lashing out.

Harpen turned his head to regard the boy, breaking off from his conversation with Mike, but otherwise not reacting. Kym, perched by the door, didn't even look up from wiping clean his knives.

"Harpen, please have the boy control his childish displays. He's giving me a headache."

Hal turned to face Kym, scowling, feeling his mind surge in reaction to the man's words. Without even knowing what he was doing, he unleashed a mental blow in Kym's direction, satisfied at the power that had been unlocked.

That satisfaction bled away as Kym simply glanced up, a contemptuous sneer on his face as he pushed away Hal's mind and pinned his body in place with a sheer wall of force. Hal bore it stoically, although the pain was mounting with every passing moment. Just as it was getting too much to bear, he heard Kym's voice in his head.

Don't for a moment think you are special in our company. You are nothing next to us, and will always be nothing if you don't rapidly rethink who you want to be.

"Enough," Harpen's voice cut through the confrontation, and Hal breathed in sharply as the pressure on him receded, gently pulled away by the whispers emanating from the older man's mind, even as he regarded Hal with an odd look, somewhere between respect and disappointment.

"You have a lot to learn Hal. Don't start by making enemies with your Brothers. Your discovery is a massive event for us, and you have the power to change a great deal. In time, you will be one of us. Until then, you will listen to everything we teach you."

Hal sat back, nodding impassively. Kym gave him one last blank look, the confrontation over and forgotten, then turned back to his knives.

* * * * * * * * * *

Several thousand miles away, in an unassuming cabin in the Balkan Mountains, a lone figure was also considering the discovery of Hal Lemirda. On the screen in front of him, powered by a small generator beneath the table – the room's only furniture beyond the chair he was sitting on – several photos and a handful of articles and reports were displayed. Sent to him from a pair of agents, one in Durban, one a short journey away, they told between them a fascinating tale.

A coven of Strigoi slaughtered. Sorcery used openly. Hunters in a stand up battle at night time. A lot of people had used and lost precious resources in an attempt to acquire the boy, and Simeon of the Fratriae knew exactly why.

He pulled a flat black stone from his pocket and tapped it several times before wiping his hand gently over the surface. The stone rippled like water, the ripples coming together to form the features of a man, seemingly carved perfectly onto the surface. That illusion was dispelled as the lips moved, the words quiet but clear in the silent cabin.

"Luna's greetings, brother."

"And to you. I have news of the Hunters that may interest us. The Lemirda has returned."

The stone's eyes widened in surprise, the mouth twisted into a feral grin as Simeon went on.

"He is young, and untrained. But the Hunters have him, and in time he will be of use to us."

"This will be well received. Do they know of us?"

"They scoured the city and found nothing."

"Excellent."

Simeon nodded as the stone returned to its smooth state. Placing it in his pocket, he gave one last look over the screen, before smashing it with one swipe of his hand and grinding it to powder beneath his boots.

* * * * * * * * * * *

The scene was familiar, a roadside cafe on a nondescript street in Durban, and Mike smiled, as he always did, to see life carrying on as normal. The people around him had no idea what went on, what the Hunters did and had done behind the scenes. The news had shown brief snippets of a burning house on a cliff top some miles from Durban, the result of an unfortunate accident that had claimed the lives of the home owners. The battle, the deaths, the wider struggle, all of it went unnoticed in the grand scheme of things.

Different Hunters reacted in different ways to this strange fact of their existence. Some were humbled, others arrogant, and most simply got on with it, becoming immune to the surreal nature of their work. Mike fell more in the former camp, his chosen way of working meaning he saw more of normal life than most in his frequent excursions, but even he was a step away from it, seeing real life as a curiosity, viewed through a window that he could close when he needed or wanted to. Rarely did his life and the real world interact in any meaningful way, and he was well versed in keeping the two separate.

Until now.

Mike had returned barely a week after they had taken Hal away, seeking to clear up a number of loose ends. Battles on that kind of scale usually left mess to clear up, and the mess in this case was a number of Vampires, drawn by the power Kym had unleashed in the conflict. Such occurrences were rare, but ideal opportunities for the Hunters, as it took time for Vampires to find decent hideaways, and their arrival usually left signs that any Hunter could follow. Standard practice was usually to deploy a team of Hunters, but Mike had volunteered, citing his up to date knowledge of the area, and Harpen had simply nodded.

That had only been part of the story, and Mike knew Harpen probably suspected the rest, the reason why, with his work complete and four new kill marks on his arm, Mike was still here, sitting at an outside table with a coffee and a bacon roll, waiting for a familiar face.

He had made a conscious choice to not think too hard about the decisions that brought him to this point, unused to these times when he had to interact with normal people. The Fortacas were the most human, the most approachable of the Brothers of the Order, but for all that, they were still that crucial step above the human race, able to remove themselves and see the world from a very different perspective.

But for all that, he had known he had to do this. He just wasn't sure why.

He rose as Steph appeared, smiling as she caught his eye, and she stopped, glancing left and right. He thought for a moment she was about to turn away, but instead she approached him slowly and sat down without a word. Her features altered several times, dull anger shifting to a wan smile and back several times, before she settled with a blank gaze.

"How are you?" Mike began, leaning forward and locking his gaze on hers.

She shrugged, her eyes meeting his for a moment, but still said nothing. Mike smiled, knowing there was a great deal they could – should – never discuss, knowing he was probably making a mistake by even being here, but knowing that his conscience would not allow him to walk away. She had suffered too much, had too much taken away, and he was all too aware of who was responsible.

She didn't react as he reached over and took her hand, but a moment later, she met his gaze and smiled.

* * * * * * * * * *

Part Two – Lemirda

Hal Lemirda pulled open the hatch in front of him, glancing around for a moment before lowering himself inside, his eyes piercing the darkness of the tunnels before him.

The radio at his shoulder squawked for a moment, and he reached up to turn it off, cutting off the voice of the Hunter at the other end, demanding to know his whereabouts. Less than a mile away, he knew a pair of Hunters were fuming at him. He knew, and didn't care.

Their report had been meant to be informative, a casual missive letting the HQ know what they had found. A pair of Vampires, occupying an abandoned station in the Paris Metro system. Nothing too strenuous for a pair of Hunters to take on, they had planned to move on them the following day, not knowing Hal had been making his way through Europe and was close enough to intervene.

Hal Lemirda, now fifteen years old, had grown considerably in the last few years. His enhanced genetics, now untapped by the knowledge of the others, had seen him grow to maturity in a little over half that time, and he could now pass for a young man in his early twenties, with a lean muscular frame and a graceless poise in everything he did. In the time since his first hunt, at the age of thirteen, he had gained a line of kill markings on his arm, and in the course of that, had discovered that he wasn't truly emotionless, that he was capable of feeling something...

* * * * * * * * * * *

"You sure you're ready for this?"

Hal simply nodded, turning the blade over and over in his hand, admiring the line of runes carved down its length. It was his, a gift from Harpen to mark his first hunt, and he was determined to put it to good use.

Across from him, Mike was grinning his habitual grin, his face half obscured by a pair of goggles. He was clad, as they both were, in a garishly coloured jumpsuit, emblazoned with slogans and the logo of a winged bear over the left breast. Outside, and far below, a vast expanse of ocean stretched away in all directions, broken only by the black hull of a ship a few miles away.

The call had come in from one of the Hunter's Bloodhounds, agents with the specialised skills of tracking and sifting through mountains of information to locate the merest trace of Vampires. This one – Hal had been told their name, but had dismissed it – had struck lucky, coming across a curious detail of a passenger requesting two rooms for one person on a transatlantic crossing, and this had been enough to pique their interest. Further looking had turned up an unusually large amount of luggage coming aboard for the use of one passenger.

This had been enough for the Hunters, their innate, almost supernatural sixth sense suggesting something amiss, and it been decided that such an operation was perfect for Hal's first hunt.

And that was why they now found themselves disguised as couriers and ready to parachute aboard the ship below. Hal had questioned the need to do this, more from curiosity than unwillingness, and Mike had simply laughed.

"We're a secret organisation, working in plain sight. Sure, we could jump aboard decked out in combats and armed to the teeth, but that kind of thing tends to get noticed. Plus, this'll be fun."

Hal shook his head. Nothing about this struck him as fun.

But then, nothing ever had.

Mike rose to his feet, reaching around Hal to connect their harnesses together. Hal had protested that he could jump alone, but had been overruled. The two of them took one more chance to check their kit was secured and hidden about their persons, before Mike handed Hal a brown parcel wrapped in string, his grin broadening for a moment.

With that, they were gone, leaping into the void and freefalling for several minutes. Hal could feel the exhilaration emanating from Mike as they fell, and noted with detachment that he felt nothing of the same, instead focusing on the landing zone below them. A handful of people had spotted them already, and Hal shook his head at that. Hiding in plain sight was not his choice, and he knew that he could have got them on to the ship unnoticed. This way, everyone on board would know of their arrival.

Mike touched down lightly, as if he had been doing this for years, waving to the stunned onlookers with a smile as he unclipped his harness. Hal simply stood, the package held in his outstretched arms, his gaze jumping from person to person, analysing and evaluating everyone on the deck in seconds. Not one of them was worth his notice.

Beside him, Mike was handing out flyers, extolling the virtues of a virtually fictitious company, and the people were lapping it up, applauding and cheering what appeared to them to be nothing but a publicity stunt.

"Ladies and Gentlemen, our thanks for your warm welcome, but now we have a package to deliver – remember, we are the Letter Bearers, and we can get anywhere."

Minutes later, the two of them were making their way down a stunningly decorated grand staircase, their jumpsuits looking wholly out of place among the well-dressed passengers. They walked slowly, casually, Hal with his features set and Mike smiling at people as they passed. Hal's hand was resting on his hip, feeling the shape of the dagger beneath the fabric of his suit, while Mike now held the package in his hands.

They arrived at Cabin 4094, and Mike stopped for a moment to glance up and down the long corridor, before producing a key card from his pocket and slotting it into the lock.

Be ready.

Hal nodded and stepped forward as Mike pushed the door open, taking in the room at a glance. Most of it he dismissed immediately, registering only those details which mattered. The thick curtains nailed over the balcony door that blocked any light from entering the room. The half dozen bottles of what could only be blood lined up on the desk. The motionless figure wrapped up in a thick blanket on the bed.

Vampire.

Hal moved quickly and silently, his years of training kicking in. With one move, he pulled the blanket away, registering in an instant the figure's eyes flicking open, the pain etched in his features. Even with the curtain blocking the sunlight, it knew, it could feel the energy leaching into his frame, and it hurt.

Which gave Hal all the time he needed to punch his blade straight into the creature's heart, feeling it scrape against bone and pierce the soft muscle beneath. Hal met the creature's gaze as it died, and for one tiny moment, he could feel a thrill race down his spine.

But only for a moment. That was...

* * * * * * * * * *

Too easy. So many of his kills had been, and Hal had grown bored. All his life he had been emotionless, feeling nothing but a blank murmur where others would become elated, despairing, depressed...

Only when he killed did Hal Lemirda feel anything at all. And only when he was challenged did he feel anything worth feeling.

Which was why he had chosen this hunt, why the Hunters in the city were bleating at him, why James Harpen would later warn him off. It went against his training, against the working practices of the Vampire Hunters, all because it took away the greatest advantage the Hunters had. Above his head, the sun was setting. Below his feet, a pair of Kappa Vampires would soon wake, and he would arrive in time to face them in open combat.

* * * * * * * * * * *

"Kappa Vampires," Joe gestured to the image before them. Hal and a handful of others, roughly the same age as him, looked on intently, although Hal's attention switched between the topic and the speaker. Joe Forjay was a Brother of the Order, and Hal could read his aura, a shimmering haze of potential that shifted slightly each time Joe manipulated the projector. His hands were resting by his sides, and had been since the lesson had begun.

"Possibly the greatest individual threat you can face, as of all the Families, these are the most capable combatants, although they tend to lack any other skills or abilities. Generally they are tough, as fast and as strong as any other Vampire, if not slightly more so, but they possess real skill in combat, not only relying on the strength and speed. This makes them a threat to us, and most Hunters tend to avoid them if there is any chance of direct confrontation. Even during the day, they can put up a decent fight if they are deep enough underground, so you should be aware of that, and when your time comes, you should plan accordingly."

His audience didn't move, focussed on his words. All of them between the ages of eight and ten, they were nevertheless mature well beyond their years, possessing already a physique and mental attributes well beyond their age. In most cases, this was thanks to a potent cocktail of enhancing agents, some chemical, some verging into the sorcerous, which made up a vast chunk of the diet of the aspirants. In the case of Hal, and the boy sitting beside him, it was thanks to their genetic heritage.

The boy leaned forward, his hand raised, and Joe nodded towards him.

"Yes Yuri?"

"Could we take them on?" he asked, gesturing to himself and Hal. There was no arrogance in his voice, and the other children did not begrudge the question, understanding their place in the organisation.

"In time, perhaps. But it should be avoided if possible. You are too precious a resource to risk."

Yuri Harpen nodded, and Hal watched him for a moment. The two boys were the same age, both gifted and capable even at their young ages, and had trained together for months now, but they could not be called friends. Yuri had never tried, and Hal had never cared. He suspected, though he had never discussed it, that Yuri had been told not to. James Harpen, who was, despite his apparent age, Yuri's great great grandfather, had known Hal's father well, and it seemed Hal shared his lack of an emotional state. It was understood without saying that one could not be friends with a Lemirda, it seemed.

"The Strigoi Family," Joe went on, flicking over the slide with a thought. Hal regarded the image carefully. Like the last, there was little to mark the man in the picture as distinguishable from any other human, but for those who knew what to look for, it was there. A tinge to the skin, eyes that seemed a little too sunken, whereas the Kappa had been a little too intense, with muscles that seemed too toned to be natural.

"Sorcerers, for the most part. Different members of the family possess a variety of skills, but this is usually due to personal preference rather than inherent skill, with one or two exceptions. You will find a range of magicks employed, including pyromancy, telekinesis, telepathy, control of natural forces including weather and disease, and also necromancy. One alone can usually be found with walking dead in attendance, particularly during the day to guard and defend them while they sleep. The greatest threat they pose, however, is down to these particularly attractive specimens."

He flicked over the slide to reveal a female Strigoi, seemingly normal in all respects, but for the fact that her eye sockets were empty.

"Some quirk of how Strigoi DNA mixes with the female chromosomes occasionally produces these Seers, Vampires with the ability to predict the future. The ability is limited and it seems, fairly random, but as you can imagine makes them a fairly potent aid. Don't be surprised if you turn up to a Strigoi lair to find it empty. This is, by the way, why the Lemirda Brother was created, to level the playing field, as it were."

Hal nodded. He had yet to receive any training in that regard.

"In a similar vein to the Strigoi, we have the Vampiri."

The image flicked over, but there was nothing depicted.

"We have no surviving image of them, and as far as we're aware, a Hunter hasn't come across one. They're included in this lesson for completeness, and..."

* * * * * * * * * *

Hal had tuned out at that point, disinterested. He cared about targets and their capabilities, and he left the rest to others. For all that, he accepted that such information, like the history of the Hunters and their place in the long war, was important, he simply didn't care himself.

Like now, for instance. He knew some Hunters made a point of studying their enemy, and it was likely that the two Hunters who had put him on this trail knew a great deal about the two Kappas ahead. As well as useful information, like their movements, supplies, and allies, most Hunters would get a name and past history in order to fit that Vampire within their extensive data libraries. While he understood why that mattered, Hal himself wasn't interested, and had always left such work to others. So far, no one had begrudged him that.

Hal moved silently down the tunnel, his senses attuned and his eyes picking out the details around him, even in the darkness. He was in a metro tunnel, empty but for himself, and some way ahead of him was the empty shell of the unused Haxos Station. Unused for the most part, anyway.

He stopped for a moment, concentrating hard, and something flitted across his mind. An image, indistinct until he focussed all his energies on it, resolving it by sheer force of will.

A vision. A prophecy. Himself, stood alone on the platform, a pair of bodies dead at his feet. As he watched himself, he saw his own head turn, arm raising to the left, posture shifting and body surging around to meet a threat, out of sight in his vision.

Then it was gone.

* * * * * * * * * * *

"Good. You're definitely getting better."

Hal shook his head. Harpen was wrong. Each vision was as hazy as the last, and try as he might, he could not will them into existence. Until he had met the Hunters, his visions had come naturally, with near perfect clarity, and at times had predicted events far in his future. But those had been uncontrolled, and to be of use, he knew he had to master them, control them, will them into his mind and read from them what he needed.

And in over a year and a half with the Hunters, it had not happened.

Day after day, Harpen and the others would come to him, individually or as a group, and seek to unlock his potential. In many ways, they had succeeded – after his first disappointing clash with Kym, he had shored up his mental defences to the point where he could shrug off all but the most powerful magicks with little effort. The Lemirda line was the most magically capable, and he found, even at his age and with little training, he could match the others in a contest of wills, and even summon powers to himself, lashing out with blows willed from his mind. He had the potential to surpass the others in might, and yet he had been warned off.

"Sorcery is easily detectable, and the more powerful and obvious it is, the further away it can be felt. It might help you in the short term, but will bring down an army on your head in short order. Better you focus your efforts on your unique gifts, the ones more easy to conceal."

And he had, but with little gain for years, until one day when Harpen produced something Hal had never come across before.

"This is an Ildraya. Rough translation, it means power, or strength. Essentially it is a sorcerous battery."

Hal took it gingerly, feeling its weight in his hand and the power leaching off it. It was the size and shape of an egg, a smooth stone with no visibly remarkable features, but he could see its aura in his mind's eye.

"I borrowed it from a friend. Karl Laumpir."

Hal grunted at the name, but said nothing.

"This is basically a cheap knock off of the same stones the Vampires use, designed for humans. It enhances natural abilities in ordinary people, and he suggested I try using it to unlock the last levels of your mind."

"What's in it for him?"

Harpen ignored the comment and lowered himself to the floor, pulling Hal down opposite him.

"You will never control your abilities fully. You cannot see everything that will happen, or even everything that will happen to one person or in one place. The best you can ever hope for is snatches of the future, but you

should be able to gain some measure of control over those."

"Is that what my father saw?"

Harpen nodded and closed his hands around Hal's, with the stone contained within. Hal closed his eyes, feeling the whispers of Harpen's aura gather around him, and he pushed out his own mind to meet it, feeling the power contained there and siphoning it into his own. In his hand, he felt the stone begin to pulse as Harpen's mind closed around it, pulling strands of Hal's with it until the energy was flowing direct into Hal's body.

"Concentrate now. Focus on the stone. Ignore what it is, ignore what it is doing. Think about where it will go. Picture its future."

Hal's brow furrowed, and he focused. Months of failure had done nothing to reduce his effort, where so many people would have given up.

A vision suddenly swam into view, hazy and indistinct, but getting clearer by the second. The stone, clasped in the hands of a teenage girl. Her eyes were tight shut, her posture relaxed. Behind her, a lone figure was sitting in an enormous over stuffed armchair, watching her intently. Hal recognised him as Karl Laumpir, a man he had not yet met but had heard a great deal about. He seemed to be training her, and Hal could faintly see the energy in the room, passing from Karl to the girl much as Harpen was doing to him now.

His eyes snapped open, the vision gone, but it had worked.

* * * * * * * * * *

From then, Hal had quickly mastered the ability, as much as he ever would be able to, and he had found that he could will brief images of the future into his mind. Occasionally, as when he had been a child, longer term visions assailed him, repeating over the course of a few days or weeks, and not coming to pass for weeks or months. He had made a habit of recording every detail of these visions, as they usually pertained to some great event that would happen in someone's life, detail for detail as he had seen it.

Mostly, as now, it was short glimpses of the near future, early warnings of what would come to pass in the next few hours, always linked to him and those around him, and always happening exactly as he had seen it. His attempts to change what would happen had met with failure, and he had stopped trying years before.

Movement ahead caught his attention, and he drew his knife from its sheath on his forearm. He knew he was practically undetectable, but if they were as old as was suspected, they would be powerful enough to know something was amiss.

In an instant, Hal exploded into life, bursting from the tunnel and launching himself up onto the platform. A pair of figures stood ahead of him, each bearing a sword, quizzical looks on their faces as they faced Hal.

Hal gave them no time to attack, swinging out his left hand, the flat of his palm smacking away the first sword blade as it thrust towards him, his right punching forward with his knife.

The blade scraped the Vampire's ribs as he twisted, turning his chest away from the blow. Hal ducked as a sword whistled over his head, reversing his knife and stabbing back under his own arm. He was rewarded by a scream as the blade slammed home in the Vampire's chest, and he spun away, wrenching the weapon free in time to meet the sword of the first. He parried half a dozen blows before finding his opening, lunging forward with his shoulder, catching the Vampire off guard and reaching around him, pushing his knife into the creature's back with a grunt. Face to face, Hal watched the eyes dull from fiery red to empty grey, before pushing the body away. It struck the floor scant seconds after the first.

His vision came to him, and he turned without thinking, his arm raising to the left in time to ward off a clumsy blow as a length of pipe swung for his head. It may as well have been in slow motion.

He didn't even bother with his knife, batting aside the pipe and punching out, his fist connecting with the man's head hard enough to shatter the skull, throwing the body back across the platform.

Hal lowered his hands slowly, feeling his body relax. Already the thrill of the hunt was receding, and he reflected that even a pair of Kappas hadn't been especially challenging. He reached up to turn his radio back on, immediately hearing the voice of the Hunter on the other end and cutting him off.

"This is Hal. Two Kappa, confirmed dead. There was a man down here too. A servant, I think."

The voice on the other end was calm, their annoyance obviously passed. No one liked to be on the wrong side of the Brothers of the Order.

"Roger that Hal, where is he now?"

"In a crumpled heap at the end of the platform."

"Dead?"

"Yes."

"Did he have to die?"

"No."

There was a pause, just long enough to let Hal know what they thought of his actions.

"Ok. Someone is en-route to get the place cleaned up"

An image flashed across Hal's mind.

"Obur?"

"Yes."

"I'll be gone by the time they get here."

* * * * * * * * * *

Hal regarded the men before him with a mixture of disdain and confusion. He had barely been in the Hunter HQ for less than an hour, and had barely begun to see the incredible scope of what the Vampire Hunters were doing here, what they were capable of and what they had access to, but here was something that threw him more than anything else.

They had landed in a cavernous hanger bay that seemed to have risen up through the trees as the plane had approached. Immediately the view, the endless forest, was disappearing as they sank into the earth, even as silent hooded technicians emerged to move the plane away to one of the side bays Hal could see lined up along the walls, stretching away into the distance.

"Where are we?"

Harpen glanced at the boy with a smile.

"Hanger One of the Hunter HQ. Somewhere under the Siberian Taiga. Couldn't tell you where, before you ask. It moves."

"The hanger?"

"The whole lot. We have miles upon miles of tunnels, store rooms, training bays, living areas, armouries...all of it hidden, and all of in constant motion. When we need access, the ground is shifted, the trees moved and the hanger raised to the surface.

"How?"

By way of an answer, Harpen led Hal to one side of the hanger, to where a thick metal door was set into the wall. Beside it, a metal staircase rose up the wall of the cavern, joining a walkway that led out to a single room, suspended from the ceiling. As Hal climbed the stairs, he glanced up and down the hanger, taking in the bewildering variety of craft the Hunters seemed to have access to.

Another metal door gave way to a small room, windowless and sparsely furnished with just a trio of arm chairs. In each sat a blank faced man with pale skin and eyes. They were motionless, their eyes unfocussed and their limbs relaxed, but Hal could feel power emanating from them. Power unlike that exhibited by the Brothers, it seemed to flow from them into the stone above and around them. As Hal watched, he saw the rock above them moving, flowing as if it were molten, gathering above them as the hanger descended into the earth, not through mechanical means, but by their control of the rock itself.

The truth dawned.

"They're Vampires."

Harpen seemed genuinely impressed.

"Yes. Members of the Obur Family, one of the six Vampire Families. The others you will learn about in time."

"Are they slaves?"

That gave Harpen pause, and he gave the boy a curious look.

"Allies, Hal. Friends."

"But we're Vampire Hunters."

"Yes. But not all the Families are targets. Some are on our side."

"But we hunt Vampires. You said. My family was created to hunt Vampires."

Harpen's voice was level, patient.

"Yes. But we have allies. Without the skills of the Oburs, we would never have survived. They keep us hidden, they build our bases, they make our weapons. We need them, and we work together for a common cause."

Hal considered this for a long time.

"I don't like it."

* * * * * * * * * *

He still didn't like it. Although not truly capable of any feelings towards the Oburs, Hal had made a point of avoiding them whenever he could. He didn't – couldn't – deny their worth and value. They were engineers without peer, and crafted every one of the weapons and vehicles that the Hunters deployed. The Obur's mastery of the physical world meant they could produce weapons that would never malfunction, shields and armour that would never break, sorcerous engines that would never require fuel. There were almost a hundred permanently living in their own section of the Hunter HQ – a section that Hal had never set foot in – and Harpen had not exaggerated when he said they kept the Hunters operating. In the field, as now, they were equally valuable, possessing a preternatural skill for cleaning and disposing of any evidence of Hunter involvement, even to the point of eliminating the bodies themselves without a trace.

But still, Hal struggled with them. For all he recognised their worth, for all he took full advantage of their skills, he could never see past their nature, never fully understand why they were not targets. Harpen had tried to explain it to him, citing the ancient histories of the Vampire Wars, the beginnings of the Families, but Hal didn't care beyond the here and now. And here and now, they were Vampires.

Movement in the tunnel made Hal raise his knife, but he lowered it almost immediately. A lone figure had stepped into view, regarding Hal with eyes that were as dead and emotionless as Hal's own. Much quicker than Hal had expected, he must have been contacted as soon as Hal had headed here.

"Greetings, Lemirda."

The voice, like the features, were devoid of any feeling. Had he been able to properly consider and understand his own emotionless state, Hal would have seen the Oburs were so like himself.

"I'll leave you to it."

Hal's voice was equally blank. For all he struggled to come to terms with the place of the Oburs in the Hunters, he was as incapable of active dislike as he was of any other emotion.

"As you wish."

Hal turned away and walked through the tunnels, heading for the hatch he arrived by. He was nearly there when a voice came through his radio, distorted by distance.

"Hal, this is Harpen."

Hal stopped.

"Go."

"We need you back here."

Hal acknowledged with a curt reply, moving off at speed. James Harpen was the only man who could elicit such a response from Hal, the only person Hal truly respected, and the only member of the organisation whose commands would be followed by Hal to the letter...

* * * * * * * * * *

Hal watched closely from the shadows, his features concealed by a balaclava, his eyes flicking back and forth constantly. He was pressed against a wall, his hands flat against the rough concrete surface, itching to be holding a weapon. He had been training for a year, and had been handling weapons for almost half that time, but this was his first time out of the HQ since he had joined the Hunters, and he was here only to observe. He was too young, too valuable, too raw to be released yet on his first hunt.

The target, a Kappa Vampire, had occupied a hideaway in an old mine shaft, and James Harpen had chosen this hunt for himself, inviting Hal at the last minute to accompany him. Things had not gone completely to plan, and they had arrived to find it empty, the Vampire having fled shortly before their arrival, and James had been forced to improvise, unwilling to let him escape. They had given chase, following Harpen's preternatural instincts to an industrial complex, half constructed and empty, arriving just as the sun was beginning to set. Hal could tell Harpen had considered pulling out or calling for support, but had decided against both.

Hal watched him now, seeing the steely resolve that was usually covered by his easy confidence as he stalked the crumbling site. High concrete walls rose on all sides, broken by window frames that had yet to be fitted with windows. On the ground, between the stacks of unpacked concrete blocks, the shadows were deepening, and Harpen was advancing, sweeping his pistol to cover each possible avenue of attack, but it was cursory, most of the work already done by his enhanced senses, and he moved across the yard swiftly. Hal followed after a moment, responding to a brief mental summons, stopping just short of a set of metal double doors.

Harpen turned to face him for a moment, a smile on his face, and Hal felt the eagerness, the anticipation in his mentor's form. Hal felt nothing of the same, his mind empty and uninspired, and he wondered for a moment at the number of hunts Harpen had been on, the number of kills he had made, and yet his energy and his passion was undiminished.

Hal felt something, a flicker of instinct, realising as he did that Harpen had obviously already felt it, turning and booting open the doors. Hal took a step forward, stopping short as he heard the other man in his head.

Stay there.

Hal nodded, unable to consider ignoring the command and unable to explain why, and watched from the doorway as James Harpen went to work.

Hal had trained with the Hunters for a year, had sparred and fought alongside them and against them time after time, honing his own skill and learning theirs. Like their auras, their styles of combat were distinct. Kym, predictably, was brutal and blunt, combining rage and power and skill in a terrifying display of martial prowess, almost unstoppable in any environment. Mike was quicker, slighter, preferring to keep his enemies at arm's reach than throw himself into the thick of it, but still capable of dizzying heights of ability, the equal to any of the Brothers despite his relative youth and his more wide ranging talents.

None of them, not even Kym, could match Harpen consistently. He had lived, and survived, for decades, and his skill was borne of genetic heritage and diligent practice, combined with year after year of hard fought experience, longer than any of the Brother's then living.

Right now, every ounce of that skill was required.

Hal watched, impassive, as Harpen was surrounded on all sides, and it became clear why their quarry had fled to this location. Half a dozen Kappa Vampires had emerged, pouncing on the Hunter as if they had been waiting for this chance, and he had simply skipped to one side, parrying the first blow to reach him and sending the closest attacker away with a vicious spin kick. In the same move, he fired a trio of shots and ducked away. Each shot hit home, the bullets burning into flesh, and Harpen darted forward to kill the first with a downward stab. He rolled away an instant later, avoiding a sweeping sword blade and lashing out as he came to his feet, felling a second and a third with a series of blows.

The Vampires fell one by one, cut down by savage but expertly placed strikes. Harpen was calm, his breathing controlled, barely breaking a sweat as he fought, and Hal felt an inkling of respect break through the void in his mind. For the first time, he truly saw what he himself was capable of, what he would become in time with the tutelage of his Brothers, of Harpen. He was a Hunter, a Brother of the Order, and in time, he would be unstoppable.

He couldn't wait.

* * * * * * * * * * *

From the shadows, Simeon watched as the Lemirda emerged into the streets of Paris, watched him glance around, feeling his mind scan instinctively. Simeon smiled, knowing he was undetectable, but feeling the power in Hal's mind. He had watched the boy from afar for years, seeing him, and his powers, grow ever stronger.

Soon he would be ready.

* * * * * * * * * *

Steph's heart raced as she entered the lobby of the Grand Port Hotel, forcing her feet to slow down as she crossed the marble floor and entered the bar, casting her eyes around.

She saw the smile first, and her own broadened as he rose from the table and embraced her tightly, before gesturing her to the seat beside him and passing her a drink. He had changed so little, still looking like the same man she had met years before, the same winning smile, the same easy confidence, the same muscular build...

She sipped her drink, smiling coyly at him. It was by now an old and familiar routine. Same hotel, same table, same drink. Every six months or so, sometimes longer, when his work brought him this way, Mike would drop her a call to see how she was getting along and they would arrange to meet for a few days. She had known, especially the first few times, he had done it out of a sense of duty after taking her brother away, but over time this had faded, and now he seemed to genuinely enjoy her company, to enjoy the refreshing break of a normal holiday.

Normal to some, that is. Most people would consider a few days in one of the most expensive hotels in South Africa to be a little beyond normal, but Mike, like Steph, didn't worry about money all that much.

The conversation was loose and easy, avoiding, as it always did, any discussion of his work or Hal – He was unwilling to talk about the former for her own sake, she the latter for the difficulty of that topic, the memory of how they had parted still bitter in her mouth. Instead, they talked about her, her life, her work as a freelance journalist and part time child carer. The wealth they had given her had allowed her to live a life free from worry, and she worked for pleasure, not because she needed to.

"Did I ever thank you?" she said, her voice suddenly serious, her expression earnest.

"Frequently," Mike laughed. "But for what in particular?"

"For what you gave me when you didn't have to. I only live this life thanks to you lot."

"I think it was the least we could do, given...everything."

There it was again, that odd look that would occasionally surface on his features for a split second, somewhere between sorrow and guilt. She had never dared press the issue.

"True," she mused lightly, before taking a deep breath. She had tried to build up the courage to raise this topic for years, each time stopping before she could form the words. This time, she just plunged in.

"Did you ever tell Hal about mum's death?"

Mike paused, clearly not wanting to discuss the issue.

"I did."

"How did he take it?"

"It was a long time ago," Mike shrugged, clearly reluctant to discuss this.

"You don't remember?"

Mike sighed, relenting.

"The same as he takes everything."

"Cold, unfeeling?"

"That's the one."

She laughed suddenly. The years had not made it any easier, and even now she struggled to talk about it, and Mike knew that.

"He saw it, you know. He told me."

Steph shuddered, remembering all too clearly the chilling pronouncement of her eight year old brother, and shook her head. She had opened the door to this conversation now.

"How is he?"

Mike laughed. "Cold, unfeeling. Do you really want to discuss this?"

"I'd like to see him again."

That seemed to surprise him, and he paused before shaking his head. She took his hand, her eyes pleading.

"Please. Just for a little while."

"Out of the question."

"Come on, how dangerous can it be for me? You meet me with no worries."

Mike paused at that, tempted to tell her of the work he put in to make these meetings safe, of the days he spent here before hand, scouring the local area, checking for any traces of a threat, ensuring she could arrive and stay unnoticed, and go home with no possible threat to herself.

"It's not for your protection. Not in that way. You wouldn't want to meet him now."

"Why not?"

She couldn't keep a note of panic from her voice, as she realised just why she had avoided this conversation for years, and was now unable or unwilling to take it back.

"He's...immersed in our world. He hunts, and that is all he knows. Other Hunters take breaks, enjoy stopping, enjoy a holiday," he glanced pointedly around the bar, "Not Hal. He hunts, and that is it."

And the only time he feels alive is when he kills, he finished to himself. Steph pondered this for a long while.

"Even so. He's my brother, my only link to my mum. I know what he's like, I think I can handle it. I'd just like to see him again."

She watched Mike's reaction, seeing that strange look, knowing that any mention of her mother would soften his attitude.

"I'll see what I can do," he said at last.

* * * * * * * * * *

Hal knew something was up the moment he arrived. Harpen was waiting for him on the hanger floor, clad from head to foot in segmented body armour, a large calibre rifle slung over his back. He didn't say a word, merely smiling as he led Hal away, winding through the labyrinthine passageways to a briefing room. Hal could feel the barest trace of anticipation, the thrill of the hunt as he imagined what kind of threat would require heavy equipment.

A feeling which only intensified as he walked into the briefing room and found the room humming with power, half a dozen distinct auras melding together. Nearly every one of the Brothers of the Order was there, and Hal felt invigorated just by being in the room. Beside James, there were the other two living Harpens, Yuri and his father Dimitri, both looking like younger versions of James, but neither sharing the sheer force of his presence. Ralph and Jason Tyler were seated, motionless, at the rear of the room, apparently bored already. Joe Forjay was in conversation with his son, a child who had not even reached maturity but who carried himself with the same quiet confidence. Kym and his son Senna were the only ones still on their feet, sparring with drawn blades despite the space they had, each blow perfectly placed and perfectly deflected. Only Mike was missing, and Hal suspected he knew why.

He halted in his reverie suddenly, his gaze snatched away as he noticed another figure near the front of room, and Hal started as he realised he hadn't registered the presence immediately.

He appeared barely older than eighteen, a young man with a confident posture and a haughty air, but then he met Hal's eyes, just for a second. In that instant, Hal was stunned by the depth of knowledge he saw there, the grim gaze of eyes that had seen far too much. Beyond those eyes, he had no aura, nothing to mark him as special, but Hal saw enough to recognise him for what he was.

Vampire. And not just any Vampire. This at last was the vaunted Karl Laumpir, last surviving member of the Laumpir family and subject of a thousand legends. Karl the immortal, Karl the destroyer, Karl the hunter without peer. Hal knew Harpen regarded him with awe, as did any Hunter who knew him. For thousands of years he had worked alongside the Hunters, guiding, supporting, and occasionally calling upon them for some great venture. The last had been only twenty years before, and had seen the death of three Brothers of the Order. For him to be here meant something was about to be suicidally dangerous.

Hal couldn't wait.

* * * * * * * * * *

Simeon strode into the room without fear, his hand resting lightly on the sword blade at his hip. He knew he didn't need it, but it paid to remind his audience who was in charge. To their credit, the gathered Vampires didn't pay his display any heed, with the exception of the Strigoi contingent, who merely shifted to move away further from him. Beside them sat representatives from the other families, even a pair of Ultors, eying him with barely contained hostility. No matter, they were here, that was enough.

"I will keep this brief," Simeon began, knowing he had no need to convince them of the importance of this meeting. They wouldn't be here otherwise. "The Brothers of the Order are gathering to answer my summons. In exchange for certain knowledge I believe you all possess, you may have the location and do with them as you wish."

There was silence for a moment before one of the Ultors rose to his feet, gleeful malice in his eyes.

"Done."

* * * * * * * * * *

"Brothers, Hunters, Greetings and thanks to you all."

Karl was smiling, revealing the barest hint of fangs in a predatory grin.

"It has come to my attention that a number of key players from the three families are gathering for some sort of conference. I suspect it is to do with another combined effort to bring me down," he grinned again. "I have a decent idea of the location and numbers involved, and would like to request your support to finish them."

Ralph Tyler leaned forward, his voice level.

"A gathering for unspecified reasons sounds a lot like a trap."

Karl shrugged.

"I know. But I would hope between us we could handle it."

Hal opened his mouth to speak, closing it again as Harpen got to his feet.

"We know the risks. With the exception of Hal, the youngest of each Line is staying behind."

The four youngest in the room, including Yuri, nodded. The powers of each line were passed onto the first born son, and they were usually carefully protected until they had children of their own.

"The meeting place is in Cumbria in England, at the Wren Castle Hotel. They're each arriving separately during the evening, and I think they're hoping to conclude by morning. Which means a night time hit, obviously, and no chance to get them all sleeping."

"How did you come by this information?" Hal spoke up, his gaze fixed on the floor. Karl ignored the gesture.

"I raided an Ultor lair two weeks ago. I recovered invitations sent and deleted from the computer."

"Definitely a trap," Ralph muttered, the smile on his face seeming out of place.

Harpen took over at that point, pulling up a schematic of the hotel on the wall and running over a basic plan of attack.

"We have no idea where in the hotel they will gather, so we need to be fairly flexible. We're assuming, based on past experience, they won't run, and in case they do, we'll have mobile Hunters on standby."

"They won't run," Karl said, a wry smile on his face.

"You seem very sure."

His smile didn't fade.

"Experience. Plus, if I was them, and I had you lot in one place, I'd give it all up for a chance to kill you all."

They took a moment to digest that.

"Any normal Hunters coming in with us?"

Harpen shook his head.

"Too dangerous."

"What about civilians?" Joe asked, and Hal noticed and ignored the tiny glance in his direction that accompanied that statement.

"Keep them alive," Karl interjected, to Hal's surprise. It seemed he had a thing or two to learn about Karl Laumpir.

* * * * * * * * * *

Hal's hands worked instinctively, fitting the rifle together with mechanical smoothness. His body armour was crafted for his form by Obur Vampires, and he barely felt it. Like all the Hunters, he had personalised it himself, adding a number of blades to the joins to turn his armour into a weapon, as well as spare knives strapped to the small of the back.

Harpen approached him, swaying slightly in the aircraft cabin, and Hal paused in what he was doing, noting the look on his face. It was a look he recognised, a look reserved for when Hal had done something especially reckless, a look that meant things were going to be said that Hal didn't want to hear. Harpen didn't disappoint.

"You're not coming in with us."

Hal resumed his work, raising the rifle to sight down the barrel. Like his armour, it was made for his specifications and to his requirements, a short barrelled carbine with a high rate of fire and no stock, perfect for close quarter combat. His voice was as blank as ever as he replied.

"You need me."

"I'm serious. You're far too valuable."

"Then why am I here?"

"I don't want to be without your sight. You'll accompany us to the house, then go into overwatch when we go inside."

"I can handle it."

"I'm sure you can. But I won't risk it."

"I've been hunting during the night for over a year."

"I'm aware, and you shouldn't do that either. But this is not a hunt. This is a battle, and some of us will probably die. We can't risk it being you. Not yet. Have a child, then you can be as reckless as you want."

Hal grunted, but made no other response. A vague sense of disappointment washed over him, replacing the thrill of anticipation, and he lowered the weapon.

* * * * * * * * * *

In the distance, he could see the reflection of the setting sun on the lake, and his pulse began to quicken ever so slightly. Behind him, hidden from view by the line of trees that concealed him, the castle was already in shadow, a towering grey walled building crested with ornamental battlements. It had never been intended as a fortress, a single glance could tell that, and he found himself wondering again what had drawn the Vampires to choose this as a meeting place.

James Harpen had spent an unnaturally long lifetime trusting his instincts, and that, and no small amount of luck, had made him one of the most successful and longest lived of his kind. Right now, those instincts were silent, and that, paradoxically, made him wary. There was some part of the picture missing, and yet he couldn't place it.

One look at Hal, lying beside him, told him that he was not the only one with concerns, although Hal was hard enough to read at the best of times, and his moods only varied between several shades of grim. Occasionally, when his eyes flicked to where Karl was concealed a few dozen metres away, his mouth tightened almost imperceptibly, but Harpen knew well enough to ignore it. Victor Lemirda had been the same.

Each one of the Brothers were concealed around the Castle, invisible from any form of scans or checks, thanks mostly to the combined presence and esoteric gifts of Hal and Karl. Harpen has considered vetoing Hal from this operation altogether, but he knew that wasn't really an option. Besides how he would react if he knew they had gone without him, without him they ran the risk of detection, even with Karl here. It had been Karl who had finally persuaded him, insisting Hal accompany them, and now they were here it made sense.

Even knowing where they were, Harpen couldn't see or even sense any of his companions. Each of them had lain for thirty hours straight, unmoving, in their own hide, carefully and swiftly constructed the previous morning.

He hoped this was worthwhile.

* * * * * * * * * *

Simeon glanced out of the hotel window as the sun set, seeing nothing but empty grounds, but knowing they were out there. They had to be.

He found himself fervently praying this would come off. A lot had been invested in this operation, from the money to buy out the hotel for the week, to the soon to be lost resources and allies he had spent years cultivating. As he strode from the hotel, locking the front door behind him, a single thought ran round and round his head.

He hoped this was worthwhile.

* * * * * * * * * *

Hal felt, rather than saw, the plane approaching, and passed it to his Brothers with a mental impulse, feeling the surge of energy in response and concentrating to hide it from detection. His hands closed around a knife that wasn't there, and he fought down the thrill building in his spine. Not this time. Despite what people thought of him and despite what he was capable of, he found he couldn't bring himself to disobey Harpen, not now with him beside him. His mind wouldn't let him dwell on that thought.

Harpen's eyes moved slightly, his senses scanning the sky. Nothing yet, but he knew Hal's instincts. A minute or two later, he saw it as it appeared over the hills. It was flying low, hugging the terrain as it approached, its engines silent and its dark hull barely visible.

Strigoi. Ultor. Kappa.

Hal's eyes were closed, and Harpen could feel the curious edge to his aura. These details were from a vision. The plane was above them, its side door sliding open.

James will get two in the main hall. Ralph will put down one in the third window from the left, first floor. Dimitri will finish him off. Joe will deflect a blow meant for Kym just after Kym's blade gets stuck.

So it continued, a litany of minor points from the coming battle, read direct from Hal's vision. The Brothers listened intently, even as the sky filled with parachutes. Almost forty Vampires were descending on the property.

Harpen watched them come, curious. Karl had said they would arrive separately, and this was a far more overt move than he had expected.

His curiosity turned to surprise as the figures landed, some on the roof but mostly on the grounds immediately outside the building. As he watched, they ditched their parachutes simultaneously, pulling weapons and launching themselves at the building. In seconds, the main door was smashed off its hinges, windows put through on all floors as Vampires leapt inside. Almost as if...

They're attacking an empty building.

Harpen could feel the confusion in Karl's words, his mind turning over every possibility. There was only one explanation for an attack like this.

They think we're inside.

Too late to back out, Karl reminded them all, and Harpen nodded, rising into view. The Brothers followed him, racing to the house with weapons drawn, launching themselves through the openings made by the Vampires. Ralph and Jason were the exceptions, taking up positions on the lawn and firing perfectly aimed shots into the house. The bullets, hand crafted and enchanted with runes of potent design, were not enough to kill a Vampire, but they caused a debilitating pain, and each Vampire they hit became an easy target for one of their Brothers in the house. Hal drew his own pistol, ready to move up alongside them, but froze, a vision clouding his mind: *Dimitri falling, a sword blade punched through his ribs.*

Hal concentrated, sending a warning, and knowing it was too late.

* * * * * * * * * *

Harpen killed the first Vampire he met without breaking step, his feet barely touching the floor as he vaulted the window and stabbed forward. There was a second Vampire in the room, an Ultor, and he seemed surprised in the split second before he was cut down, a wooden stake lodged in his heart. Harpen didn't slow down, moving out into the corridor and glancing left and right as Yuri and Dimitri appeared on either side, their blades dripping with blood. Ahead of them, an elaborate grand staircase led down to the ground floor and the main hall, and Harpen headed down, Hal's prophecy in his head. Sure enough, he found a pair of Vampires there, their backs to him as they traded blows with Kym and Joe. As he approached, they sensed him coming, one of them lashing out with a savage kick that sent Kym's blade into a wooden column with such force that it stuck fast, then turning to face Harpen while his fellow swung for Kym, who ducked, knowing what was coming. Joe swung his knife above Kym's head, deflecting a blow and sending the Vampire spinning away, straight into the path of Harpen's blade. The two Vampires hit the floor as Hal's voice sounded in their heads.

Dimitri is about to die. Rear Kitchen. The attacker will try to escape.

Harpen turned, knowing they had all heard the warning. Dimitri was heading down the stairs, and Harpen just nodded to him. There was no sadness, no farewell, just a resigned acceptance to the fate they would all eventually share, and Dimitri smiled as he kicked open the kitchen door and dived inside.

Harpen followed, knowing it was no good, pushing through the door in time to see Dimitri fall, his attacker pulling a sword free from his chest. There were three of them in the room, all of them Kappas, and Harpen knew they were the last survivors in the building by the silence elsewhere.

There was no sentimentality for Dimitri, and there would be very little mourning beyond what was expected from losing a valuable Hunter from their forces. What there was, and what Harpen demonstrated now, was furious vengeance.

He smashed his fist into Dimitri's killer, shattering his jaw and sending him reeling to the floor. Drawing his handgun, Harpen emptied it into the prone Vampire, watching him writhe in agony as the bullets burned into his flesh. Around him, his Brothers surged forward to engage the remaining two, but they were too slow, the Kappas already diving headlong through the windows and out into the night.

Cold fury in his eyes, Harpen stabbed down with his knife.

* * * * * * * * * *

Hal saw the two Kappas emerge from the house and was running before he had even processed the thought, unwilling to let them escape and feeling the familiar surge of the hunt course through him. Unlike Harpen, he had no desire for revenge, merely a desire to kill.

One of the Kappas went down suddenly, an expert shot from Ralph clipping his ankle and throwing him to the floor. Hal was there before the wound could heal, holding the Vampire in place with a boot before killing him with ease. The second had fled into the trees, and Hal made after him, determined to reach him before the other Hunters caught up.

Branches whipped by his head as he ran, his heightened reflexes allowing to him to dart through the wood without hindrance, but he found his quarry much sooner than expected.

He broke into a clearing suddenly, halting himself as he saw the body of the Kappa on the floor. A sickle shaped blade protruded from his chest, pulled free a moment later by a lone figure, who even now eyed Hal with a grim smile. He was not a Hunter, Hal was certain, but not a Vampire either. He cast out with his mind, but found nothing, no aura, no energy, not even a heartbeat, nothing in fact to confirm that he was even standing there at all.

For the first time in his life, Hal was hesitant. The man's skin was dark, his eyes darker still, and Hal could feel his gaze upon himself, an intense stare that somehow carried a trace of glee.

The man moved, the spell broken, and Hal leapt forward, determined to know who he was. Despite Hal's speed, the man avoided him, dodging away impossibly quickly, then seeming to change his mind, reaching back with his arm. Hal latched onto him...

And the world went black.

* * * * * * * * * *

Steph stirred in her sleep as Mike rolled from the bed, reaching for his phone. Padding silently into the bathroom, he flipped it open, knowing this was likely bad news.

The tone in Harpen's voice left him in no doubt, and he listened with mounting panic before hanging up and stepping back through to wake Steph.

"I have to go."

"Already?" she said sleepily, raising herself onto her elbows and glancing at the clock. "I thought you said they wouldn't need you..?"

He nodded grimly. "Hal has been wounded. We don't quite know by what, and he hasn't woken up."

"I thought you said he couldn't be badly hurt?" she was awake suddenly, sitting bolt upright.

"Apparently I was wrong."

He paused for a moment, watching her climb out of the enormous bed and begin to throw her things into a bag.

"What are you doing?"

"Packing to come with you," she replied distractedly, pulling on her clothes without meeting his gaze.

"I don't think that's..."

"I don't care if it is possible. Or wise. Or whatever else you're about to say. I don't care who he is, or who you are right now. He is my brother, my only living relative," she stressed that part. "And I intend to be there to help him."

"How can you help?" he said gently.

"How can you? You said you didn't know what was wrong."

Mike shook his head, and she knew she had won. For all his vaunted skills, she knew him only as a good friend, and he reacted as she expected. It was against his better judgement, but as he climbed into the car and headed for the airport, she was seated beside him.

* * * * * * * * * *

Simeon pushed open the door with a triumphant air, nodding greetings to his siblings around the room. One of them detached himself from the group and stepped forward to embrace him, his own face twisted into an approximation of a smile.

"Is it done?"

"Nearly Julius," Simeon replied. "Enough has been done. He would never have joined us willingly last night, but now he will come to us."

* * * * * * * * * *

Steph was bowled over by what she had seen since stepping from the aircraft, the sheer scale of it taking her breath away, the audacity and ingenuity it took to hide something like this...From the hanger they had landed in, she had been led through a narrow corridor, passing a pair of men who had eyed her warily until Mike had said something in a language she didn't understand. This seemed to satisfy them, and she had quickly become lost in the maze of passages she found herself in. Mike led her unerringly, her hand in his, through passageways that looked like they had been grown from solid rock, smooth surfaces with no sign of machinery or tools on every side. Passages led off in all directions, and metal doors were set into the stone every dozen metres. Many were closed, but the few that were open gave her a glimpse of the scale of life down here. Storerooms, bed rooms, open spaces filled with men locked in combat, firing ranges, even rooms that seemed to be overflowing with plant life, all of it passed her in a blur as Mike led her onward, stopping eventually outside a doorway identical to the rest.

"James knows you're here, and he understands, but he's not happy. And neither am I. Be careful with what you touch, and what you say, but most of all with what you look at."

With that, he opened the door, and she felt her rising panic fade away as she realised it was just a hospital ward. She had expected all manner of esoteric devices from his warning, but instead there were simply rows of beds and blank walls. Every bed was empty bar one, and they made their way over to it. James Harpen was leaning against the wall beside it, and Steph gasped as she saw Hal's form in the bed. His flesh was emaciated and tight against his bones, his black eyes wide open, although he showed no sign of life.

"This is how we found him. He went after a Kappa in the woods, managed to kill him, but somehow he was brought down."

Mike immediately went to work, running his hands over Hal's body, his eyes closed as a purple mist seemed to flow from him into Hal. After a moment, he stopped, his eyes open and confused.

"There's no wound."

"There never was," Harpen shrugged. "This isn't a conventional attack. Something drained him of all his power and left him exhausted without killing him. Our normal doctors had a look at him as soon as we arrived, and there is nothing to heal, as far as we can tell. We hoped you might have an alternative."

He meant that as a remark to Mike's skills as a healer, but he couldn't help glance at Steph, not unkindly but rather more...bemused.

"Hello again. How's the car?"

She ignored him and leaned over Hal, staring into the black pits of his eyes. She had no idea what she was doing, no idea what she had hoped to do once she got here, but needed to do something, anything to justify to herself why she had all but forced Mike to let her come. Hal didn't react, and she felt like she was back with her mother, overseeing a body that may as well have been dead for all the life it contained. She looked up at the two men.

"Will he recover?"

Mike shrugged. "If the attack had been meant to kill him, it would have, I think. It takes a lot to bring one of us down, especially a Lemirda. He should recover in time, but it might help if you talk to him. A familiar voice and all that."

Is that true? Harpen's voice sounded in his head, unknown to Steph.

Possibly. Probably won't make a difference, but it's good for her. She needs a connection, some closure.

It won't do her any favours when he wakes up.

I know, I'm hoping we can spare her that when it comes. We've done enough damage.

I hope you know what you're doing.

Even in his head, Harpen's voice sounded unsure.

*　*　*　*　*　*　*　*　*　*

Steph stayed at the HQ for several days, catching a few hours of fitful sleep here and there, eating food that was brought to her each day by Mike. After a day she had begun to see through him, knowing that he was doing this for her benefit. From what little she was allowed to see of their operation down here, she very much doubted that they needed her help with anything, but she pressed on, content to take the opportunity when it was offered, regardless of why it was offered.

She spoke at length to Hal's oblivious form, sometimes with Mike, mostly alone, about her life and her pursuits, telling long stories with the most trivial detail, knowing he wouldn't care if he was awake, but selfishly enjoying the connection with him denied to her when he was young. She steered away from anything to do with him, but she wasn't entirely sure why.

The fourth day began like the others, and she rolled from the bed next to Hal's with a yawn. She picked up her story where she had left off, already nattering away as she reached over to rearrange his bed sheets, recoiling instantly as his hand shifted. She paused, not sure if she had imagined it, but certain when she saw it again, the fingers closing into a clenched fist.

She looked up into his eyes, seeing life there for the first time, seconds before she was thrown back across the room, an invisible wall of force striking her like a freight train and slamming her into the far wall hard enough to break bones. She hit the floor hard, crying out in pain before her vision begin to grey out. Through dimming eyes, she saw Hal walk from the room without a backward glance, before she felt into merciful unconsciousness.

*　*　*　*　*　*　*　*　*　*

Mike dropped his fork as he saw Hal enter, calmly picking up a roll from the shelf by the door and chewing it as he glanced around.

"Where's James?"

Mike regarded him before answering. He was healthy and whole, no trace of the illness that knocked him out for four straight days, and Mike couldn't quite believe the change.

"On his way, I would imagine. Where is Steph?"

"In the medical bay, unconscious. My mind flared as I woke, knocking her back. I think it was a reaction to whatever attacked me."

His voice was calm and unconcerned, no trace of guilt or emotion in his face, and Mike had to remind himself just who he was dealing with. Without a word, he was gone, passing Harpen in the doorway on his way to Steph's side.

Harpen stepped aside to let him pass, moving to sit beside Hal with a smile.

"You're looking well. Do you remember what happened?"

Hal nodded. "I need to go after him."

"After who?" Harpen asked, puzzled.

"The man who attacked me. He was...he had the power to drain me with a touch. We can't let that kind of power get away."

"A Vampire?"

"Yes," Hal lied, though he couldn't tell why, not even sure if he was lying. No one else could have that kind of power.

"You've just woken up. Give it some time..."

"No time," Hal shook his head. A vision was in his head, the man, the stranger with the terrifying power, sitting alone on the ground with a smile on his face. Behind him, skyscrapers loomed, a long artificial skyline of buildings in the distance. The man leaned forward, his smile wider, and Hal heard his voice in his own mind. *Six nights.*

He told Harpen none of this, unwilling to dwell on the reasons why, and refusing support as it was offered.

"I need to do this alone. Need to bring him down alone."

Harpen nodded after a long while, accepting Hal's pride as a reason for him to chase down this mysterious figure who had been able to best him. Hal knew, and he told Harpen, that it would not happen a second time. This seemed to be enough. Plus, Harpen knew that if Hal wanted it, it would happen with or without his consent.

Within an hour of waking, Hal was gone.

* * * * * * * * * *

Mike lifted Steph slowly into the bed, careful to avoid jarring her newly healed limbs. He had gone to work the moment he had found her, healing her broken bones in a matter of minutes but leaving her unconscious. Although substantial, her injuries were nothing to him, and he knew Hal had not intended to hurt her. If he had, she would have been in considerably worse shape. Or dead.

Harpen found him as he left the room, explaining briefly what had happened, and Mike simply nodded. Without permission, Hal would simply have gone anyway.

"You want me to follow him?"

Harpen shook his head. "I think it's best you're here when she wakes up. I've got Hunters on alert, they'll keep us posted, and Ralph is packing to follow him, just in case. Whoever this is will probably be dead by tomorrow."

Mike nodded, neither of them knowing how wrong he was.

* * * * * * * * * *

Hal had been still for a very long time, a cold mug of coffee in his hand and a pistol concealed beneath the hem of his jacket. The waitress had left him alone, accepting his money with a scared look and leaving him to his thoughts as he sat by the window to wait.

To watch.

Six nights, the man had said in his vision, seated on a street in Frankfurt City Centre. That street was now outside, and that sixth night was tonight.

Hal was flexing his mind, building up his mental defences with a series of meditations, readying himself for the inevitable confrontation. The memory of the attack was strong in his mind, and he analysed it, unpicking it and observing the energies within it piece by piece. It was not a Vampire, he was certain, although it carried a taste of familiar power that he couldn't quite place. What he was certain of was that it wouldn't bring him low again, his defences bolstered far above their normal levels. He was running a serious risk of detection, but he knew it was worth it, and he hadn't felt a Vampire nearby since his arrival.

The sun had slipped behind the horizon, the streets plunged into artificial light, when Hal, ejected from the Cafe after hours of waiting, felt something approach. People had passed him all evening, some crossing the street to avoid him, but he had paid them no heed, their presence barely worth his notice. This new presence was, however, and he concentrated, concealing himself and casting his mind out simultaneously. He realised belatedly that he had no visions of what was coming, not sure what that meant for him, but knowing he was committed now.

A man was walking down the street across from where Hal was seated, his hands in his pockets and a cigarette in his mouth. There was nothing remarkable about him at all, but Hal could feel the energy around him, a barely tangible air of power. Not a Vampire, he was certain, and also not the man from the Castle...

The man froze as Hal rose to his feet, drawing his pistol without ceremony and aiming it squarely at the stunned figure. His hands flew into the air, panic clearly written on his face, but Hal wasn't fooled. The power coming from him was unmistakable now, and no amount of play acting would fool Hal into thinking otherwise. Without a word, he gestured to the floor.

The man nodded, lowering himself carefully to the ground, pressing his face into the pavement. Hal stepped forward cautiously, hearing a strangled sob come from the man as he turned out his pockets, desperately throwing the contents at Hal's feet.

"This isn't a robbery," Hal began, but he faltered as something bounced against his foot, something round and dark. He glanced down, seeing a smooth black rock coming to rest on the street, and feeling the energy coming off it. His eyes shot to the man, and he realised his mistake. The energy had been coming from an Ildraya in the man's pocket.

Hal had just held up an ordinary man, with no trace of any power at all.

"Where did you get this?" he asked, picking up the stone while keeping his pistol trained on the man, not taking any chances until he was sure.

The answer was lost as Hal turned suddenly, his instincts screaming at him to duck without him being sure why, and he did so just in time as a sickle shaped blade flew over his head.

The man from the woods was smiling at him from a doorway nearby, and Hal would give him no chance this time. With a snarl, he gave chase.

* * * * * * * * * *

Simeon turned and ran back into the building, kicking open a door and darting through. His mind was working frantically as he ran, rapidly replanning as he realised he had no time to hide. He had underestimated the strength of this one, knew now that he would be perfect for their purposes, providing he passed the final tests.

Simeon passed through the building in seconds, diving from a first floor window and rolling to his feet. The Lemirda was close behind, and Simeon ran, widening the gap slowly, knowing that if he could reach somewhere more crowded, he would buy himself the time he needed.

* * * * * * * * * *

Hal was tireless in his pursuit, sprinting headlong through the streets, dashing through a wide open square and out onto the river bank. He veered right onto the path, watching as his quarry effortlessly vaulted a railway engine on display at the side of the road, and went after him. Despite his efforts and his own superhuman physique, Hal was falling behind, but he kept doggedly on, dodging the few people out at this hour of the night, ignoring their curses as he went.

The man veered off again, leaving the river behind and heading back into the city. Hal followed, but faltered after a short while, his mind reeling. The man was gone, lost in the crowd of people outside the railway station in front of him, and Hal realised that he couldn't even sense him, that there was nothing to differentiate him from any other person.

He slowed to a walking pace, his breathing controlled despite the frantic chase, and his eyes scanning the crowd around him. The smile was visible for a moment, and Hal went for him, dashing down a set of stairs into a wide open shopping concourse beneath the station. It was closed and deserted at this time of night, and Hal spotted his target immediately, standing with that bland smile and blood on his fist.

The body of a woman lay at his feet.

Hal paused, thrown by this bizarre development, knowing that if he gave chase the man would simply flee again and unsure of how to proceed. The answer was taken from him when the man turned and vanished around a corner.

Hal covered the ground in a few steps, glancing left and right down the concourse and seeing no movement. He spared a glance for the dead woman, and was about to head off again when a voice cried out a warning behind him. Hal turned, belatedly noticing the two men pointing weapons at him. Local law enforcement, their faces hard, yelling at him to get on the floor. He glanced again at the body by his feet, realising how this looked and just how cleverly he had been set up.

His options had been reduced massively by this move. His best course was to surrender now, give himself up in the confident knowledge that this could be overturned in a matter of days by way of any number of faked documents issued by Hunter HQ. He had done it before, but he did not have several days now. He could just run, knowing he could outpace them and heal any damage they might cause him in a matter of hours. But he was in the city centre, and even now he could hear sirens as more police closed in on his location. Escape undetected, unharmed, and most importantly, quickly enough, would be impossible, even for a man of his talents.

The logical course was clear, the only way he could continue this chase, knowing that if he didn't the man would be lost forever.

Faster than the two men could follow, Hal pulled out his gun and fired.

* * * * * * * * * *

James Harpen shook his head as Ralph cut the link, staring at the blank screen for a few moments. Not Hal. Not him.

This was not good.

He found Mike where he expected, alongside Steph in the medical centre. He reflected briefly that he had let this go on too long, but he was passed that now, all his attention on Hal.

"Hal has gone rogue," he said without preamble, not caring that Steph was awake, his normally unflappable demeanour gone. Mike rose to his feet, concern on his face, but not, Harpen noted, disbelief.

"What's he done?"

"Robbed a man in Frankfurt, beaten a woman to death in the railway station, then shot the two police officers who tried to bring him in. He disappeared after that. Ralph just let me know. The trail is getting cold, and we need to go. Get your things."

"I don't believe it," Mike said firmly. "Not Hal. He couldn't..."

He turned as Steph took his hand, seeing the look in her eyes. He had explained to her how and why she had been injured, and she seemed to have believed it, but now that faith was shattered. Her voice was weak as she spoke, more from emotion than her injuries, he suspected.

"He could."

"He had a damn good reason then," Mike said, and to Steph's surprise, Harpen nodded in agreement.

She didn't react as Mike kissed her and ran from the room.

* * * * * * * * * *

The chase had ended suddenly, an anti-climax after all he had gone through. Hal had slipped through the web of law enforcement with ease, picking up the trail so easily he suspected it had been deliberately left for him to follow.

When he came across the smiling man seated on a park bench waiting for him, he was sure.

His first reaction was to go for his gun, but the man waved it away dismissively, gesturing to the seat beside him.

"You have tried attacking me, you know how it ends. If you lay a hand on me you will be unconscious again, and I will disappear. Forever, this time."

Hal sat, on edge, but the man made no attempt to attack. His posture was casual, his hands resting in his lap, and even this close, Hal could detect nothing from him. He was, as far as Hal could tell, an ordinary human. But that was impossible.

"Who are you?"

"My name is Simeon of the Fratriae. You are Hal Lemirda, son of Victor, the great seer of the Vampire Hunters and a terrifyingly potent killer. My greetings to you."

The man bowed his head slightly. Hal didn't react.

"You know a great deal."

"Secrets are my business. Many of yours, mostly mine," he said, his smile broadened for a moment.

"Let's start with yours then. This...chase. Everything since the castle. A challenge, a test. For what purpose?"

"To test your worthiness."

"Worthiness for what?"

The man didn't answer at first.

"You have a great many talents, Hal Lemirda. As do we. We share a common enemy, after a fashion. We can help each other."

"Why?"

Simeon seemed surprised by the question.

"Because we share a common enemy. Or if you prefer, because we can offer you knowledge and power beyond that which you already possess. We can even offer you what you most wish for."

Hal raised his head. "And what is that?"

"The same thing your line always seems to have wanted. A challenge worthy of your skills. A challenge that will give you the exhilaration you crave, the thrill denied to you in so many of your hunts."

Hal leaned back.

"And in exchange?"

"Information."

"Regarding?"

Simeon's smile faded. "The Vampiri Family."

"They're extinct," Hal said, remembering his training. No Hunter had met one in hundreds of years.

"So your people believe. We know better."

"Then you know better than me. I can't help."

"You have a unique gift, Lemirda. One shared only by your bloodline."

"Prophecy." Hal said, beginning to understand. Simeon nodded.

"Our offer to enhance your powers benefits us as well as you."

"What happens if I say yes?"

"You come with me now, and we will strike an accord. You may name your terms, within reason, and we will endeavour to meet them. All we ask at this stage is a guarantee of complete secrecy."

Hal thought for a moment, then nodded.

* * * * * * * * * *

Simeon led him to an unassuming car nearby, not saying another word as he drove them away. The sun had risen as they left the city, and Hal noted that his companion was not troubled by it.

"I am not a Vampire," Simeon said, clearly noticing his gaze. "And in my own way I hate them more than you do. My hatred is just more...localised."

"To the Vampiri Family."

Simeon refused to say another word, and they drove for several hours towards the East. It was midmorning when Simeon stopped the car inside a thick forest, turning to Hal with a smile.

"Now you may meet the Fratriae."

Hal stepped from the car warily, sensing nothing in the forest around him. Simeon laughed.

"We are very good at hiding. Siblings, the Lemirda is here to meet you."

Hal watched as figures appeared from the woods, ordinary men and women in every respect, all of them sturdily built and dark skinned. Their eyes regarded him closely, and he met each of their gazes one by one, seeing just a hint of the strength of each of them. One man he recognised, the man he had robbed the night before, and Simeon laughed.

"Julius is one of us."

Julius nodded and smiled. "Greetings, Lemirda. I believe you have something of mine to return."

Wordlessly, Hal passed him the Ildraya, before seating himself on the ground. Around him, the thirty brothers and sisters of the Fratriae sat also, their attention riveted on him. He couldn't bring himself to accept that they were of the same breed as Simeon, but as he looked around, he realised that now he couldn't sense them, even with them sitting right there.

"Tell me who you are. You cannot be human."

"We are not. We are creatures of the Vampiri, bred as weapons, as the ultimate warrior. Unkillable, immortal, possessing great strength and an immunity to sorcery – as you yourself have seen," Simeon smiled again, and Hal felt vividly the memory of the blast that had knocked him out.

"The Vampiri were masters of creation, fashioning beasts and monsters with ease, twisting people into ever more creative forms. After the Laumpir rebellion, the Vampiri turned their genius to different ends, and created the Fratriae as servants, slaves, agents who could pass undetected among humans and do their bidding in the daylight."

Hal made no reaction.

"What went wrong?"

"We chose another path."

Hal could feel a chilling undercurrent of tension in his voice, wondering how long they had carried this anger against their creators, knowing it must be hundreds if not thousands of years.

"You rebelled?"

"We defended ourselves. The Vampiri set out to wipe us out, to destroy us, and we fought back. They had designed us too well, and we broke from confinement and destroyed our creators."

"It seems you did a good job..." Hal began, but Simeon cut him off.

"The Family exists still. We killed but a fraction of their most able, and the rest fled, fearing us. They went underground, and disappeared. We have hunted them ever since. We have no interest in your war, no interest in the other Families. I will make no secret that we have allies there, scattered across the five families. We trade knowledge for knowledge and we do not care where that knowledge comes from. We care only for our task."

"If your only loyalty is to yourselves and your task, how can I trust you?"

"You cannot, but you are of more value than anyone. That we gave up some of our most valued allies to lure you in should be proof enough. And be reassured, we have no reason to turn against your people unless you choose to side with the Vampiri."

"That isn't likely," Hal said drily.

"Just so," Simeon rose to his feet, followed by the others. Hal remained seated.

"There is one final test Lemirda, then we may be allies. We will give you power, allow you greater control of your visions, and a challenge worthy of you, and in exchange, you will furnish us with locations as you see them, and you will keep our very existence a secret from even your closest fellows. You may accept this as a sign of our good intentions."

Hal caught the Ildraya as it was thrown, feeling the power contained within.

"We recovered this from your father's body in the remains of a hotel in Italy fifteen years ago. It is designed for your bloodline."

Even then, Hal couldn't look surprised.

"You are by no means the first Lemirda we have worked with. We will see you in one week."

With that, the Fratriae were gone, disappearing into the trees without a sound. Hal considered going after them, but knew it would be a wasted effort.

He rose to feet and headed for the road, pondering this strange turn of events. There was no guile in his new allies, no trickery that he could see. The Hunters were unaware of them, that much was true, and their story seemed to add up. Hal could feel his body course with anticipation at the prospect of a challenge, and he reasoned rightly that what they offered would benefit the Hunters immensely. And as Simeon had said, the Vampiri were common enemy, even if the Hunters had stopped fighting them a long time before.

Hal paused suddenly, his senses warning him of figures ahead, but he was not unduly concerned in the middle of the day. A moment later, he realised what it was as a familiar face emerged from hiding ahead of him.

"Hello Hal," Mike said, his voice strangely quiet. Hal glanced to one side, seeing Ralph Tyler training a weapon on him, then realising there were others behind him. One by one, the Brothers of the Order emerged, surrounding him.

"Are you here to kill me?"

"No Hal," Harpen said from behind him. "Just to understand. Will you come with us back to the HQ?"

Hal nodded, but didn't say another word.

* * * * * * * * * *

He was left alone for a full day after their return, kept but not locked in his own room. He did not try to leave, understanding their wariness around him, but he knew he could not explain.

He had only one visitor in that time. Steph walked timidly into the room, seemingly unwilling to stray too far from the open door. Hal supposed he couldn't blame her.

"They told me you killed people, Hal. Normal people. Innocent people."

Hal locked his gaze on hers, shrugging.

"I did."

That seemed to hit her, as if confirming what she had hoped was a horrible nightmare or lie, and she burst into tears.

"What did these Hunters do to you to make you like this?"

Hal shrugged again.

"Nothing."

* * * * * * * * * *

Harpen came to see him eventually, and Hal didn't have to ask what had caused the delay as he dropped a thick folder on the table. Hal opened it, finding witness statements, CCTV photos, police reports, blood samples, all of it from the supposed crime scene and all of it pointing squarely at him as the one and only culprit. The Fratriae covered their tracks well.

"Will you explain this to me?"

Hal didn't reply. Harpen sat down heavily.

"Hal, we have executed Hunters for less than you have done. You should know that some have suggested that. A few are in favour of locking you up permanently. Collateral damage is one thing. We could overlook that, but outright murder? This is beyond you."

"What do you think?"

Harpen looked perplexed. "What?"

"Some want me dead. Some locked up. I can see why. But not you. What are you thinking?"

Harpen sighed. "I think there is more going on here. I think, despite your mental state, or maybe because of it, you aren't a murderer. And I think you have friends in high places."

Hal inclined his head slightly, the closest he came to puzzled.

"Karl Laumpir contacted me. He told me to trust you, and to not ask questions."

Harpen paused, and the hurt in his face was clear as he went on.

"And he told me there are powers that even I cannot be made aware of."

Hal was silent, unsure of what to say. Harpen just smiled grimly.

"Lucky for you I trust him. Lucky for you I believe in you. Whatever you do from here, don't give me a reason not to."

Hal considered this, then nodded once.

* * * * * * * * * *

Mike watched as Harpen strode into the common room, a smile on his face that didn't reach his eyes. Wordlessly, Mike passed him a drink, and he downed it before turning to Steph, a sympathetic look in his eyes.

"I think it's best you went home. You've stayed too long here anyway, and I think that as long as you're around Hal..."

"What will you do with him?" she interrupted suddenly, her voice cold. Mike looked at her, confusion evident in his eyes.

"What do you mean?"

"A trial. A...court martial. Something other than just sitting him a room. Something for murdering those people."

"What would you have us do?"

"I don't know. But you can't just cover this up. Can you?"

She saw the look in their eyes, and she didn't need an answer.

"Oh my god...you've done this before, haven't you?"

Mike met her gaze and held it.

"Yes."

"But...how can you do that? You can't just be above the law!"

"We can and we have to be," Harpen said quietly, conviction in his voice. "We are Vampire Hunters, we do this to protect people..."

"From what!?" she cried suddenly, her voice cracking. "All I've seen is the damage *you've* done! Murders, cover ups, your oh so fancy tricks as you swan about swimming in money. How is that any better? How can you be so arrogant as to think you're above everyone else, that the rules don't apply to you?"

"You have no idea," Mike said gently. "What they're capable of. They kill, they enslave, they feed. They steal people and force them into servitude..."

"Like you did with Hal."

Mike shook his head.

"We do this for the right reasons. Our enemy is ancient and powerful, and they are a very real threat. Is my word not enough for you?"

"Not anymore," she whispered. "How can I possibly forgive this? How can I go on loving you when I know you *can* forgive this? I was willing to put up with so much. You took my brother from me and I forgave you. I even forgave you for what your people did to my mother..."

"I don't know what you mean," Mike said, too quickly, and Steph was amazed at just how poor the lie was.

"I'm not an idiot Mike. You knew what was wrong with her when you first saw her. Every time I mention her you look guilty. I may not know what killed her, but you do, and I suspect it is closer to home than you dare admit."

Mike fell silent, unable to meet her gaze, and she knew it was true. She had pretended to ignore it for years, hadn't intended to bring it up now, but a part of her was glad she had forced him to admit it at last.

"What is she talking about?" Harpen muttered, one eyebrow raised. Mike sighed deeply.

"Steph's mother had been given Clairian root."

"Ah," was all Harpen said.

"It's a degenerative poison," Mike explained to Steph, clearly unburdening himself. "Hal's father must have given it to her to ensure she delivered Hal to whoever was supposed to meet her. She would have been given the antidote then, but she never met him. By the time I met you, it was no good."

"And you think this is ok!?" she screamed, storming across the room and turning back to face him, red with anger.

"No," he said firmly. "But Victor must have thought that was the best way to keep Hal safe."

"There it is again! The rest of the world can rot as long as you get your way. Never mind laws, or decency, you're all so far above that!"

"I don't expect you to understand."

"Good! Because I don't! And don't you dare try to talk to me about Vampires or danger. You turned my brother into a monster. You killed my mother. My whole life has been ruined because of you, and then you just hide it all away because it suits *you*!"

She slammed down into the chair, tears running down her face. This had been pent up for years, and now she had unleashed it all in a single storm of fury.

Mike was genuinely crushed, knowing her accusations were all justified, but knowing that she could never properly understand. It wasn't arrogance, just a proper realisation of the threat. But he knew he could never explain that.

"I'm sorry," he said sincerely, but she just stared at him with hatred in her eyes.

"Let me out. Send me home. Then never contact me again."

* * * * * * * * * *

Hal knew none of this, already having departed once again. This time, he was allowed to go without anyone tailing him, and he acknowledged how much easier that made his work. He knew he could slip away from any one they sent after him anyway.

He considered how easily Harpen had let him go, knowing how close he had come to censure or execution. For all the Hunters were above the law, they were still self-regulating, and those Hunters that occasionally went off the rails were invariably brought back or brought down in fairly short order. Karl Laumpir's word carried great weight, however, and Hal knew that was the sole cause of his freedom to act. He had no idea how deeply Karl was involved with the Fratriae, and he didn't much care.

He spent a week in limbo, travelling aimlessly from place to place. He made no attempt to contact the others, no attempt to hunt, merely waiting for the contact he knew must come.

Seven days to the hour from his last meeting, Simeon was waiting.

Hal had passed through Europe slowly, moving from country to country with no real sense of direction. The Fratriae had given him no details, and he was content that they would find him, given the aptitude they had so far displayed. He was not disappointed. As if it was purely a coincidence, as Hal strode through a tiny building onto a rundown Romanian railway platform, Simeon was there, leaning back with a smile on his face.

"Greetings Lemirda. The final test is passed."

Hal nodded.

"I accept your offer."

* * * * * * * * * *

They boarded the next train to arrive, and Hal found himself wondering just how they had planned this when they alighted several stops down and Simeon led him to a deserted factory complex near the railway line. Inside, they made their way through rusting machinery to a large open space on the top floor, where several of the Fratriae were waiting. Hal resisted the urge to draw his weapon when he saw a Strigoi Vampire with them, realising immediately she was chained securely to a massive stone pillar in the centre of the room, her gaze fixed on him despite her having no eyes with which to see him.

Now he understood.

"This is Vicky," Simeon said lightly, waving the Fratriae away from her. "She will be helping us today."

"I served you," she hissed suddenly. Hal felt the build-up of power, watching as a black mist erupted from her outstretched hands and enveloped Simeon, but he was unconcerned as it seemed to just dissipate around him.

"And you serve us still," Simeon's voice was condescending, as if speaking to a child. "Please do not attack me again, you have seen what will happen, and it demeans us both."

"What is going on?" Hal asked, more curious than anything else.

"We need power, Lemirda. Life force is needed for what we require, and who better to provide it, who better as a statement of our commitment to you, than one of your own enemies?"

Hal just nodded, feeling nothing for the victim or his new allies. Without ceremony or ritual, Simeon took a sickle shaped blade from one of his men and decapitated her with one blow.

"This will unlock the potential in your mind. Your people know of your gifts, but it seems that they do not know how to properly utilise them. We will show you how you may do so."

Hal could feel the power in the room suddenly grow, feeling the Fratriae harness it and direct it, passing from the body of the Strigoi through Simeon's mind and into his, refined and altered into a form he had never known, as different to his Brother's auras as they were from the energy of the Vampire families.

"This will hurt," he heard Simeon say dimly, the roaring of the energy around him reaching a thundering crescendo, and he just nodded, steeling himself.

With a sudden shift, the energy plunged into him, lancing pain into every cell of his body, and he cried out involuntarily as agony he had never known burned through him. Just as he thought he would black out, the pain was gone, and with it, the world around him.

* * * * * * * * * *

He found himself standing by a river, a thick leather cloak wrapped around his body. His hand was enclosed by a heavy gauntlet, a stone spike protruding from either side of his fist. He glanced around, noting the figures around him, cautiously stepping out onto the river bank, equally archaic weapons in their hands. They were young, so young, but he could feel the power in them, knew they were more than they appeared. He turned to his companion, a perfect likeness of Kym Malum, and the two of them stepped forward and waded into the river. They were up to their waists when Vampires appeared on the far bank, launching themselves into the river. Hal and the Malum Brother turned to flee, even as their companions launched projectiles across the river.

* * * * * * * * * *

He was running alone through a tangle of rocks, effortlessly leaping from tor to tor as he made his way higher up the moonlit hillside. Ahead of him, a deeper shadow resolved itself into a cleft in the rocks and he ducked inside, finding a web of tunnels extending downward. He didn't break step, dashing through the darkened tunnels until he came across a cave, empty but for a single Kappa Vampire. He smiled as he attacked.

* * * * * * * * * *

He was standing atop a wall, armoured in some sort of light weight alloy, a sword in his hand forged from the same dull material. He saw the world through narrow eyes slits in a full face helmet, seeing the hordes of armed figures manning the walls around him. Many of them were children, and he realised who they were as Karl Laumpir appeared beside him, younger than Hal had known him. These were the Laumpirs before their extinction, when Karl himself had been young.

He understood.

* * * * * * * * * *

On and on the visions came, brief flashes of the lives his ancestors had known, of the visions they had had. He lived through hundreds of the Lemirda prophecies in a matter of minutes, and with each one, he could feel the visions become stronger as he understood the power, seeing it through the eyes of his ancestors. His mind reeling, he saw the final image, a yellow flag fluttering before a sun that was just beginning to set, a baby handed to a woman, a vial of poison given with it. The image shifted suddenly, and Hal saw fire and the flash of blades, felt the blow that had killed his father.

His eyes snapped open.

He could feel a humming in the back of his head as the power Simeon had unleashed receded. He rose to his feet, not remembering sitting down, and saw the Fratriae staring at him.

"What now?" he asked, knowing this could not be over, barely feeling any different.

"You will find you have greater control of your visions, be able to pull them to mind with greater ease, and see more than you previously could. But to be of any use to us, you must be linked to my brothers. By seeing their future, you will shape it."

Hal understood perfectly, not even flinching as Simeon took the blade, still dripping with the blood of the Strigoi, and sliced the tip down the length of Hal's forearm. Hal felt his skin begin to heal immediately, but not before Simeon had repeated the process with his two acolytes. Hal watched as the flat of the blade was pressed against the open wound on his arm, the blood of the two men passing into his own even as the cut closed. Not even a scar was left.

He concentrated, willing his mind to see, and almost immediately, a vision appeared in his head.

* * * * * * * * * *

It took them almost two days to reach their destination, and in that time Hal had built up a decent impression of his new companions. Iago and Hector were focussed and driven individuals, completely subservient to Simeon, but they were capable combatants, as he found out in the midst of a hectic sparring session in the bowels of a ship. It seemed to Hal that the Fratriae had no means of travel of their own as the Hunters did, but they seemed to do fine without it. When Hal asked, Simeon had merely shrugged.

"It is very hard to find us, no matter where we are. We go where we will."

In the time Hal spent with them, he found nothing that made them stand out, nothing to mark them as extraordinary in any way.

Until they arrived.

Hal's vision had guided them to Italy, taking them straight to the remains of a rural church in the hills east of Rome. The ship they had travelled on had docked on the east coast, and a car had been waiting for them, unlocked and with the keys already in the ignition. Hal had furnished them with the details of his vision, and they had simply known where to go from his description of the surrounding area, apparently recognising the features he described without any trouble, despite their claims to have never been there. Yet another mystery to go unsolved.

As he had seen, Hal raised a flagstone seemingly at random, revealing an entrance to catacombs that had clearly been sealed for centuries. Even to Hal's inexperienced eyes, the tunnels seemed to predate the church that had been built over them, and he realised what was amiss.

How do they feed?

His companions didn't reply, and Hal realised they could not hear his thoughts when he projected them, their immunity to sorcery being apparently total. Instead, he tapped Simeon lightly, seeing a furious gaze turn on him sharply. Hal was unthreatened by it, but shook his head nonetheless, leaving the issue for later. As it happened, the answer was waiting for him anyway.

The three Fratriae had changed when they drew close to the lair, their posture and features becoming twisted, quivering with barely restrained rage. Hal could see the blood pounding beneath their skin, see their fists clench and unclench in anticipation of the killing to come, and he began to see the depth of loathing these men had carried with them for centuries. They began to run as they drew closer to the end, loping along with bounding strides, their eyes flashing in the darkness, and Hal ran with them, feeling the thrill of the hunt course through him. They reached a door, clearly put in place hundreds of years before, but the Fratriae didn't slow, smashing it to kindling with feral howls and bursting into the room beyond.

Hal's trained eyes took it all in in moments, taking in every detail of the vast circular room without even pausing in his charge. At its centre was a fire pit, dormant now but with a large black cauldron suspended above it. Around that, arranged in a series of concentric circles, rough stone blocks were laid out, and on each of them was the remains of a different creature. Some Hal recognised, but most were either too alien or too mutilated for him to even begin to guess what they were. Here and there among the blocks were pillars the height of a man, topped with bulbous fleshy mounds that seemed to pulse and shift as if alive. Suspended from the ceiling were dozens of cages, each one containing a living creature, but of these, Hal didn't recognise a single one, seeing a bewildering array of feathers and scales and fur, some with tentacles, some with wings, all of them screeching at the slaughter taking place beneath them

And slaughter it was. Hal had caught glimpses of it in his vision, and had seen years of combat, but the scene before him was unlike anything he had witnessed.

The Vampiri were half starved mockeries of the Vampires he had fought and bested, elongated limbs ending in hooked and calloused hands, faces pinched and hollow. Their mouths were empty but for a pair of fangs, their lips and gums bloodied and raw. There was almost twenty of them, lurching from alcoves around the room, and Hal noticed with interest that they made no attempt to fight, instead screaming and fleeing for the door, apparently willing to run out into the sunlight rather than face their killers.

But the Fratriae were everywhere at once, seizing their victims with bare hands and dashing them against the walls and the floor, shattering limbs and ribs and skulls, tearing chunks from their flesh and devouring it raw with howls of savage glee. One by one the Vampiri died in agony, and Hal watched as they were consumed, not just their bodies, but their very life force taken by the Fratriae in an orgy of murderous rage.

He was impressed. Twenty Vampires in a matter of minutes was no mean feat, even starved as they seemed to be, even in daytime. He felt no emotional reaction to the horror of the scene, merely seeing a vanquished foe and a victorious ally.

Simeon was smiling again, his body relaxed and his features calm, despite the blood and gore smeared across his body. The change was instantaneous as the last Vampiri fell, he and his two companions straightening up and resuming their unassuming demeanour as simply as flicking a switch, only a slight frown on his face as he glanced upward to where the creatures were still screeching in fear or hatred or hunger. This twisted suddenly to his killing face, and he leapt, tearing the first cage from the roof and dashing it to the floor, the killing resuming for a few moments as the works of the Vampiri were destroyed.

Only then did he turn to face Hal.

"They are a blight to life. They build mockeries of creatures in their workshops with no regard to sanity or decency. They feed on the scraps of their own creations, experimenting with ever more twisted forms of life, and we will destroy them wherever we can find them."

Hal said nothing, wondering if Simeon noticed the contradiction posed by what he said and what he was.

* * * * * * * * * *

Mike killed without enthusiasm, pinning the Vampire to the floor with one foot, watching the smoke curl from the bullet hole in his neck for a second before stabbing down with a wooden stake. He waited for a moment until the body was still, then shifted his foot, glancing up at the terrified face that peeked out from behind the bed.

The target site was unusual, a well-kept ranch house in Colorado, one of two properties that lay side by side in a valley, miles from the nearest main road. He had come alone, leaving his car beyond a nearby ridge, approaching during the night and lying up in wait, but he had been forced to engage sooner than he had hoped, hours before the sunrise. Lights had come on in one of the buildings, a wooden ranch house that had obviously been converted into an attractive retreat for some wealthy family, given the cars that were parked outside. Mike hadn't reacted, until he had heard the screams.

He knew most Hunters would have ignored them, willing to sacrifice for the greater good, and knowing how dangerous it was to run headlong into the unknown.

He was not most Hunters.

The door had been hanging open, the lock smashed, and Mike had gone straight in, trusting in his instincts to keep him safe. The Vampire had been upstairs, unaware of him, along with three humans, one of them seconds from death by the flickering shadow in his aura.

He had taken the stairs in three bounds, pistol and knife already in hand, vaulting a dead adult male with a fractured skull and a broken arm, turning on one heel and bursting into the first bedroom. The bright blue walls were sprayed with blood as he entered, arcing from the neck of a girl as the Vampire had pulled away from her, his mouth stained with crimson.

Mike had fired, dropping the Kappa with a throat shot, killing him a moment later before turning his attention to the girl behind the bed. She was shaking, terrified, her hair unkempt and blood dripping from the wound in her throat, staining the pale shirt she was wearing.

He faltered for a moment. She was the same age Steph had been when he had met her, and he was painfully aware that this could have so easily been her, a nameless victim, brutalised by Vampires and covered up by Hunters. He saw himself as she must see him now, as Steph might easily have seen him, a murderer who had emerged from the night standing over the body of a creature who should exist only in nightmares.

Most Hunters would have fled at that point, using their web of contacts and cover ups to conceal everything, pervert the witness accounts, and lay false trails to remove them from existence. Some, like Hal or Kym, would have been more direct, using threats to keep the story covered. Harpen, uniquely, could have just reached into their minds, removing any trace of the incident and leaving the family with nothing with a blurred memory.

None of these were Mike's way.

He sheathed his weapons, holding up his hands, palm outward, as he stepped forward. The girl flinched, backing away on all fours into the corner, whimpering to herself. He heard screaming behind him as the third person, the mother, emerged and found her husband dead in the passageway. Mike ignored her and spoke to the girl, his tone soothing.

"If you let me, I can help, and stop the bleeding in your neck."

She didn't react, but didn't resist as he reached forward and brushed his hand over her throat. At his touch, her neck was healed, smooth skin still marred by the dark blood stains, and her face calmed a little. A second later, Mike ducked, warned by the widening of her eyes, easily avoiding the bat swinging for his head.

He resisted the split second urge to go for his weapons again, instead simply catching the bat as it swung for him a second time and pulling it away from his attacker, a slim middle aged woman wrapped in a thick dressing gown. She stepped away from him, tripping with a scream and crawling to where her daughter lay, still cowering on the floor.

Mike looked at them both sadly, knowing this one night had changed their lives forever. He thought, as he always did, about staying for a while, helping them to piece their lives back together, but knowing ultimately that such a decision was not the right one. Nothing he could do would make things any better.

That was the story of his life, an endless tide of suffering that he couldn't prevent, and for a moment, he pictured Steph as the girl on the floor, feeling the guilt of the damage he had done to her. That thought made up his mind, and without a word, he picked up the dead Vampire and walked from the house.

It was better that he left now: Better for them, better for him, better for all the victims of this war that he kept them at arm's reach. Although he had known that all along, Steph, more than anyone, had made it clear.

That still didn't make it easy.

* * * * * * * * * * *

Hal remained with the Fratriae for several weeks, guiding them in that time to two more lairs, each as well hidden as the first. He found that he could feel nothing even when right outside, feel no trace of the Vampires within, and he saw clearly why the Hunters never found them. Each time the Fratriae would go berserk, tearing into the lairs with an animal rage and destroying everything within, sucking the lifeforce from their hated enemies and destroying their physical forms. Never once did Hal see them take a wound, and each time they would revert to normal the moment the last Vampire fell.

Between Hunts they were content to simply travel, moving from place to place with no real purpose, sleeping where they could and passing unnoticed wherever they went. Hal never once saw them eat anything other than Vampiri flesh, and yet they seemed not to notice, apparently not requiring any other sustenance than their irregular feasts. They were not especially interesting company, but neither was Hal himself, and they worked well together, although he was beginning to grow weary of the aimless wandering, even punctuated as it was by short bouts of vicious slaughter. He was not permitted to kill any Vampiri, the Fratriae reserving that right for themselves, and he missed the thrill. At the same time, his visions no longer contained the

Fratriae or Vampiri, instead reverting to what they had been before, albeit clearer and longer, visions of his own hunts.

Simeon seemed to notice, nodding as if he had expected this and dismissing Hal as they left the third lair.

"You leave with our thanks, Lemirda. Please, accept this as a token of gratitude."

Hal took the box as it was offered, raising an eyebrow. It was unadorned, a blank metal tin with no visible markings, and Simeon gestured him to wait.

"We promised you challenges in return for your aid," Simeon said simply. "This will guide you thusly. Return to your life, use the gifts we have granted, but be aware – You will see more in time that will be of use to us. When you do, we will find you, and you will be compensated for your time."

With that, he was gone, leaving Hal alone with the box. Removing the lid, he found a shard of glass inside, with a map precisely inscribed upon its surface in what could only be blood. At the centre of the map was the Kappa Family crest.

A vision came unbidden into his mind, himself locked in a fierce struggle with half a dozen Kappas, surrounded and pressed on all sides. He could see from a glimpse this would be a battle worthy of his skills, a battle that would let him feel something worth feeling.

The thrill was addictive.

* * * * * * * * * *

Part Three – Lemirda Unleashed

James Harpen surveyed the scene before him with a critical eye. Many of the details were familiar by now – The bodies, the wreckage, the lack of any evidence to point him to the killer - with only the setting being different each time. They only knew it was Hal because of the messages they had received, a few curt lines passed to Hunter's in the area and from there to Harpen himself.

This was the fourth such scene Harpen had attended in a little over two months, and he was beginning to be troubled. The lairs were well hidden, even by the standards the Hunters were used to, and contained more Vampires than usually could be found in one place. That Hal had found them was remarkable, that he had walked away miraculous, but Harpen's concern came from the fact that he *had* just walked away. There had been no attempt to clean up, to dispose of the bodies, or to even hide them. Hal had never cared much for that side of their work, but these were not normal hunts – the bizarrely roundabout communication and Hal's curious reticence to return to the other Hunters made that clear – and Hal was being more reckless than usual. He had no support, no back up, no one who even knew where he was from day to day, but he seemed to be throwing himself into the most dangerous hunts and just assuming others would pick up the pieces.

The fact that they were doing just that was beside the point.

Harpen idly picked his way through the building, an abandoned petrol station somewhere in northern Russia, noting the key features of the fight with a detached air, piecing together the sequence of events with an ease of long experience. The front door was smashed off its hinges, lying against the wall where it landed, on the far side of the room. The room had been occupied, a pair of Vampires reacting immediately, but they had barely held Hal off. The rest had put up a stronger fight, holding a series of rooms in the rear of the building, as attested by the upturned and shattered furniture scattered around. In the rearmost room, however, Harpen found one chair righted again, a notch in the wall beside it where a knife point had been stuck. Hal had sat here to wait for another Vampire to return, which suggested he had known how many were meant to be here.

Interesting.

He turned as Ralph appeared in the doorway, his face its usual mask of bored complacency, his voice equally so.

"Quite a hit, this. At night, too,"

"He's done well," Harpen agreed, although his features betraying his concern.

"What are you thinking? Do we bring him in?"

"He's done nothing wrong," Harpen shrugged. "And would you like to try?"

Ralph made no response, and the two men went about disposing of the bodies, dragging them together and sprinkling them with purpose designed fuel. A concoction of the Oburs, the substance burned the bodies in minutes, leaving no trace of ash or even a scorch mark on the floor, and they left the building empty.

Harpen paused outside, barely noticing the cold wind, examining the marks in the snow in front of the building. Any foot prints were long covered up, but a set of parallel grooves was still visible.

"He's got his own transport then," Ralph nodded, clearly following the same train of thought. That was one question answered at least. Hal hadn't made use of a single Hunter transport since their aircraft had dropped him back in Frankfurt.

Harpen had to admit that there was too much here that didn't make sense, and he hated the enforced ignorance. Hal's achievements were incredible feats of skill, worthy of praise and recognition and accolades if he brought them to light himself. Instead, he was moving on in secret, acting as if he had something to hide, leaving only a trail of clues that allowed them to follow at a distance and nothing more. It would all make perfect sense if he had gone off the rails and was slaughtering innocents, but as far as Harpen could tell, he was doing exactly what he was supposed to be. Unless there were piles of corpses Hal *was* disposing of, he thought darkly. He dismissed the thought immediately, knowing they would be aware if that was the case, but still he was concerned. Hal had been away far too long without contact, and Harpen knew what he was capable of. It was time to get him back, but there was only way he could think of to make that happen.

"Let's get going. I have to speak with Karl Laumpir."

* * * * * * * * * *

Harpen had served as a Hunter for decades, and had been face to face with hundreds of Vampires in that time. Most, he had been trying to kill, locked in a life or death struggle that few men could survive. Many had been Oburs, who with few exceptions were blank, single minded of purpose and lacking in any depth of personality.

Karl Laumpir was the exception. As driven as the Oburs, capable of heights of rage and passion that no human could match, he was at the same time capable of great charm, intelligent insight, and appreciation of the finer things in life.

It was the latter that was most obvious to Harpen as he sat in an elaborately appointed study in a beautifully built mansion, a glass of wine in his hand and a log fire burning at the end of the room. Only the crystal sword hanging above the fire and the goblet of blood in his host's hand gave away the truth.

Karl was, to all appearances, a young man of indeterminate age, a smiling youth dressed in a collarless shirt and white linen trousers, leaning back with an easy going attitude and a confident air.

Harpen knew better of course, knowing that even a fraction of Karl's achievements outshone his own many times over. He had survived the death of the whole Laumpir family, holding together the Vampire Hunters by sheer force of will for hundreds of years, and surviving who knew how many attempts on his life by a Vampire family that had been created to kill his.

Harpen felt nothing but awe.

"Sorry I delayed you," the Vampire was saying as he settled into his armchair. "I've had a few things to clear up here."

"Ralph told me a little," Harpen nodded, having heard something of events nearby.

"I assumed you were here to discuss those events," Karl said, faint curiosity in his voice. "Is there another matter?"

"There is," Harpen nodded, choosing his words carefully. Karl had been clear about the need for secrecy. "I wanted to ask you about what has happened to one of my men. Hal Lemirda."

"The Hunters are your business, James. I would hate to presume knowledge beyond yours."

His tone was friendly, his face open and honest, but Harpen wouldn't be put off.

"Not in this case, I feel."

Karl leaned forward suddenly, placing his glass down and steepling his fingers as he fixed his gaze on the Hunter. Harpen met it without flinching.

"There are secrets here, James. You understand better than anyone how important that is."

"I am aware of the importance of secrets. However, I also have a Hunter who has cut himself off entirely after killing innocents pursuing a secret agenda, with no guarantee he won't do it again."

"Would my guarantee be enough?"

"Can you give it?" Harpen countered immediately.

Karl pondered this for a moment, then shook his head.

"The Lemirda's have always been difficult. Too much glee in killing, no colour in the rest of their lives. They have never been psychopathic, but it could happen, I suppose, if the targets dried up, or if they became too easy."

"They're becoming too easy," Harpen said, thinking of the battle sites he had found so far. "And Hal is not like his forebears. They never killed innocent people. Not directly."

Karl paced the room for a moment, pondering this, and Harpen waited patiently. He struggled to imagine the life Karl had known, struggled to come to terms with just how much he had seen over the years. The Vampire sighed suddenly, undecided.

"You have been a good friend to me, James, as has your family. They will not thank me for this, but you deserve better."

"Who?"

"A well kept secret, one that I and others have kept for many generations. They live in secret, known only to those whom they choose. But perhaps it is time someone broke their rules. Perhaps it is time the Fratriae were revealed to you. Times are changing, after all," He said this with a knowing laugh, but Harpen didn't know what he meant.

"I will do this for you, but be warned, you may find you wish you had never asked. They will not be pleased that you know of them, and they may cause you problems. They are a law unto themselves, and capable of a great many things."

He smiled suddenly, his fangs gleaming in the firelight.

"But then, so am I."

* * * * * * * * * *

Simeon was outwardly calm as he read the message before him, but the enormity of what Karl Laumpir had done was ringing in his head. Thousands of years of secrecy, undone by the arrogance of one man. Simeon was tempted to simply kill him for this, but he knew that would require a great deal of effort, and the benefit of Karl's friendship was still worth the inconvenience this posed.

With anger boiling in his mind, Simeon arranged the first meeting in his long life that wasn't on his terms.

It would be the last.

* * * * * * * * * *

Hal's blood was singing as he forced his way into the railway carriage, his mind high on the adrenaline and the thrill and killing to come. The days and weeks between each hunt had passed as a blur, inconsequential and without interest, only broken by his visions, now stronger and more frequent than ever, and the frenzied bouts of killing.

He saw the blow before it was even struck, turning it aside with contemptuous ease and striking back, inflicting a punishing wound on the Vampire before him but not killing him. The Kappa rallied, the wound healing as it came at Hal again, and the two of them duelled for several minutes, blades clashing faster than a normal eye could follow. Hal inflicted another deep cut on his opponent before deciding enough was enough, finishing him with a single stab to the heart.

He lowered his weapon, feeling the excitement ebb already. He shook his head, unwilling to admit the truth. He had enjoyed gloriously difficult fights, taking on incredibly powerful beings on their own turf, but the thrill was waning each time. As much as it pained him to admit it, each time he felt a little less.

He needed a greater challenge.

Crouching in the middle of the devastation he had wrought, he concentrated on the foreign blood running through his veins, calling up an image of the Fratriae, calling up an image of their prey.

* * * * * * * * * *

The first thing Harpen noticed was that the man was seemingly ordinary in every respect. Even to his enhanced mind, there was nothing that made this man different from any other human on the planet, and yet even Karl seemed to treat him with a wary caution, leaning over to whisper in his ear as the stepped from their vehicle.

"Don't let him touch you."

Harpen nodded, his hand resting lightly on the pistol at his hip. He glanced around, seeing nothing but darkness in any direction, noting with surprise that the man before them seemed to have no means of transport, despite them being deep in the woods in the middle of the night. He had driven the jeep direct from the Hunter hanger, following marked paths the Oburs had cleared in advance, and he found it strange that the Fratriae had picked a meeting place so near the Hunter HQ, guessing it was merely to prove that they could come and go as they pleased. Honestly though, he couldn't care less.

"You are of the Fratriae," Harpen said boldly. The man nodded, and Harpen went on.

"I understand you are holding one of my men in thrall. Hal Lemirda. I wish him to be returned to me."

"He has no similar wish."

Harpen blinked, not letting his surprise or anger show.

"He is one of my men. He will..."

"You have misunderstood, Harpen, and you have made a grave mistake. My business is my own, a secret, and not yours. Likewise, our dealings with the Lemirda are our business..."

"And his business is mine," Harpen said evenly, meeting the man's steel gaze without flinching.

"You vastly overestimate your importance in the world, Harpen. I could crush you with a flick of my hand."

"But you won't, Simeon," Karl said quietly. "James is more valuable to me than you are. Just as I am more valuable to you when you haven't tried to kill my friends. Give him what he wants, or our accord will be done with."

Simeon seemed to war with himself for a long while, and Harpen wondered just kind of deal these two immortal beings had struck with one another, what pacts kept them tied together. Eventually, the man nodded, anger written clearly across his face.

"What is it you wish?"

"I want to know where my Hunter is."

Harpen narrowed his eyes as Simeon began to laugh.

"Done."

* * * * * * * * * *

Harpen kicked down the door with a snarl, firing into the room. Two of the shots hit home, sending the Vampire to the floor, but he didn't stop to finish him, hearing the sound of pursuit closing in on him and darting through the room. Mike lingered a moment behind him, tossing a grenade back the way they had come, but it barely slowed them.

This had gone badly wrong. Harpen had brought the two of them to the location furnished to him by the Fratriae, and had quickly realised his mistake. He should have expected a trick, and now they were going to die. He cursed Simeon's treachery as he ran.

It had taken several days, but the Fratriae had contacted them, via Karl, and Harpen and Mike had gone immediately, expecting to find Hal waiting for them.

Instead, they had found a single Strigoi seer, laughing even as Mike killed her, knowing she had seen him coming and had warned her companions. She had, and they had descended on the two Hunters with fury.

They had given a good account of themselves, dropping two before they were forced to break off, a jagged cut on Harpen's leg making him realise it was unwise to stay, and now they were making their frantic way up the main stairs of a high rise office block, knowing even as they did so they would eventually run out of building and be forced to turn and fight. Still they ran, hoping at least to ensure that was on their terms.

Harpen picked a floor eventually, breaking out of the stair well and into an open plan office, picking a spot where the two of them could have their back to something and heading for it, darting between rows of desks and potted plants to the pillar in the centre of the room.

A moment later, they saw Hal Lemirda step casually around it, his pistol already firing over Mike's shoulder, his knife in his hand as he darted forward. The first Vampire went down easily, then Hal was in the thick of it, surrounded on all sides. Harpen watched for a moment, amazed at how differently he now fought. Only his heightened awareness could pick it out, but Hal was reacting perfectly, moving to block attacks almost before they were struck, parrying everything that came at him with barely an effort. In return, he swung for empty space before a Vampire moved into it, almost as if he was predicting every second of the fight before it happened.

Harpen and Mike swung in beside him, but they were not needed. Alone, Hal butchered the coven that had nearly killed the two of them together, and the three men were regarding each other over a pile of bodies.

"Hello James," Hal said quietly, as if he had only seen him that morning, rather than months before.

"I thought the Fratriae had set a trap."

Hal gave no reaction to that.

"Who are the Fratriae?"

Harpen raised an eyebrow, unconvinced.

"I met Simeon."

Again, Hal showed no surprise.

"Then you know I can tell you nothing."

"Did he tell you to meet me?"

Hal seemed to consider this for a moment.

"No."

"Then why are you here?"

Hal shrugged.

"For the fight."

Harpen paused, confused.

"Did you know we'd be here?"

"No."

"Will you come back with us?"

"No."

"Hal, where have you been?"

Hal turned to face Mike as he addressed him, looking as if he didn't know who he was.

"Fighting."

"Hal you need a break. What you have done is...astounding, but you need to stop."

Hal cocked his head.

"Why?"

Mike had no answer, knowing there was nothing they could say to reason with him. Uncertain, they simply watched him leave, knowing the only way to stop him was to fight him, and knowing that would be a colossal mistake.

Hal turned suddenly in the doorway, staring into space for a moment, then fixing his gaze on them.

"You have a meeting to go to. Great changes in the war, artefacts retrieved. An Obur council. A gathering of leaders. But it will go wrong. Ultors will attack from the front of the house, and the basement, and the Obur Family head will be killed."

With that, he was gone.

* * * * * * * * * *

Days later, Harpen was still reeling from Hal's chilling pronouncement, all but dismissing it as the ravings of an unstable mind. Family Heads were the oldest, the strongest, the first of their line. All Vampires ultimately descended from one of the six Family heads, and all were in essence a diluted version of the original, the powers passed on by the total exchange of blood, and as power then increased with age, the Family Heads were all but unmatched. To his certain knowledge, the rare occasions a Hunter or even a Brother of the Order met one, it ended in their death. Harpen had never met William Obur, but he knew enough. He was not a warrior, by any means, but his sheer raw power should be enough...

But then, apparently not.

When Harpen received the invitation several days later, he was not surprised.

* * * * * * * * * *

Outside of those Oburs who lived within the Hunter HQ, it was a distant relationship shared by the two groups. Their work overlapped, obviously, and they were trusted and welcome allies, but for the most part they kept to their own affairs. Most Oburs were not warriors, instead devoting their lives to engineering works, constructing weapons or vehicles or buildings, many for the use of the Hunters, some simply to satisfy their innate desire to create and build, which meant that the Hunters had little need to interact with the bulk of the family.

There were exceptions, of course. Joseph Obur was well known within the Hunters, a high ranking Obur with authority over one of their largest cells, his power second to the Family Head himself. Unlike many of his kind, he was a skilled combatant, as capable of wielding a range of weapons as he was of constructing them, and Harpen, having worked with him before, was pleased to see him as they arrived.

The same could not be said in reverse, of course. Like all his Family, Joseph was dour and expressionless, only moved by the most extreme emotions. So like Hal, Harpen thought darkly.

Joseph asked them to leave their car, directing them up the road to where there lay a run down three storey farm house, set back behind a high mesh fence and nestled in a clump of trees in the foothills of the Drakensburg mountains. Harpen and Mike moved up casually, unconcerned by the armed figures they could sense all about them, and passed through the gateway, heading for the house itself.

Inside the vast entrance hall, the two men kept to themselves, sitting out of the way in a pair of the many large arm chairs that were the room's only furniture, besides a long table at the end. Outwardly, they were calm and relaxed, but inside, Harpen was agitated. He would have rather not been here, would rather be finding a way to bring Hal back to his senses, but he knew this occasion was too important to miss, and Karl would be here to offer his advice. Plus there was the other matter…

Hal's prophecy came back to him, and he stood suddenly, resolving to act while he had the chance. Waving Mike back to his seat, he strode through to a side room, greeting the two Oburs he found there and asking for their leader.

William arrived a moment later, and Harpen felt instantly the sheer force of his presence. Like all his kind, he was blank and unsmiling, but that covered an undertone of sheer, elemental power.

Harpen bowed low.

"My Lord Obur, I…"

"Am troubled," the Vampire finished for him, and Harpen simply nodded, unfazed.

"My Lemirda Brother has had a vision. It pertains to your Lordship, and your…death."

William Obur's face didn't change.

"When is this to occur?"

"Tonight, My Lord. I came to warn you, to ask you to take measures…"

He trailed off as the Obur raised his hand.

"Has a Lemirda ever been wrong?"

"No my Lord."

"Then what measures do you suggest should be taken?"

Harpen met the Vampire's gaze for the first time, forcing himself to hold it.

"Safeguard your men. And their future."

William Obur just nodded, he and his bodyguard apparently unconcerned.

"Your counsel is good. You may aid me, by not repeating this revelation. If I am to die, then it should be alone. There is no sense in others dying to prevent an ordained death."

Harpen returned to his seat, knowing he had done all he could, and he managed to relax a little despite what he knew, even cheering up when Karl Laumpir arrived. He had a girl in tow, and Harpen went to greet them, exchanging a few words with the two of them before taking his seat again. Knowing William was right, he said nothing of what was to come.

William entered a moment later, and Harpen listened as he began to speak.

He had barely finished his introduction when the alarm sounded.

Like everyone else in the room, Harpen felt rather than heard it, a dull buzzing that seemed to be just beneath his skin. He sat for a moment, seemingly unconcerned even as his mind and body came alive. Hal's words came back to him, and he despatched Mike to the basement with a thought, before following the bulk of the Oburs out into the grounds.

Karl was waiting for him, sword in hand and a smile on his face that belied the seriousness of the situation.

"You know James, this might not be the time for this conversation, but I suspect the Fratriae want you dead."

"What gave you that impression?" Harpen said drily, drawing his own weapons and standing alongside the Vampire. He glanced back and forth, noticing that there was no sign of any attack, but confident the Oburs had matters in hand.

"A decent working knowledge of their methods," Karl said, his voice suddenly serious.

"Did you know they had set us a trap?"

"They tried to kill you?" Karl said, looking genuinely surprised.

"Not them, but they may as well have. A coven of Strigoi were waiting. We only survived because Hal was there. Of his own accord."

Karl didn't reply to that, lost in contemplation, and any reply he did have was quickly forgotten a moment later.

Harpen saw figures suddenly emerging from the gloom, armed with short blades and stubby machine pistols, clad in mud-stained coveralls and goggles with abnormally wide lenses. They were coming from the gateway, and Harpen narrowed his eyes as he realised there had been no warning, that the guards on the gate must have been killed instantly. He cursed at Hal's absence, knowing he would have provided them with an early warning...

Harpen hesitated a moment before the Ultors reached the Obur line, knowing it was too late. Battle was joined.

Karl was the first to engage, dashing forward with a battle cry on his lips, his sword accounting for three Ultors in a matter of seconds. The others turned to follow him, the bloodlust clear on their faces as they strove to reach the Laumpir, and this proved to be their downfall. Joseph led the Oburs forward in a furious charge, and Harpen went with them, swept along by the tide of combat and rage, crashing into the Ultor line and tearing it asunder.

Harpen faced off with a single Ultor, firing his pistol even as he darted forward, causing the Vampire to double up with pain, but Harpen gave him no time, slamming his knee into his opponents face, then stabbing forward as his body jerked up. The timing was perfect, the knife hitting home, and Harpen let the body fall as he skipped backward, narrowly avoiding a line of bullets where he had just been standing. The gunman was eviscerated a second later, Joseph's sword carving upwards into his chest, and Harpen nodded his thanks.

He turned his attention to the wider struggle, seeing only isolated pockets of Ultors being cut down, and he lowered his blade as Karl approached at a run, a stern look on his face.

"That was a diversion. I don't know how, but they've taken the cellars."

He paused, holding his sword aloft.

"Oburs, with me!"

Harpen ran with them as they charged, already knowing the outcome.

* * * * * * * * * *

The house was silent again, the damage already repaired by the Oburs in a matter of minutes, and Harpen was seated once more in the main hall of the house. Joseph was seated nearby, cleaning his weapons, entirely unaffected by the death of his leader. All of the Oburs had been the same, acting as if it was no great loss. Not that Harpen had expected any different from them, of course, but he had at least expected an acknowledgment of the loss. Instead, they carried on as if all was normal. Only Karl was different, suddenly more animated. In the aftermath of William's death, he had announced himself the supreme authority, and the Oburs had accepted it without objection. The curious hierarchies of the Vampire Families meant that Karl was senior even to Joseph Obur, and by default had inherited command of those Obur Cells that were present. Great changes indeed.

Harpen listened for a while as Karl and Joseph conversed, discussing the damage that had been done by the surprise attack as well as how it had been pulled off. Little was said of William's death, as if it was an inconsequential footnote.

Karl turned to Harpen after a while, a thoughtful look on his face.

"Tonight is a momentous occasion in more ways than one, James. I have plans in mind that have waited centuries to come to fruition. Soon, very soon, things will change. I sincerely hope I can count on the support of you and your men."

"As always," Harpen nodded.

Karl smiled at that, ideas clearly forming in his mind.

"You knew of tonight's attack. More specifically, Hal knew."

Harpen nodded again, noting that neither of the Vampires seemed especially bothered by his secrecy at the time.

"He warned me the last time I saw him."

"His gifts would have been invaluable tonight. With him here, fewer men would have died."

"He saw William's..."

"I know that," Karl said hastily. "I mean others. Hal, more than any of us, has the power to change a great deal."

"He is...beyond my control."

Karl leaned back in his chair, nodding to himself knowingly. Harpen found himself wondering just how involved Karl had been with the Fratriae, how much he knew of their actions.

"Then we must bring him back. Too much rests on him. The Fratriae have outlived their usefulness to me, I think, and something must be done at last."

He rose, and Harpen felt the glee in his voice.

"A reckoning is in order."

* * * * * * * * * *

Hal stalked through the tunnels without enthusiasm, his knife held loosely in his hand and pistol still holstered. He couldn't remember when he had last drawn it.

The fight to come was passing across his eyes, every detail of it laid bare by his vision, each strike and thrust and parry predicted before he even reached them. He barely felt any of them.

Hal had realised something in the midst of the grey life between hunts, something that had not occurred to him before. All his life, he had felt only the joy of the kill, a moment of colour as he did what he was created for. Since meeting the Fratriae, that thrill had declined, kill by kill, until he barely noticed it. Now he felt the absence of the killing thrill as keenly as he had ever felt the thrill itself, and every fight was just an attempt to regain it, to feel something again...

To no avail.

The Fratriae had given him targets, increasingly tougher Vampires from across the three families, but it had done nothing for him. Whole covens lay dead in his wake, dozens of Vampires slaughtered and his pulse had barely elevated.

Perhaps today.

* * * * * * * * * *

Joe Forjay flexed his mind, spinning his knife in the air before him absent-mindedly, watching it turn lazily over and over, the dim light glancing off the edge of the blade. Beside him, seated on a mass of pipework, Ralph and Jason Tyler were slotting rounds into magazines simultaneously, each movement perfectly in time with each other. A pile of already filled magazines lay beside them. Across the tunnel, Kym Malum was pacing from side to side, stopping periodically to punch another hole in the brickwork buttressing. Mike and Harpen looked asleep.

Apparently, waiting beneath a water treatment plant was boring.

"How much longer?" Kym growled suddenly, causing all of them to stop and glance at him for a moment.

"Patience, Kym," Harpen said without opening his eyes. "He'll be here."

"You said that yesterday. And meanwhile, the Order sits inactive in a half ruined tunnel. We all have places to be."

"It would be less ruined if you didn't keep punching it," Joe grinned.

"And we have nowhere better to be. A few days not hunting won't hurt, and we need Hal back."

"All of us?"

Harpen opened his eyes and sat up at that point.

"He's taken out whole covens by himself. Given that, of all of us, only you would even try to pull that off unaided, we reasoned that perhaps a combined effort would be best when it came to pacifying him. Besides, that was Karl's request. I suspect you will get your chance to tear chunks out of something other than a wall soon enough."

"You're not wrong."

Weapons were suddenly in hand as they reacted to the new voice, holstered immediately as Karl swung into the tunnel from a hatch in the roof. He was clad in thick leather body armour, reinforced by strips of dark metal, and his sword was sheathed over his shoulder.

"Expecting trouble, my Lord?" Kym asked, a smile on his face letting them all know what he hoped the answer would be. Karl nodded.

"Not just yet, but later certainly. If this works, the Fratriae will become...unpleasant."

The Brothers were silent at that. Karl had told them what they were dealing with, outlining just who these men were, and even the Order baulked at taking them on.

"But there are things to be done first. We can drop the veil now, he's in the tunnel network."

There was an audible sigh in the room, and a shift in the air pressure. Each of the Brothers felt the weight lift from their mind, as the energy they had been siphoning into Karl stopped flowing, and the section of tunnel they were in became visible again.

They all knew time was of the essence, and they moved with speed, silently traversing the tunnel system, moving further and lower as they went, until Karl veered off, ducking through a ragged hole that had been smashed in the tunnel wall, immediately adjacent to a thick metal door. A set of steps ran down on the far side, and they came out into an empty room.

Empty, except for the half dozen bodies on the floor, and Hal Lemirda, crouching amidst them with his eyes tightly shut. He didn't even notice them until Karl stepped forward, tapping his foot once. Hal's eyes snapped open, and he regarded them all with a blank recognition as he rose to his feet.

"Hello Brothers."

"Hi Hal. How's it going?" Harpen said lightly, very aware that they were blocking Hal's only exit. Hal didn't respond, his eyes fixed on Karl Laumpir. Karl simply nodded as if suddenly understanding something.

"It's time this finished, Hal. The Fratriae are controlling you. They're directing your visions to suit them, and twisting your blood to keep you addicted and dependent."

Harpen watched closely. Karl had explained this to him over the last few days, and at first he had fumed at the scale of the deception the Fratriae had been running through the years, had even fumed at Karl's implicit allowance of this to continue. Karl himself had been apologetic, insisting it had never been this extreme, and Harpen had had to concede the point. The Hunters would have surely noticed this if it had happened before.

Hal didn't seem to react, still standing with his gaze locked on Karl, and the Vampire continued slowly.

"Think about it. The only visions you have are of the middle of fights. There are no warnings anymore, no long term foreshadowing. You don't even have visions of your Brothers anymore, just you and the Fratriae. They gave you more power, but only to see the fights you would have, and the fights they wanted. They took over your mind..."

As he had been talking, Karl had inched forward, but now he faltered, his eyes scanning Hal's form, resting eventually on his jacket pocket. Without warning, Karl struck, a blade suddenly in his hand cutting neatly through the corner of Hal's jacket, sending a small stone bouncing across the floor. Hal went after it, but it had already moved, whipped up into the air and dropped neatly into Joe's hand. Hal simply stood still, his gaze back on Karl.

"Well that's new," Karl muttered, taking the Ildraya from Joe and holding it up to the light, examining it closely. "And that certainly explains a lot."

"What is it?" Harpen asked, still watching Hal warily.

"The reason Hal has been acting a little more irrationally than his family in the past. An Ildraya, keyed for his genetics. Overriding the usual killing urge and replacing with it a hunger, a need. Made him more susceptible to the blood control, more malleable…That reminds me."

Karl's voice was casual as he struck, plunging the point of the blade into Hal's forearm.

* * * * * * * * * * *

Hal barely felt the blade hit home, but he felt its effects as blood started flowing from the wound, his body's natural abilities doing nothing to prevent it. He watched in fascination, feeling a foreign energy leach from his form, before raising his head again to meet Karl's gaze. A moment later, the Vampire, and the Brothers behind him, were gone.

* * * * * * * * * * *

He could see the moon rising on the horizon, reflecting off the surface of the sea. In the distance, too far to see them clearly, a trio of ships lay at anchor, unlit and barely visible.

Hal was walking the line, seeing the pits carved from solid rock, the barricades and obstacles built above them, and the men manning those pits. Many of them were Hunters, faces Hal recognised, heavily armed and armoured as if for a battle, not a hunt.

But a battle was what had come, he knew. Thousands of Vampires were set to descend on these shores, set to clash with the full force of the Vampire Hunters on this insignificant island. A reckoning, a battle to settle things once and for all, a last ditch effort by both sides to wipe out the other.

Obur Vampires were spread among the line, some still constructing the defences even as the enemy ships bore down on the island. Others were armed, standing motionless and staring out to sea, their faces unfathomable.

Hal walked on, finding a handful of his Brothers waiting for him at the mouth of a cave, each of them greeting him warmly. They were clad as he was, in heavy body armour and visored helmets, every one of them armed to the teeth and smiling in anticipation of what was to come.

Hal paused suddenly, glancing upward to the cliff top, raising his blade in salute. Karl Laumpir stood there, clad in segmented body armour of clearly ancient design, his sword held loosely in his hands, and he nodded once to Hal.

The vision shifted suddenly and Hal was plunged into combat, feeling his limbs act without his command, feeling his own mind as two vast armies came together in a chaotic whirl of death. His own mind, certainly, but something was different…

* * * * * * * * * * *

Hal awoke as if from a daydream, the vision fading before his eyes but the memory of it still vivid. He had felt his own mind, felt the detached calm there. No apathy. No boredom. No desire for a greater thrill or a more challenging kill.

Free.

He felt the wound on his arm close as Karl stepped away. The ache in his mind was fading, the need to kill a dull murmur. Still there, but no longer all encompassing, all consuming.

"That will help. I've taken away most of their influence, but that is all I can do."

"How do I get rid of it forever?" Hal asked. He felt more himself than he had in a long while.

"Only they can do that, and I doubt they will agree. They will probably try to kill you all for this."

"Then we will have to kill them first," Kym said grimly, a smile on his face, but that faded as Karl shook his head.

"Have you not been listening? These creatures outclass you. They're sorcerous voids, and they're unstoppable. Any fight and they'll knock you out instantly and dismember you."

"There is a way," Hal said evenly.

* * * * * * * * * * *

Simeon felt the urge pulse inside him, the all-encompassing rage that descended each and every time he drew near to his quarry. He felt the power in his limbs, the hunger in his soul as it prepared to receive the pure life force of his most hated victims. Three of the Fratriae ran with him, all of them equally enraptured by the prospect of what was coming.

His rage flooded out of him as he burst through the solid stone wall into the Vampiri lair. He screamed in rage as he saw a dozen Vampiri dead on the floor, with Hal Lemirda seated casually among them.

Simeon couldn't help himself, needing to sate his bloodlust, barely comprehending how the Lemirda felt he could do this, launching himself forward with his arms outstretched...

And spinning away as he was struck by a sledgehammer blow, an enormous chunk of solid rock smashing into him from the side. His companions fell beside him, each of them struck by a hail of shot. None of them were injured, their flesh undamaged, but the sheer force of the blows was enough to knock them down.

Simeon was the first to recover, readying himself to strike again when he properly noticed the room for the first time, noticing the scent of power in the air, and the grim faced men gathered around its edge, all of them heavily armed and cradling massive shotguns. In their midst, Simeon saw Karl Laumpir, and he cursed out loud.

"Don't waste your time," Hal said quietly, the threat clear in his posture. "I've seen this conversation already, and I know how it goes."

He swung a massive length of pipe downward, catching Simeon square in the face before he'd even begun to leap.

"So I knew you would do that," Hal continued. "Your time with me as your play thing is up. I spit on your deal and demand you get your blood out of my body."

Simeon ignored him, venting his rage on Karl Laumpir instead.

"You swore to keep our secret. You swore to serve us."

"It suited me then," Karl replied. "Times have changed."

Simeon spat and turned back to Hal.

"I reject your demands. You have nothing to offer."

"This isn't a deal, Simeon. You no longer hold the power. I've seen the life you will live and I've seen your end. You will do as I say, or I will use my gifts to hunt out every Vampiri lair I can find, and kill them all one by one. You and your Fratriae will be left starved and broken, and then I will destroy you."

"We cannot be destroyed," Simeon replied, but the confidence had gone from his voice.

"Would you test that with the extinction of your prey?"

Simeon shook his head, defeated.

* * * * * * * * * *

Hal stepped out into the night air with a curious sense of peace washing over him, breathing in deeply as he felt the last trace of the Fratriae control dissipate from his mind. They had given him up for good, but he knew he had not finished with them as brief snatches of visions flashed across his mind.

Karl Laumpir stepped out behind him, his armoured jacket unfastened and hanging open, revealing a fine shirt of chainmail. He smiled at Hal, revealing his fangs for a moment, and Hal nodded his head in greeting. His hostility towards Karl had gone.

"You have my thanks, Lord."

"I have let them work for too long. I suspect if James knew what freedoms I have allowed them he would be considerably less...pleasant."

"You may be right," Hal nodded.

"And this Ildraya is a disturbing development," Karl turned it over in his hands. "I have never heard of one being used like this. I didn't even know it was possible."

"They said they retrieved it from my father."

"They lied. This is newly made, fresh. The power within it is still raw."

"Did they make it?"

"No, they haven't the means to do so. Only Strigoi are capable, and even then only the most powerful. But then, the magic required, the energy, the power...Whatever the Fratriae offered them...it must have been huge. The Fratriae were more highly connected than I thought. And far more persuasive, it seems. Still, the matter is done now. I will keep this safe."

"No. I will."

"Even without their blood control, it can still affect you," Karl warned.

"Exactly why I should keep it where no one else can find it."

Karl hesitated, then passed over the stone. Hal felt the energy within, seeing it now for what it was doing to his mind, and he dismissed it, his mental defences casting out the few tendrils of pure thought he could feel worming into his being.

"I see you have work ahead," Hal said suddenly. Karl smiled again.

"You see correctly. Times have changed. This war will change. I have need of your services, Lemirda. If you wish to give them."

"I was born for this life," Hal shrugged.

"Quite. Thank you."

"I suspect there is something you will do for me in return."

"Oh?"

"I had a vision. You, the Hunters, the Order. A battle. I was fighting, yet I felt no joy in killing. It was...liberating. I think you're going to help me achieve that."

Karl raised an eyebrow, puzzled.

"I have no plan for a battle. At least, not yet. As to your thirst for killing, the Fratriae did not cause that, they simply hijacked and enhanced it for their own ends. That is in your blood, that is how all your line have lived. The Lemirda feel no emotion, save the joy of the hunt, that is the way it has always been. As far as I am aware, it cannot be undone. It is how you were made. I'm sorry, but your freedom from the Fratriae was my only goal here tonight."

Hal nodded thoughtfully, noting how clear his mind was now that it wasn't plagued by visions of combat. He knew better, it seemed, but would not press the matter. For now.

"Perhaps not then."

"Perhaps not."

He made his farewells, and Hal watched him leave, his mind clear. He knew what was coming, better even than Karl Laumpir.

He was content to wait.

* * * * * * * * * *

Part Four - Fortaca

As he always did, Mike Fortaca was smiling a curious half smile as he sat and watched the world go by. Unarmed, clad in scruffy jeans and a long jumper, he sat in an airport departure lounge, a can of cheap cola in one hand and a dry sandwich in the other.

The months since Hal's return had been bloody, to say the least. As if responding to the death of William Obur, Vampire covens across the planet had been more obvious, feeding more openly, leaving ever more clues for the Vampire Hunters to follow, and they had been kept busy. Mike had hunted less than most, his skills as a healer being called into play more and more, but he had made his fair share of kills.

As far as any of them could tell, the upsurge in activity was not a deliberate act in itself, but rather a reaction. William's death had shifted the balance of power in more ways than one, and it seemed the other families were railing against the success of the Ultors, jockeying to improve their own power and standing in the subtle, subterranean world of Vampire politics. To the Hunters, that merely meant more targets in the short term, but many, the Order in particular, were wary. Shifting power was fine until it settled and one Family found itself on top.

What made many of them more wary was the absence of Karl Laumpir. Contact with him was sporadic, and although they knew he had some great matter in mind, he was keeping his own counsel, at least for the time being.

Mike snapped from his thoughts as Hal sat down next to him, looking slightly incongruous and very uncomfortable with a half-eaten pineapple in his hand.

"What the hell is that?"

"A pineapple," Hal shrugged, no trace of sarcasm in his voice.

"But where the hell did you...? You know what, never mind. Feeling relaxed?"

Hal shrugged again, and Mike sighed. It had been worth a shot.

Hal's return to the Hunters had been greeted with enthusiasm by most. For all he was emotionless and seemingly unfriendly, he was a part of the organisation, an accepted and vital part, and he was held in high regard, especially after his achievements while under the thrall of the Fratriae. The more negative aspects had been forgotten, swept away by his return unharmed, and he had gone back to hunting within days, showing clearly that his skills had been honed to a knife point in his absence. Only his visions had waned, no longer coming to him day by day, reduced now to the levels he had grown accustomed to before the Fratriae. Still, they painted a vital picture, guiding the Hunters to key battles, warning them of hunts and risings and deaths to come, and they were glad of his aid, even if what he predicted was not always what they wanted to hear. After a particularly large scale Hunt, in which three Hunters had died, two of them foreseen and forewarned, Mike had all but forced Hal to take a break, and to his surprise, Hal had agreed. Mike had found it odd at first – he still did, really – but had found the experience of Hal's company a completely new one.

"I don't feel anything."

"You must feel something. Besides the joy of killing," he added as Hal immediately opened his mouth to reply.

Hal seemed to consider this for a long while.

"No. But sometimes I know when I should feel, when others would feel something. I just don't."

This was news to Mike, and he leaned forward, his interest piqued. As far as he knew, no one had got a Lemirda to open up like this.

"Like when?"

"When I wasn't killing for the Fratriae I felt the absence of killing. When I killed those police officers, I felt that I should feel guilty. And when Steph left..."

Mike flinched, causing Hal to stop. He should have expected that, should have known it was coming, but he had been too drawn. It was still too recent for Mike, too raw...

"She's going to yell at you," Hal said quietly, and Mike blinked, realising his companion was seeing this.

"What?"

"That's it," Hal said, raising his head again. "That's all I saw. You're in a kitchen, and she's yelling at you."

Mike sat back heavily, not sure what to think. Hal took a thoughtful bite of his pineapple and leaned back next to him.

"Should I feel something now?"

* * * * * * * * * *

Harpen lowered the blade as Mike walked purposefully into the room, nodding to his Obur opponent and stepping off the practice mat. His bare chest was marked with half a dozen minor wounds, all of them healing slowly, all of them taken over seven hours of solid sparring. He was barely out of breath.

"You look...pissed off."

Mike nodded his head to one side, only half agreeing.

"I looked Steph up."

"That would do it," Harpen nodded, sighing.

"She has a child."

That made Harpen stop in his tracks.

"Yours?"

"I would think so."

"And you want me to make the decision to take him for you," Harpen said kindly, knowing full well Mike knew what was at stake here, and was quite able and willing to order a team to accompany him to retrieve the baby himself. But Mike shook his head.

"A team is prepping now. I just thought you'd want to know."

"Right. Thanks," Harpen said with one eyebrow raised. There was more to this, he could tell.

"And Hal said you're coming with."

"There it is."

* * * * * * * * * *

Steph felt her heart begin to pound as she heard the doorbell ring, and without even thinking she went to work, the routine now familiar. The windows were all locked and barred anyway, but she checked the larger ones, not bothering with the rear doors, happy that they were sealed. Her son she hid away with a smile and a kiss, knowing he would make no noise in his concealment. She walked to the door slowly, jangling keys to disguise the sound of her unlocking the drawer where she kept a gun.

She did all this in under a minute, having practiced many, many times, and even though she felt stupid every time, she had never been able to stop, convinced that the one time she didn't, she would find...

There her mind refused to continue, refused to admit that she was scared of Vampires appearing on her front door step to steal her infant son. Over time, she had begun to convince herself it had all been a lie, a fabrication...There were no Vampires, no superhuman Hunters, just a scumbag boyfriend who had used her and dumped her and...

Was now standing on her doorstep.

Steph stepped back from the peephole slowly, unsure of what to do, jumping as the bell rang again and Mike's voice came through the letter box, calling her name.

"Go away," she whispered, inching slowly up the stairs. She had no idea what she doing, no idea what she was going to do, only knowing she needed to get her son away. She reached the top of the stairs and turned the corner, throwing open the cupboard where the basket was hidden, pulling the child from hiding and cradling him in her arms. Frantically she rushed to the stairs, knowing she would have to unseal a back door to get away, then freezing as she looked down and saw her front door wide open, Mike standing alone in her hallway. He wasn't looking at her, admiring instead a handgun, her handgun, she realised belatedly as she saw the empty drawer.

"Get out," he looked up at the sound of her voice, a hurt look on his face, but she wasn't having any of it.

"I see the house is secure," he said mildly, ignoring her anger. That just made her more furious, as all the memories came flooding back.

"I said get out. You aren't welcome here."

"I came to see my son."

She paused for a second, hearing the genuine emotion in his voice, her anger faltering as she looked into his eyes. But only for a second.

"Is that all?"

He didn't answer, and she knew he didn't have to. Pushing past him, she headed for the kitchen and pulled a bag from atop a cabinet, holding the baby with one arm as she began to fill it with food. Mike followed.

"What are you doing?"

"What I should have done months ago. Going somewhere you can't find me."

"Why?"

"Because I know why you're here Mike! You might not have thought about me, but I've done nothing but think about you. What do you think all this is for?" she swung her free arm, gesturing around the house. "The security, the weapons, the constant, constant panic? It's not for Vampires, or werewolves, or ghosts or aliens or any other supernatural crap. No, it's in case you ever turned up to steal my baby."

She faltered again, seeing the agonised look on his face, the hurt in his eyes, and she was so close to bursting into tears, to apologising, to flinging herself into his arms and...

"I have to," he said quietly. "You know that. I explained...so much more than I should have."

"Have you forgotten, Mike? I've heard this before. But you know what, it isn't dangerous. Hal was with me for eight years, and the only bit of danger was a few days after you turned up. Me and Cal have managed fine, and you won't take him. Not this time."

"Cal?" he smiled, looking at the baby for the first time, and she fumed even more as she realised that was the first attention he had paid to the child.

"You see? You don't even care about him as your son. He's just a weapon to you, someone you can take away and turn into a monster. I won't let you. The only danger in his life that I can see is what you're offering."

"Listen to me," his voice was hard suddenly, his features still showing his hurt. "This has to be this way. I'm sorry for everything, your mum, Hal, our life...I should never have let it get this far, but it did and I can't change it. The chi...Cal is a Hunter, a Brother of the Order, and he needs to be with us. I know this is hard for you, I know you have had it rough..." She spluttered an angry retort, but he cut her off. "I know you've had it rough, but there is no choice here. He has to come with us."

"And I have to suffer," she said quietly. Her mind was reeling. She had expected this since before the boy was born, waking up every day to wonder if that was it, time up.

"If there was another way..." he began, but he stopped when he saw the look in her eyes, a dark, haunted look. Her voice dropped to barely above a whisper, and he noticed her hand resting inside a drawer.

"I could kill him."

Mike froze as she pulled a long kitchen knife from the drawer, holding it threateningly over the baby's head. The child didn't react, his yellow eyes fixed on his mother.

"No you couldn't," Mike said quickly, softly, his hands raised in front of him. Her facial expression didn't change.

"Why not? What are you offering that is better?"

Mike didn't answer, knowing nothing he could say would persuade her.

"He'll die anyway with you, why wait?" her voice had a maniacal tone as she went on. "You made Hal into a soulless killer. Why would I want that for my own child? Better he die now than have to live that life."

"Steph, I...there's nothing I can say to make this better, nothing I can do to take back what I've done to you," his voice was soft as he spoke. "But you can't possibly understand what we do. We have saved thousands from slavery, from death..."

"By enslaving and killing?"

"We save the innocent. We carry the burden of that so normal people don't have to. We do what we do so the rest of the world doesn't have to suffer."

"I'm suffering. My child will suffer."

"He was born to. That's why I'm sorry. I'm so sorry this has to happen."

She saw the look in his eyes a moment too late, realising he wasn't just talking generally. The knife jerked in her hand, slamming down on the countertop of its own accord, and she cried out as it was ripped from her grasp. A moment later, an invisible force took hold of her arm, pulling it gently away and holding her immobile as Mike stepped forward and took the child from her. She felt sick as she saw the baby reach out and grab Mike's shirt front, nestling into him with fondness.

"Thanks Joe," Mike said as another man stepped into the room, his eyes a curious shade of amber, his arms folded casually. Behind him, another figure was standing, and she gasped as she recognised him.

"Hello Steph," Hal said, his voice as blank as she remembered. She felt no fondness for her brother, just pity and loathing in equal measure. He regarded her for a moment, a faraway look on his face, and she thought for a second he was going to reach out to her, to open up, to apologise...Instead, he simply shook his head and turned to Mike.

"She'll never understand. But she will be safe."

Mike sighed, meeting Steph's eyes for the last time.

"Have a good life. Try to forget us. You'll find it quite easy."

His voice was devoid of any emotion, and she didn't understand until she realised a fourth man had entered the room unnoticed and was sitting down at the table. She felt his eyes fix on her, felt his gaze boring into her skull, the icy touch in her brain, the whispering voice in her ear. She swayed, suddenly confused and disorientated, and her vision began to grey. Before she blacked out, she heard a voice, a voice she recognised, a voice she loved. He was looking down at her, and holding a baby. Their baby.

"I'm sorry. I wish things were different, but there was no other way this could have gone."

* * * * * * * * * *

Mike watched from the car as Harpen stepped from the house and shut the door behind him. He looked tired, and Mike knew he must have been exhausted by the effort he had just expended.

"It's done," he said as he got into the car. His voice was low, laden with weary emotion. "All trace of us is wiped, and she remembers only the good bits of you. Later on today the police will call to tell her that her boyfriend and baby son were killed in a car accident."

Mike nodded gratefully. "Thank you."

"It was the least we could do. Will you be ok?"

Mike nodded again, holding his son closely.

"It had to happen this way, Mike. You did the right thing. And she'll be better off this way."

"I know."

"Now what's up I wonder?" Harpen said, his voice back to its normal level. Outside, Hal was striding up from the other vehicle, his face unreadable.

"Go. Now," he said as soon as he reached the window. Mike was alert immediately, casting out with his mind, scanning for threats.

"A vision?"

Hal shook his head. "A call from a Bloodhound. We're in trouble."

"Hal, it's daytime."

"Not Vampires. Fratriae. It seems my threat didn't work."

* * * * * * * * * *

Simeon closed his eyes and breathed in deeply, feeling the power nearby. The Brothers, and the child with them. More than enough for his purposes. He refused to be cowed, to let them control his destiny. He was of the Fratriae, a killer like no other, and no one who challenged him would survive. Damn the Lemirda's threats.

The Order would be sundered.

* * * * * * * * * *

The Brothers made good time, the three car convoy leaving the city behind in their attempt to outrun the approaching Fratriae. All of them were tense, alert for any threat, weapons held ready just below the sight of anyone they passed. The Fratriae had been spotted by a Bloodhound in the city centre, recognised by the descriptions Hal had circulated in the weeks since his return, but had not been seen since. It seemed too lucky, and Harpen was beginning to suspect they had allowed themselves to be spotted, which if so meant this was probably a trap.

Nothing we can do then, he shrugged to himself. They had chosen to avoid their safe house in the city itself, reasoning the Fratriae would have second guessed that move, and they were heading away from the Obur cells for the same reason. Instead, their destination was Port Elizabeth Airport, where a Hunter aircraft would be waiting for them. It would mean driving into the night, but they couldn't risk heading for Durban airport on the off chance it was also guarded. In the circumstances, an ambush by Vampires was preferable. None of them were willing to face the Fratriae head on, less so with Mike's son with them.

Hunters had begun to respond, the handful that were nearby heading to join those Mike had brought with them in the mad dash to the airport, and Harpen had been tempted to send them away again. He would have without question had it not been for the child, knowing that, if came to it, he had to throw away lives to slow the Fratriae, to keep the young Fortaca alive. The human Hunters wouldn't stand a chance, and he hated the Fratriae for what they were forcing him to do.

The cars were racing at speeds that were not just illegal, but downright impossible for any car not driven with superhuman reflexes and Obur tuned engines. They weaved between what little traffic there was, skimming past vehicles that seemed to be stationary in comparison, watching as the city gave way to open country side, the sea still visible occasionally on their left in the distance. More than once, sirens began to blare then quickly recede as they left the authorities behind before they could even begin to chase them down. Through it all, the child remained silent, his eyes moving from Brother to Brother in the car, his limbs still.

In the car behind, Hal flicked the steering wheel casually, sending the car veering around a pickup truck that had swerved at the last minute, his foot pressed firmly to the floor. The view outside was overlaid by visions, most of them of the road ahead, and he blinked as his mind sorted one from the other, picking out the routes that all three cars would take and communicating with Harpen and Joe in the other two. Besides the four Brothers, each car carried human Hunters, all of them armed to the teeth. They had come ready for a fight, knowing someone might attack them when they picked up the child, knowing that he was an irresistible target to every Vampire out there while he was still too young to defend himself. He hadn't foreseen the Fratriae, and he now saw yet another facet of their seemingly limitless power, knowing for a fact what he had long suspected, that they could somehow control his visions and keep themselves hidden even from his mind when it suited them.

A voice came tersely from the radio, and Hal glanced at the Hunter beside him. They were less an hour out of Durban, nowhere near their target, but it seemed their support was closer than they thought.

"Hunters Hunters, this is airborne. We have visual on you, four vehicles travelling at speed on the R61 heading west. We are set for pickup, please advise."

"Airborne, this is Harpen," the reply came immediately. "Confirm four vehicles?"

There was a pause.

"Confirmed."

Hal swung the wheel immediately, wrenching the car around, bringing it to a halt after a long skid down the centre of the main road. He could hear Harpen in his head, calling for immediate pickup, and behind that, the distant sound of VTOL engines as the aircraft descended. He knew it was already too late, watching Joe's car pull up nearby, the Hunters spilling out with weapons in hand, and behind them, veering through the civilian traffic, a single vehicle was racing, dodging slowing and stationary vehicles with an ease that betrayed the driver. Hal took a moment to consider the scene, pressing down the urge to kill in his mind, feeling his thoughts rebel as it surfaced. Dozens of cars were slewing to a halt all around them, many of them crashing into other vehicles now littering the road. People had already begun to flee the scene, whether from the danger of the imminent pile up or the armed men now spread across the road, but Hal ignored them, focussing on what mattered. The aircraft would be landing in a matter of minutes, but that was too long. Harpen and Mike had abandoned the vehicle and were running, almost invisible in the gathering gloom, knowing their safest bet was to not be seen, hoping the Hunters would be enough of a threat to distract the Fratriae. Barely a hundred metres away, the Fratriae car had slid to a halt, its four occupants leaping out and dashing forward, and Hal saw immediately their path was taking them straight for Mike, saw immediately he had no choice. A vision flashed across his mind, breaking through the Fratriae control, Joe falling in a spray of blood, Hunters dead around him, but Hal gave the order anyway.

With a cry, firing as they went, the Hunters charged.

* * * * * * * * * *

Mike turned and glanced back as gun fire ripped through the air, seeing no discernible reaction from the Fratriae. Above, the aircraft was looming, its side door already open and a single figure leaning out, but too far away. Mike looked back again. Most of the Hunters were already dead, the remainder standing beside Joe and Hal as they held off three of the Fratriae. The fourth had passed them and was heading straight for Mike, hatred in his face.

Harpen dropped his pistol and pulled his knife free, walking slowly towards the approaching figure, not glancing back as he spoke.

"I'll slow him down."

"He'll kill you."

"Probably. Save the boy."

* * * * * * * * * *

Hal felt the urge to kill rising, threatening to overwhelm his mind as he fought. He knew it was an urge that would go frustrated, knowing he couldn't possibly kill the two figures before him, his speed and agility barely keeping their hands from him. He had a knife in each hand, hacking and slashing, forcing back their limbs undamaged. They were unarmed, complacent, and confident they knew how this would end. Hal, for a change, had no such certainty, his visions darkened with the Fratriae around him. He would be dead in less than a minute without drastic measures.

Joe fell unceremoniously, his limbs rigid as the third Fratriae grasped his wrist. Hal was powerless to act, watching from the corner of his eye as Joe hit the floor and the Fratriae's boot stamped down, crushing his throat and snapping his neck with one savage kick. Hal felt Joe's power extinguish, the aura of life that surrounded them all released, and in that instant he knew what he needed to do. The Fratriae were immune to any damage he could cause, but they could at least be halted.

Hal leapt back, putting himself out of their reach for a precious second before the third could reach him. His mind was churning furiously, barely controlled as he harnessed the power leaching from Joe's dead body and turned it to his own ends. His more extreme powers were rarely used, too obvious to go undetected and so making him a target, but that meant nothing here and now. Without this, he would be dead in moments.

He felt some of the power dissipate, absorbed by the triumphant Fratriae, but it was not enough, the full force of Joe's mind and spirit dragged into Hal and wielded as a blunt force. He knew he couldn't attack them directly, knew such an attack would simply fade as it struck them, but he had a better idea.

Brute rage washed from his form, the condensed energy ripping out from him in a radiating arc. It was unsubtle, clumsy even, but it did its job. The ground around him was wrenched into the air, the road torn from its foundations and smashed with terrifying force into the three Fratriae, burying them, alive and still unharmed, beneath chunks of solid concrete. His mind was alive, fully unleashed for the first time, and he revelled in the power, feeling something akin to the killing urge but so much sweeter course through him, sheer joy at his own capabilities. He flexed his mind, instinctively wielding with ease the strength that had lain almost dormant all his life, and lashed out again, crushing the rubble around him with the wrath of an angry god, smashing down again and again, crushing the still living Fratriae beneath the surface. He realised he was smiling, laughing with a savage glee for the first time in his life, his arms spread wide.

A cry alerted him and he turned, seeing Harpen locked in combat with the remaining Fratriae, holding out impossibly against the odds. Hal's smile was still on his face as his mind reached out, plucking a car from the side of the road and hurling it. The Fratriae was smashed from his feet and Hal hit him again and again, mangling the vehicle as it forced the body into the ground, cracking the road surface with the force of the repeated blows. Harpen was breathing heavily, his endurance pushed to the limit by the fight, and he was looking at Hal with a mix of awe and horror, seeing the smile on a face that had always been blank.

"We need to go. Now."

Hal nodded, the power draining from his form, the last vestiges of Joe's mind leaving him. He could feel the earth shift as the Fratriae forced themselves free.

"They can't be killed," he said, disappointed. Harpen shook his head.

"Bring Joe. Leave the others. We have to get the boy out of here."

* * * * * * * * * *

Mike was silent as the door slid shut and the aircraft rose, cradling Cal in his lap. Hal and Harpen were sitting nearby, the only survivors of the fight, the latter already sealing a bag around Joe's body. This was a lot of deaths to save one boy, and he wondered for a moment if Steph had been right, if they were just senseless killers. He banished the thought almost immediately, but the idea lingered for a moment in the back of his mind, mixing with his feelings for Steph. His eyes were blank as he banished her from his mind as well.

* * * * * * * * * *

The journey home had been mercifully safe, and Harpen was glad to be back in the hanger, doubly so as the earth closed around it, sealing them underground. Hal headed off without a word, and Harpen watched him go thoughtfully, knowing he would have to address the events of the fight soon. He shivered involuntarily as he remembered Hal's face, a smile where no smile had ever been, and he knew something would have to be done.

"He's tasted power now," Mike observed, nodding towards the door Hal had just left by before turning to face his friend, his son sleeping in his arms. Harpen inclined his head, the concern evident in his features.

"We just got him back. We can't lose him again."

"Why would we?"

"You didn't see him Mike. He was laughing. Hal doesn't laugh."

"He used his powers to the full. You know what that's like."

Harpen nodded, remembering the few times he had been forced to do the same, to unleash his mind in a furious display. Such an undertaking was draining and dangerous, for so many reasons, not least the beacon it created, a magical lure to anyone who could feel it. He had no doubt every Vampire in southern Africa was heading south to find whatever had released such sorcery.

"We know to curb it. Hal has no such feelings. And the Fratriae gave him an addictive personality."

"Which Karl cured. He'll be fine."

Mike walked away, turning in the doorway.

"Thanks, by the way."

Harpen nodded, a weary smile on his face, following a few moments later, heading for his own room within the HQ. Like most of the complex, it was personalised to the owner's tastes, a large open plan suite, simply furnished with a broad couch and a low table, laid with bottles of drink and a row of bladed weapons. One wall was taken up by his armoury, a wide open fronted case that held his weapons and several sets of armour, and a walk in wardrobe took up the other wall. There was no need for a bed, the couch sufficing for what little rest he took.

He removed his torn uniform and pulled on a pair of light linen trousers, laying out his weaponry on the table and beginning to meticulously clean each component part. He flicked on the TV as he worked, cycling through the channels until he found what he was looking for, a link to a South African news network. The twisted remains of the road he had been fighting on hours before filled the screen.

To his satisfaction, the story was simple. No explanation was forthcoming for the fighting that had occurred, and no one had been able to identify the bodies of the men involved. The dead had been taken to a police morgue, and Harpen made a mental note to have the Hunter's corpses retrieved as soon as they could. Several figures – the Fratriae, Harpen guessed – had been observed fleeing the scene, and were wanting by police for questioning. Eyewitness reports of an aircraft hovering over the road had been dismissed when no radar had detected anything, but as yet police had no explanation for how an explosion had ripped up the road but left no scorch marks...

Harpen turned off the TV, content their secrecy had been maintained. There was nothing to trace the events back to the Hunters, and he allowed himself a sigh of relief. Only a couple of things remained to be sorted from the day.

Some were easier than others, he mused as he finished his work, returning the weapons to the armoury and pulling on a shirt as he left the room. He wandered with purpose, heading for Hal's room, picking up Mike on the way. The rest of the Order were away, engaged on hunts elsewhere, and the three of them would have to do.

"What is it?" Hal asked as Mike and Harpen entered his room. It was smaller than Harpen's, bare but for racks of weapons and armour and a single high backed chair.

"There's something we need to do, and you should be there."

"Why?"

"You should see where we all end up."

* * * * * * * * * *

There were whole stretches of the HQ that were unused, tunnels that had been created but never utilised, rooms which had been left empty. Many were waiting for a time when they would be required, or had simply been created as an exercise by the Obur's. Some were deliberately abandoned, left to crumble and then used as training areas, although most Hunters preferred the purpose built sections of the HQ for such exercise. A few areas were forgotten by all but a few, and it was one of these that the three men headed for now, carrying between them a plain wooden coffin with a simple inscription on its lid. A single Obur came with them, one of the residents of the HQ who had crafted its halls for centuries.

They were far beneath the rest of the HQ, miles underground, the air and pressure and temperature maintained by arcane means. They walked through the pitch darkness in silence, the lack of light no hindrance to them, until they reached an ancient wooden door, encased by metal strips. A heraldic device was embossed in its centre, a crest of a design unfamiliar to Hal as he reached out on Harpen's instructions and rested his hand on the metal. He felt it react to his touch, the door swinging open silently, revealing a long passage. He stepped inside, glancing to his left and right, seeing alcoves in the walls, one after another, stretching out into the distance. Above each one was a stone slab, engraved with a short epitaph and the name of one of the Brothers of the Order. Hal read the first few, the lives and deeds of the earliest Brothers. In each alcove, a coffin was lain, some wooden, most of them stone, all of them perfectly preserved.

"We're all buried down here. Every Brother whose body isn't destroyed outright is recovered and interred. The Obur's have maintained this tomb for thousands of years, moving it when they needed to, expanding it every time one of us falls."

Hal knew he should feel something, but it just wouldn't come. He was a part of this Order, but he couldn't even feel that.

"Why?"

"What?"

"Why do we recover them?"

"We are the pinnacle of humanity, Hal, beyond evolution. The secrets and power that went into our creation should never get out. Especially not to the Families. Think what they could do with access to our power, our blood."

"Then why keep them at all? Why not destroy them?"

Harpen sighed, knowing he should have expected this, that he had seen it before in Hal's ancestors. Hal couldn't understand the importance of their kind, couldn't even understand his importance in their history.

"Respect."

Hal simply nodded and they walked on, following the corridor as it went on and on, passing down sloped passageways and long corridors, crisscrossing deeper into the bowels of the earth, following the history of the Order from its inception to the present day.

Eventually they reached the end, Hal running his eyes over the epitaph for Victor Lemirda as they passed. The passage stopped abruptly, the last alcove in line bearing Dimitri Harpen's name. Opposite, the wall was blank, and the three Hunters waited as the Obur went to work, placing his hands on the wall. It softened as if melted at his touch, and flowed away into the surrounding rock, forming a perfectly squared off alcove in a matter of moments. The coffin was placed inside without ceremony, and Harpen recited the epitaph that appeared in the stone above the alcove as the Obur ran his hand along the wall. They waited while this was complete, then returned to the surface in silence.

* * * * * * * * * *

Hal returned to his room and sat down, his mind empty. Like all the Brothers, he had no need for sleep, but he took rest when he could, not because he needed to, but because it gave him time to think, gave his mind time to work, and his powers the opportunity to surface. Even after all this time, it was still not an exact science, coming at random intervals, but he could feel his mind churning. Some of it, he knew, was the after effects of the battle and the torrent he had wielded, but among that was a familiar feeling, a vision creeping to the surface of his thoughts...

He shut his eyes.

* * * * * * * * * *

He could see the moon rising on the horizon, reflecting off the surface of the sea. In the distance, too far to see them clearly, a trio of ships lay at anchor, unlit and barely visible.

Hal was walking the line, seeing the pits carved from solid rock, the barricades and obstacles built above them, and the men manning those pits. Many of them were Hunters, faces Hal recognised, heavily armed and armoured. Obur Vampires were spread among the line, some still constructing the defences even as the enemy ships bore down on the island. Others were armed, standing motionless and staring out to sea, their faces unfathomable.

Hal walked on, finding a handful of his Brothers waiting for him at the mouth of a cave, each of them greeting him warmly. They were clad as he was, in heavy body armour and visored helmets, every one of them armed to the teeth and smiling in anticipation of what was to come.

Hal paused suddenly, glancing upward to the cliff top, raising his blade in salute. Karl Laumpir stood there, clad in segmented body armour of clearly ancient design, his sword held loosely in his hands, and he nodded once to Hal, before turning away, walking to join a girl Hal vaguely recognised.

Hal turned back to his Brothers and led them into the cave, plunging into darkness. The walls were rough and uneven, a natural cave network twisted in places by Obur artifice into a warren of tunnels that led down into the base of the island. He had walked them before, committing every inch of them to memory, and he led his Brothers now to the lowest levels, where the tunnels opened out onto a broad moonlit beach. Above them, a sheer cliff face loomed, dotted with small openings, Hunters placed in each one, weapons trained on the beach. Above that, on the cliff top, lay the defences Hal had walked minutes before.

He and the Brothers were to be the first line of defence, luring the attackers into the tunnels and holding them there. It would be tight and brutal, close quarter killing in the confines of the tunnel network. Hal caught a glimpse of himself in combat, locked in a death struggle in the darkness. His mind was clear, blank, composed, no thrill or urge clouding it.

Free.

* * * * * * * * * *

Harpen and Hal pushed their way through the revolving doors, striding confidently over the marble floor, dressed in sober black suits and gleaming shoes that clicked as they walked. Hal's eyes were hidden beneath a pair of tinted glasses, the cut of his jacket concealing a handgun resting on his hip and his knife strapped to his forearm. Harpen was similarly armed, and he smiled as he handed over a business card to the receptionist, declaring them to be representatives of a security firm. She smiled in return and directed them to a waiting area, picking up the phone and dialling a number.

The two men sat side by side, unmoving, patient.

It had been little more than a day since their return to the HQ, and already they were active once again, engaged in the endless pursuit of their calling. A lone Kappa, masquerading as a security guard, identified by a work schedule that saw him on permanent night duty. Harpen shook his head. It was little wonder the Hunter's kill tallies had increased dramatically in the last decade or two, when finding targets could take little more than a clever or lucky internet search. Firewalls and passwords were nothing to the Hunters, the Obur's mastery of technology extending easily to computing, and they had at their fingertips any information they could require.

He knew, as Hal knew, this hunt did not require a Brother of the Order, let alone two, but neither had referenced the fact on the journey here. Harpen wanted a chance to converse with Hal in an environment in which he was comfortable, and that really meant a hunt. Quite why Hal had gone along with it, he wasn't sure, but didn't care to enquire.

"We need to work out if something can be done about the Fratriae," Harpen began, unwilling to dive straight in with his main concern. He spoke quietly, but he knew Hal would be masking their conversation from curious ears.

"How?"

"I'm not sure. But they are a danger to us now. We can't afford losses like that every time we meet them."

Hal nodded in agreement, and Harpen had a sense he was about to say something, but didn't. He ignored it and went on.

"Did you do any damage to them?"

"No. They were crushed, and buried, but they weren't hurt. I don't think they can be."

Harpen nodded, seeing his chance.

"About that. What you did was..."

He was interrupted by the receptionist, resolving to wait. He had no idea how Hal would react. He seemed to have returned to normal, or at least what passed for normal for a Lemirda, and Harpen wondered if Hal's insane display of power had been a one off, an aberration brought about by extreme circumstance. His concern about Hal becoming addicted or affected seemed so far to be unfounded, but he knew he needed to confront it soon, before Hal found himself in a position to deploy his powers again. He was thankful Hal had agreed to come on this hunt, where there was no such danger.

The two men followed the receptionist across the main hall, entering an office and introducing themselves to the head of security for the building. The conversation was inconsequential, uninteresting, and, from Harpen's side at least, completely fictitious, but it got them what they wanted. As the sun began to set, and the building began to close for the night, Harpen and Hal were led on a tour of the building.

They viewed a series of security arrangements, all of them bland and dull, neither of them really listening as they scanned around, their senses working to detect a hint of Vampire. There was nothing, and Harpen began to wonder if they had made a mistake.

He felt Hal's mind brush his own, and a moment later he caught the scent, a dim inkling of something on the far side of the building. Their guide noticed nothing as Harpen reached into his head, leaving suggestions that made him alter his tour route, bringing them closer to the source of the power, now unmistakably a Vampire.

They pushed open a fire door and stepped into a grey walled stairwell that stretched above and below them. Silent now, their guide led them down and along a long blank utility corridor. Harpen detached himself from the man's mind and left him lying unconscious beneath the staircase, leading Hal away. Almost immediately, a door ahead of them opened and a man emerged, wearing a blue security guard's uniform and whistling nonchalantly as he headed for the stairs. The Kappa stopped suddenly, noticing the two men and immediately realising something was wrong.

Hal pulled his knife free and hurled it, but the Vampire had already gone, dropping his bag and disappearing back through the door he had entered by. The two men gave chase, seeing him flee across an underground car park, and Harpen slowed down, drawing his pistol casually and firing a shot, the bullet catching the Vampire across the calf and slowing him down enough for Hal to catch him, finishing him with one swift stab to the heart. Harpen watched, seeing a curious look on Hal's face as the Vampire died, but it was gone almost immediately. Less than a minute later, the body was gone, burned into nothingness, and the two men returned to the unconscious head of security. He awoke without realising anything was amiss, and the two Hunters went with him, heading for the reception and his office, the tour concluded.

As they pushed open the door, they found themselves facing a number of men, all of them armed, all of them pointing weapons at the two Hunters, and all of them looking very pissed off.

"Can we help you, gentlemen?" Harpen said calmly, his hands raised. These men were not an obvious threat, all of them ordinary human beings. Beside him, he could feel Hal tense almost imperceptibly, and he shot a note of caution through his companion. There would be no murder here.

"Who are you?" one of the men demanded, and Harpen almost laughed. He had been threatened by Vampires and wounded in ways these men couldn't even conceive. The man was trying to sound tough, but it just wasn't working.

"We are security reps from..."

"Cut the crap. Your firm doesn't exist."

Harpen raised an eyebrow. This had never happened before. The Hunter's covers were expertly weaved, with accounts, personnel, records, portfolios, statements, legal documentation, the works. Each Hunter had dozens of identities, all of them verifiable with national databases, census records, and employment histories. They were solid, cast iron covers that had never failed them. Until now.

"There must be some mistake."

"No mistake. He showed us. He told us who you really are. So I suggest you drop the pistol concealed under your jacket and get your hands against that wall. I will shoot you if you give me the slightest excuse."

Well this is interesting. Harpen sent to Hal. *When you're ready. Don't kill any of them.*

The two men didn't even pretend to drop their weapons, leaping forward simultaneously. It seemed like an age before the guards opened fire, but Hal knew it was just how long human reflexes took to react, and he and Harpen were already among them, lashing out with carefully controlled blows, knocking the men to the floor. It was laughably easy, neither of them even thinking about what they were doing, and the final man was curled up on the floor nursing a broken wrist in a few seconds. Harpen reached out for a moment to remove any trace of them from the men's minds, and for the second time raised his eyebrow, puzzled. Their thoughts were thick, sluggish, and he couldn't penetrate them without considerable effort.

Someone has been in their heads. They have defences.

"Fratriae," Hal muttered, and Harpen turned. Outside, visible through the window, a single man was standing watching them, his features composed.

"Are you sure?"

"I've seen him before."

Harpen opened his mouth to respond, but Hal was already moving. The power was building up in his body, and Harpen knew he had already missed his chance, seeing that chilling smile on Hal's face again as he prepared to unleash fury.

The window did nothing to slow him, smashing into fragments as Hal ran through it, and he didn't even give the Fratriae time to act. Harpen had barely opened his mouth, barely begun to call Hal off, before the ground beneath the Fratriae split open and an invisible force smashed him down, pressing him into the earth. Harpen watched as Hal raised a hand, and a whole section of wall was ripped from the front of the building opposite, crashing down on the figure rising from the crater, burying him beneath tons of rubble.

Harpen despaired, feeling the aftershock of the power washing from Hal. He knew they should just run, but he had to clear any trace of them, and he resumed his work, grunting with the effort of clearing the memories from the men lying around the reception, leaving the suggestion of their injuries being sustained by the falling building. It was clumsy work, but it would have to do. The minutes it took was time they could not afford.

He was done at last, but as he stepped through the smashed window, he realised it was too late. Figures were approaching them along the street, drawn by the power Hal had unleashed, armed and ready to fight. Harpen glanced at Hal, seeing the fading hint of a smile as he drew his blade.

Time was up.

* * * * * * * * * *

Hal felt the familiar thrill again as he killed, but it was nothing compared to the joy he felt when he pushed his powers to their full. Almost a dozen Vampires were around them, most of them dead already, all of them drawn by the sorcery, and Hal knew more would be on their way, arriving from ever greater distances to meet whatever threat they perceived in the power unleashed. Beside him, Harpen fought grimly, and Hal recognised the look on his face, the look that said a conversation was imminent, the look he recognised from his years of training. It was a look of resigned disappointment, and Hal realised that for a fleeting moment, he cared about what Harpen thought. The thought was gone and forgotten in an instant, but for that instant, Hal was shaken.

He faced off with the remaining Vampire, slashing twice before landing the blade home. This one was a Strigoi, and as he fell, Hal felt the exhalation of energy from his form, a pale imitation of the power that he had siphoned from Joe's body, but there nonetheless, tangible, a taste on the tip of his tongue.

Like the previous thought, this realisation was gone in an instant, but unlike the previous thought, he allowed it to linger in his mind as the two men fled into the night.

* * * * * * * * * *

Cal was silent, and Mike smiled as he leaned over the basket, dropping empty bullet cases over his son. Each one was batted away by a clumsy swipe, Cal's yellow eyes fixing on them in turn, and Mike saw the focus there, even at this young age. Mercifully, there was nothing of his mother in his looks, not that Mike had thought there would be, and as he played with his son, a calm settled in his mind.

This was the turning point for him, the moment from which he could afford to hurl himself headlong into every challenge, confident that his line was now safeguarded. In the short term, Mike would teach his son, train him, bring him up as a Hunter and help him to take his place in the organisation, but in the long term, his future was written, as surely as if Hal had seen it. With his son alive, Mike could fight without hindrance, knowing he would eventually die in combat. No one knew how old the Brothers could live to be, as none of them had ever died a natural death, and Mike knew what fate awaited him. As he looked down at his son, he felt confident, and that confidence was borne of the certain knowledge of his place in the long war.

Despite his humanity, despite his conscience, even despite Steph, he knew that if he had had the choice, he wouldn't have changed a thing.

In time, and especially in the days to come, he knew he would need that certainty.

* * * * * * * * * *

"The Fratriae are a danger to our operations, that much is clear. At this stage, we have no idea how much, but we know they managed to second guess a hunt and influence forces to stop us, as well as destroying fabricated information. If they can roll this out on a larger scale, we could see our entire organisation shut down, or worse, exposed."

Harpen met the eyes of each of the men in the room, before glancing at the camera mounted on the desk. On the wall of the conference room, a large screen was divided into dozens of images, each one of a Hunter somewhere in the world. This threat was serious, and Harpen had contacted all the key players in the organisation, either in the HQ or via web link. Karl Laumpir was also visible in one of the screens, along with half a dozen Obur cell leaders.

"We need a way to shut them down before they can do serious damage."

"They cannot be killed," Karl spoke for the first time. Behind him, Harpen could see the interior of his study. "And after this, it's not likely you can make a deal with them. I have no goodwill left with them either."

Harpen paused, wondering if there was a 'however,' but apparently there wasn't.

"Can you see what you can do?"

"I will try, but I am doubtful. I will ponder the problem."

With that, Karl was gone, and Harpen faced his men.

"We have no choice. For the meantime, go dark. Shut down all operations and stand down, but be alert. We don't know what they know, or how they know it, or what they might do. Keep hidden, keep safe, and call in anything unusual, or any ideas."

Harpen cut the link, knowing he should have finished with something slightly more inspiring, but he couldn't bring himself to do it. The revelation that the Fratriae could effectively expose their operation was a greater worry than he let on, especially as they knew the location of the HQ. He half expected some country's military or secret service to appear above them, was tempted to have the Oburs move the entire HQ, but even that they might detect. By one low level action, the Fratriae had paralysed the Vampire Hunters. He wondered what they were getting in return, if anything, knowing this was a seriously high stakes game, and that any of the Families would have given up a great deal to achieve this result. Even if this was resolved with the Fratriae, the Hunters could re-emerge to find their enemies stronger than ever.

And Harpen was powerless to do anything about it.

* * * * * * * * * *

Part Five – Lemirda sated

Hal was walking the line, seeing the pits carved from solid rock, the barricades and obstacles built above them, and the men manning those pits. Many of them were Hunters, heavily armed and armoured, and a good number of Obur Vampires were spread among the line, some still constructing the defences even as the enemy ships bore down on the island. Others were armed, standing motionless and staring out to sea, their faces unfathomable.

Hal walked on, finding a handful of his Brothers waiting for him at the mouth of a cave, each of them greeting him warmly. They were clad as he was, in heavy body armour and visored helmets, every one of them armed to the teeth and smiling in anticipation of what was to come. Mike clapped him on the shoulder, a gesture that was meant to be reassuring but was lost on Hal.

He paused suddenly, glancing upward to the cliff top, raising his blade in salute. Karl Laumpir stood there, clad in segmented body armour of clearly ancient design, his sword held loosely in his hands, and he nodded once to Hal, before turning away, walking to join a girl whose aura shone with power.

Hal turned back to his Brothers and led them into the cave, plunging into darkness. The walls were rough and uneven, a natural cave network twisted in places by Obur artifice into a warren of tunnels that led down into the base of the island. He had walked them before, committing every inch of them to memory, and he led his Brothers now to the lowest levels, where the tunnels opened out onto a broad moonlit beach. Above them, a sheer cliff face loomed, dotted with small openings, Hunters placed in each one, weapons trained on the beach. Above that, on the cliff top, lay the defences Hal had walked minutes before.

He and the Brothers were to be the first line of defence, luring the attackers into the tunnels and holding them there. It would be tight and brutal, close quarter killing in the confines of the tunnel network. Hal caught a glimpse of himself in combat, locked in a death struggle in the darkness, his mind clear, blank, composed.

He killed without feeling, each blow landing without rage or hate, until something seemed to strike him, an invisible force that left him shaking, leaning on the wall for support as his Brothers surged into the fray around him. A moment later, he was...

Gone.

Hal opened his eyes, the vision cut short. He shook his head and rose to his feet, restless. The confinement was telling on all the Hunters after just a few days, the inactivity rendering them bored and edgy, especially the Brothers. The same vision was plaguing him, foreshadowing some great event. He wanted to tell Harpen, but knew there was nothing that could be done, and that Harpen himself had enough on his mind, directing their forces to find some way to catch and shut down the Fratriae. Hal had tried to help, tried to direct his visions to the Fratriae, but nothing would come. Whatever they had done or by their own arcane powers, they kept themselves from his visions. He had even considered wearing the Ildraya again to try and galvanise his mind, but so far he had resisted.

He knew he needed to act, needed to do something other than wait, and only one thing occurred to him at this time. He rose to his feet, pulling a selection of weapons from his armoury, and walked purposely through the halls of the HQ, passing Hunters on the way. Most were hard at work, poring through local news and scattered reports for some trace of the Fratriae, galvanised by Harpen's orders into digging out some detail that would help them, but so far the search was proving impossible. Some Hunters, the less subtle, were leaving the search to others more suited to the task, honing themselves for the time when their skills would be called upon, and it was to one of these groups Hal headed, finding Kym at its centre, sparring with a team of Hunters who came at him two or three at a time. Kym dropped them all in seconds, over and over as they came back at him, only stopping when he noticed Hal standing there.

Their eyes met for a moment, neutral and even. Hal had had very little dealings with Kym over the years, each of them content to work with their own company, but they had at least a degree of respect for each other. Of all the Brothers, Kym had been quickest to forgive Hal's transgressions, seeing instead the martial skill that had been displayed, and they had at least a frosty but cordial working relationship.

Nothing needed to be said. Kym picked up his knives and followed Hal, knowing there was only one reason Hal or anyone else came to him. He was a blunt instrument, a killer among Hunters.

Hal wanted to hunt, and Kym was happy to oblige.

* * * * * * * * * *

Simeon smiled to himself, but his eyes were angry as he directed the brothers and sisters of the Fratriae. The web they were crafting was intricate beyond measure, a thousand strands of insignificant detail that combined would bring down the Hunters piece by piece. The Fratriae had watched them for centuries, seeing them grow, using them as a weapon, a cover, an unwitting ally, but those days were over. Simeon had enough information to bring them crashing down, and all that had prevented him from doing so was the scant aid they could provide. No longer, it seemed.

Under his direction, confidential reports were being sent, addressed, via a long and untraceable series of intermediaries, to police officials across the world, each by itself a small detail that would go unnoticed in the grand scheme of things. When it came to fruition, only those who knew, those who cared, would notice the elaborate and unconventional attack, and Simeon knew the Hunters were smart enough to see the threat, but would be unable to counteract it.

The smile finally reached his eyes.

* * * * * * * * * *

Harpen was drumming his finger on the desk, reading a stream of reports from cells across the world, all of them turning up nothing but dead ends. The whole organisation was dedicating itself to finding some trace of the Fratriae, but it was as if they didn't exist.

He looked up as Hal and Kym entered the room, two of the most dangerous men on the planet, both of them armed to the teeth.

"Going somewhere nice?" Harpen asked wryly.

"I want to make good on my threat," Hal replied, and Harpen smiled as he realised that was almost Hal asking for permission, but he shook his head.

"We need you here."

"I'm no use here. The Fratriae keep out of my visions. If I kill Vampiri, it will hurt them. They may even come to me."

Harpen nodded once, tempted to go with them, feeling a brief moment of concern at the thought of Hal unchecked and unleashed, but he knew the danger of Hal losing it was much less than the danger posed by the Fratriae.

"Good hunting."

* * * * * * * * * *

They travelled for a day or two before Hal felt the familiar surge in his mind as a vision came to him. Harpen had been unwilling to let them take an aircraft, forcing them to head for the nearest commercial airport, but that had given Hal the time he needed, and the two men had boarded the next available flight, hopping via a number of cities, following Hal's visions and making their way to Santiago. They didn't say a word to each other, content with silence, content to wait until the next hunt.

Hal guided them unerringly, snatches of visions moving them forwards, striking out of the city and making for the hills in an Obur tuned truck. The scenery was lost on them, the grandeur of the landscape and the ruins meaning nothing to them, and they drove through the night to reach their destination.

As the sun rose, Hal led them away from the road, walking for a short while, stopping seemingly at random. The landscape was barren and rocky, only a few scattered shrubs here and there, and only Hal's visions let him know they were in the right place.

"Now what?" Kym asked, glancing around, his knives drawn and ready. There was no threat they could sense, but he wasn't capable of switching off.

"Now we dig."

Several hours work uncovered a circle of stones, and further digging revealed that these were just the top of much taller columns, at the centre of which lay a flat stone, unmarked but clearly hand carved. It was the work of a moment for the two men to pull it aside, revealing a vertical shaft that disappeared into the earth. One glance at each other was all it took, and the two men jumped.

They landed lightly, despite the height of the drop, and immediately moved, both of them silent and alert, feeling the presence of Vampires nearby and reacting on instinct. They advanced as one, Kym leading, crouched low with his knives held in front of his face, Hal holding his carbine over the other man's shoulder. The tunnel was low and narrow, carved from solid rock, and by the look of it the work had been done by some massive creature, leaving clear claw marks in the walls. It was old, clearly unused for some time if the layers of undisturbed dirt were any indication, but they were tense as they advanced.

The froze as the floor shook beneath them, a low rumble that made the smaller stones skitter along the floor, and Kym shifted his feet, widening his stance and turning his knives so they pointed downwards from his fists. He was barely aware of what he was doing, reacting to a threat that hadn't yet manifested itself, and Hal followed suit, taking a few steps back to cover the tunnel around Kym.

The floor split suddenly, throwing a cloud of dirt into the air, and the two men caught a glimpse of claws and teeth emerging from the gap. It snapped at Kym, who ducked and rolled away, leaving Hal the room he needed to open fire, a burst of rounds stitching a line of bloody holes up the creatures flank. It crawled further into the tunnel, swinging a claw again, and again Kym rolled away.

It seemed to have been based on a mole, grown and enhanced to insane proportions and with multiple claws protruding from its shoulders, all of them grasping and waving as if independent of each other. Its mouth was held open by row after row of blade like teeth, and it regarded them with milky eyes that were set far behind its pointed nose. It was a monster, a terrifying product of the Vampiri family, all at once the creator and guardian of these tunnels.

It didn't stand a chance.

Hal fired again, emptying the clip into the thing's eyes, eliciting a snarl that died away suddenly as Kym struck with both of his blades. The first was turned away by a swipe of a chitinous claw, but the second bit down, lodging in place in the monster's cheek. It snarled again, the tip of the blade visible in its mouth, and Hal swept in, cutting a bloody welt from its eye to the base of one of the claws. He leapt back, narrowly dodging a swinging claw, only to see Kym dive forward, taking advantage of the opening and pushing the longer of his blades up into its chest, piercing its heart and cutting away with one savage blow, ripping a long gash in its body. It thrashed for a few moments, then lay still.

They said nothing, pausing just long enough for Kym to tear his knives free, then they took off, running down the tunnel, abandoning silence for speed. The tunnel was long, and pierced with side passages, but Hal led them to a section that suddenly widened out into a long chamber. Half a dozen figures were moving, rolling sluggishly from narrow alcoves in the walls, and the two men were in amongst them without hesitation, dropping three before they could react. Kym duelled two more at once, pinning the first to the wall and killing the second instantly with a single thrust to the heart. Hal didn't even engage, merely throwing his dagger with a backhanded flick, watching as it landed squarely in the back of a fleeing Vampiri, piercing his heart. He fought down a mental impulse as he felt the spirits of the Vampires seep into the air, realising this was the first time he had killed Vampiri without the Fratriae there to absorb the power, and he found himself intoxicated by the energy leaching into his form, having to fight to keep it contained. He glanced at Kym, seeing he was clearly unaffected, and that allowed him to break the spell, reasserting his own mental control.

He paused for a moment, seeing the single still living Vampire and realising that Kym had offered him a chance he had never had before. He stepped lightly across the room, grabbing Kym's arm as he raised it to strike, aimed at the chest of the remaining Vampiri. The Vampire was held suspended and immobile by Kym's blade in his shoulder, and Hal had to drag Kym away to stop him making the kill.

One moment.

Kym scowled, his red tinged eyes glaring at Hal, but he relented, turning away and venting his anger on the creatures that littered the floor of the tunnels. Most of them were stunted and malformed, no threat as far as they could see, but it kept Kym busy.

Hal ignored him and turned to the Vampiri, gazing impassively into the face of his prey. Its skin was deathly pale and pulled tight over its bones, its fangs clearly visible in a mouth that was bloodied and raw. Only its eyes, dark and sunken, revealed its power, burning with a fierce intellect and boring into Hal's mind. He dismissed it with a thought, and raised his knife over the thing's heart.

"Tell me about the Fratriae."

At the mention of the name, the creature flinched, but showed no other sign of understanding. Hal pressed the tip of the blade against its chest, and spoke instead straight into the creature's mind, reinforcing his words with graphic images of the kills he had witnessed.

I served the Fratriae as a Hunter. I have led them to your fellows and watched them die in fear and agony. My Brother and I have killed your coven, but that is a mercy we need not grant you. We will leave you as an offering to the Fratriae, to be consumed and destroyed, unless you tell me what I want to know.

The creature relented, and Hal felt the easing of pressure from the Vampire's mind as it dropped its defences. Its voice when it spoke was curiously at odds with its bestial appearance, a low monotone speech that was devoid of accent.

"You will kill me."

"Yes."

The creature seemed to consider this.

"Then you offer me nothing but a choice of deaths."

Hal nodded. His hand was itching, his grip on the knife just a little too tight, and he fought down a sudden urge to carve it into the Vampire's chest. He realised his breathing was quickening, his heart beginning to race, and it took force of will to step back and lower his blade before he killed. That made it no better, and the power of the dead Vampiri, the power that he had forced out, rushed back into his form as if sensing weakness. He felt the thrill run through his veins, felt the urge to release it all in one devastating attack that would shatter the Vampire's form and bring the tunnel down on top of him.

He staggered, dropping his knife, not noticing that Kym was watching him. The other Hunter made no attempt to come to his aid, merely looking on, uncomprehending, as Hal suffered, his body wracked by the urge to kill, the urge to channel his powers and the energy around him into a dizzying frenzy of rage and sorcery. It was addictive, self-destructive, and Hal felt himself giving in, feeling the anticipation and the thrill.

Kym saved him. Just as Hal was on the brink of breaking, his Brother lashed out, slaying the final Vampiri and throwing its body to the floor. Hal convulsed, fighting down the split second desire to turn the destructive force of his mind onto his Brother for denying him the kill, before the power dissipated, the foreign energy earthed and Hal's mind once again in control.

He nodded once to Kym, who ignored him, and Hal felt an absence in his mind where guilt should have been, seeing the disapproval Harpen would show over this lapse in his mental control.

He wondered at that for a while, allowing his thoughts to drift in a rare moment of introspection. He couldn't articulate the thoughts on James Harpen, much less talk to him, knowing that any move that way would lead inevitably to the older man's censure of Hal's ways. Although he felt no guilt, Hal was aware that his displays in recent weeks had been excessive, and that Harpen was waiting for a time to confront him over it. Something wormed away in whatever passed for Hal's conscience whenever his thoughts drifted this way, and he couldn't dwell on it for long.

That addictive feeling was still there, boiling away in the back of his mind, the desire to release raw power and realised potential coursing through him, and he itched to repeat it. The urge was still nothing next to the consuming hunger the Fratriae had put him through, but was still a potent force, a goal, a target he wished to reach again and again. He knew, even if he couldn't admit it, it was only Harpen's inevitable criticism that somehow held Hal in check, his respect for his mentor ensuring he kept himself in line.

For how long, he couldn't foresee, and he knew something would have to be done. He had no wish to return to the state of addiction that had claimed him and nearly ended his work and his life. His mind was already being hijacked, the thrill threatening to take over again, and he knew he could not afford to let that happen. The next fight he was in could see him descend further into a joyous rage, and would drive a wedge between him and his Brothers. He had no need for their companionship, felt no warmth towards them, but still, somehow, the thought troubled him.

He gestured to Kym, and the two men departed, making their way back into the tunnels and out onto the surface. The vehicle was where they had left it, and they made the return journey to the airport in silence. Once there, Hal turned to his companion.

"Head back. I need to carry on alone."

He expected some objection, seeing again Harpen's disapproval, but Kym just nodded and climbed from the cab. Hal sighed, then inclined his head as he heard Kym in his mind.

I will tell James what happened in that cave.

Hal nodded to himself.

So be it.

* * * * * * * * * *

Harpen was sitting quietly, his features impassive as he read the latest reports to reach him, none of them bearing good news. Almost a hundred Hunters were fleeing, heading into hiding with local law enforcement on their tails. Sections of the Hunter's fake business empire had been exposed, courier services, security agencies and transport firms revealed to have non-existent assets, or to simply exist on paper. Accounts were being frozen in dozens of countries as the scale of the deception was made clear, personnel accounts that contained only fake IDs and alter egos were being seized as police and auditors were made aware of what was going on.

Harpen nearly laughed. The crackdown was pathetic compared to the size of the organisation they had created, and the money and business' that were being shut down barely scratched the surface of what the Hunters had access to. No one in the world could possibly draw the links between these disparate frauds in dozens of countries, as there was simply no visible connection between any of them.

What was worrying him was the implications. The cover stories were perfect, the secrets unbreakable, and yet ordinary human authorities were achieving the impossible. This was the Fratriae's doing, the attacks too perfect, too precise to be anything else, and he knew this was just a warning, the first step in an attack that he had no idea how to fight. He knew nothing of this enemy, had no idea what they knew of his organisation or how they knew it. If this continued, they could shut down and ground every business, every vehicle the Hunters operated under the cover of one business or another. There was information, details of actions that could see them all arrested and executed for crimes across the planet, and he saw for the first time just how they would look to the rest of the world, how they had looked to Mike's girlfriend. Mass murders, thefts, cover ups, conspiracies – The Hunters worked outside the law, behind the backs of governments and law enforcement. If they were revealed, a lot of people would be out for their blood.

And still he had no idea what to do.

He glanced up as Kym entered the room, then raised an eyebrow. Kym had sent a typically terse report on his way here, and now Harpen listened, a grim look in his face as the Hunter relayed the details of the Vampiri cell. His scowl deepened when Kym described how Hal had convulsed, turning to concern when he realised Hal had departed alone. There had been no word since, and Harpen shook his head at the thought of losing Hal again, but knowing he couldn't spare the resources to find him this time.

"How's it going here?"

Harpen shook his head in response.

"Not good. The Fratriae are presumably pissed at your little display and have orchestrated a crackdown. A handful of business have been shut down, a dozen or so arrests for fraud and embezzlement."

"That doesn't seem so bad."

"It's just the beginning. If it carries on like this, we could be stuck with murder charges, terrorism, even genocide. The Fratriae have us in a vice, and in the meantime, the Families are loving it. With Hunters going into hiding, they're acting out. Bloodhounds are calling in murders and attacks that have left bodies drained of blood and left in the open, and we're stuck, scared of human authorities."

"What can we do?"

"For now, nothing. But if it carries on, we may have to do something we regret."

Kym just smiled his humourless smile.

* * * * * * * * *

The creature was afraid, its bewildered eyes regarding Hal as he sat unmoving on a floor awash with gore from his latest kills. Four Vampiri lay dead around him, carved and butchered, and a fifth was cowering in one corner. Hal's knife now lay on the floor out of reach, his pistol empty and thrown away after the fighting was done. His chest was heaving, not from the exertion of the fight but the effort of now controlling himself, feeling the energy from the dead leaching into him and forcing it out of his body, feeling his mind open up to it, inviting it in, the craving to harness it and rend the remaining Vampire with it almost overwhelming.

He took a deep breath and met the eyes of the creature in front of him, not believing it had come to this, but knowing he had no choice if he wanted to return to his Brothers.

I will destroy the Fratriae if you tell me how.

The Vampiri's eyes widened, a flicker of hope visible for a moment, but it made no reply. Hal raised his hand, feeling the energy run through him, a smile on his face as he ripped off the Vampire's arm with a thought.

You will die here regardless.

"They cannot be killed," the Vampire rasped suddenly, barely affected by the wound. "We made them perfect."

That is not what either of us wanted to hear.

"It is the truth. They need no sustenance, no healing. They have no weakness."

Hal convulsed again, conscious of the energy around him, knowing he had little time before it overwhelmed him.

"I have seen them eat the flesh of your kind."

"Spite. Malice. Nothing more."

Hal could stand it no more, and unleashed his rage on the Vampiri, smiling grimly as sheer force smashed the life from its form, feeling the spirit invigorate him against his will, unwilling to stop, unable to control his own mind.

The power was spent suddenly, and Hal collapsed, his breathing shallow and his mind reeling. There was a void in his thoughts, a growing desire to push himself to ever increasing heights of violence.

This could not go on, he realised, and for the first time in his life, he found he was able to admit something to himself.

He needed help.

* * * * * * * * * *

The room fell silent as Harpen entered, the assembled Brothers and Hunters waiting patiently as he walked to the front of the briefing room. His face was grim, his green eyes hard as he faced them, pausing to cast his gaze across the room before speaking.

"I'll keep this brief. The Fratriae have outplayed us. Our organisation has been shackled by their actions, and we need to do something before we're shut down. I've delayed this, hoping we could find them and stop them, but every lead has come up short. The best we can manage is to slow them down, and hope something turns up in the process."

He paused as the Hunters took this in, looking out on a sea of stony faces, starting as he saw Hal's among them. He must have just arrived, leaning alone on the back wall, avoiding everyone's gaze.

"The Fratriae cannot be stopped directly, but Bloodhounds have traced their agents. Vampires, mostly Kappa but some Ultor, are directing the police activity, feeding information on our dealings from the Fratriae to police forces across the globe. They need to be stopped to protect our interests in the short term."

"And the long term?" Mike asked, articulating the thoughts of everyone there. Cal was nowhere to be seen, safe in Mike's quarters.

Harpen just shrugged and shook his head.

The meeting broke up, the Hunters heading for armouries with a subdued air, and Harpen watched them go, wishing there was something else he could do.

Hal approached him slowly, and Harpen noticed he was walking upright, his body stiff as if wounded or in shock. Harpen looked in his eyes for the first time, seeing something there, a flicker of pain, there and then gone.

"Welcome back," he said, unwilling to enquire further. "We could use you now."

Hal shook his head.

"I came back to get something. There are things I have to do."

Harpen made no reply, unsure of what to say. Hal had never explained himself before, and there was something different about him, some air or aura about his person that Harpen recognised. His eyes travelled down Hal's arm, seeing his hand in his pocket, feeling the energy emanating from there, and he met Hal's gaze suddenly, shocked by the haunted look in his eyes, shocked by the eyes that despite their emptiness seemed almost human.

Hal didn't resist as Harpen pulled his arm free, revealing the Fratriae's Ildraya in Hal's hand. Neither of them spoke for a long while.

"We need you with us," Harpen said quietly. "Whole, and undamaged."

"I know. Let me go now, and I will be."

Harpen began to shake his head, but stopped as Hal spoke again, a word he never thought he'd hear from a Lemirda, his voice barely above a whisper.

"Please."

* * * * * * * * * *

Mike kicked open the door and fired on instinct as two figures moved to attack. The room, a luxurious penthouse apartment on the top floor of a high rise hotel in Shanghai, was in darkness, heavy drapes nailed over the windows allowing no light to penetrate, and Mike knew immediately the call had been a good one.

Hunters were at his back, swarming into the room, clad in featureless black body suits and full face hoods, only their eyes visible as they advanced. Vampires were waking, grabbing weapons and rushing forwards, but the sun was shining outside and they were snarling more in pain than anger. Mike didn't even bother firing again, instead stepping over to the window and dragging the drapes away, letting brilliant sunshine wash into the room. The half dozen Kappa's still standing collapsed in agony, writhing on the floor, scratching at their own flesh as it burned, and the Hunters went to work, ending the suffering of each with a single stab.

Mike surveyed the room, seeing that the elegantly appointed furniture had been pushed aside and the bed overturned, clearing space for a bank of computers. Hunters were already working, attempting to gather any information left on them, but one glance told Mike it was no good. Each one had been wiped, their screens blank and the drives smashed beyond repair, destroying any information that might lead them to these Vampires' shadowy overlords.

This scene had so far been repeated in a dozen raids across the planet.

The Hunters had acted with characteristic flair, striking hard and fast against every location identified by the Bloodhounds, a dozen separate teams hitting almost simultaneously across four continents. Most had gone smoothly, each band of Hunters finding and killing a handful of Vampires in short order. From the scattered reports Mike was already receiving, only Kym's group, the only one to have a target that was still in full darkness, had met any real resistance, and Mike grinned as he pictured his Brother locked in a furious struggle.

The point of similarity between all the raids was the total lack of information any of them had recovered, every trace of the Fratriae or even other cells expunged, and Mike almost laughed at the absurdity. The Hunters had pulled off a major coup, launching a series of pinpoint raids against a dozen targets, killing dozens of Vampires in one beautifully orchestrated assault, and yet it was simply not enough.

He dreaded to think how the Fratriae would react to this.

One of the Hunters called him from the doorway, and he headed out into the corridor, pleased to see his men had been unharmed in the attack. His mood shifted as stepped through into an emergency staircase, moving from the stunning opulence of the guest areas to the utilitarian grey of the back rooms, glancing down a dizzyingly high stairwell. Figures were visible far below, clad in blue and black, and even at this distance it was obvious they were armed.

"Seems we pissed them off."

Mike nodded, heading back into the apartment, satisfied that the bodies had already been disposed of and any trace of their attack removed.

"Pack up and get ready to run. Local police are heading this way."

He watched as his men quickly gathered their few belongings and ran for the stairwell, heading upward to where their aircraft was waiting on the roof. Mike paused and glanced down again, seeing the police officers pounding up the stairs, knowing they must have been warned to have arrived so quickly, and he breathed a sigh of relief as he departed.

He would have hated being forced to kill them.

* * * * * * * * * *

Karl's mansion was one of the most secure places on the planet, more so even than the Hunter HQ, protected from attack and detection by any means, conventional or sorcerous. It was a luxurious estate of sweeping grounds, surrounded by high walls, at the centre of which lay a stone manor house, dotted with high windows and fronted by a thick wooden door.

Hal approached slowly, walking along a broad gravel drive bordered on each side by thick forest. He had left his car beyond the walls, after making his way across Europe and into England by ferry, avoiding air travel as much as possible. From Dover, he had driven down the coast to the city of St Aldhelms, and from there to Karl's mansion, hidden in a forest a few miles from the city.

The door ahead of him opened, a long rectangle of light shining out onto the darkened drive, and a figure was silhouetted in the doorway. Hal stopped some way from the door, raising his hand in greeting but going no closer, unwilling to stand near Karl Laumpir in his present state of mind.

"Hello Hal," Karl said, his voice even. "Welcome to Sayfaven Hall."

Hal accepted the greeting with a nod, taking the Ildraya from his pocket without preamble. He could feel its influence, feeling his mind begin to yearn for killing, for power, for addiction itself, the proximity of a Vampire making it so much worse.

"I want to know how this was made."

Karl regarded him for a moment.

"To what end?"

"I want to remake it."

"That would be quite a piece of work," Karl said, his tone light, almost playful, but laced with curiosity.

"I was hoping you could help."

Karl paused at that, a look of surprise on his face for a moment before he stepped back and invited Hal inside. The room was all deep reds and dark woods, and Hal was drawn by the displays of weapons that decorated each wall, most of them ancient and ornate, but all of them still potent weapons of war. Several doors led from the room, one of them on a first floor gallery at the far end, and Karl led him to one of these on the left of the main door, opening it to reveal a room lit by flickering firelight. A number of thick armchairs were spread about the room, all of them unoccupied apart from one. There was a girl there, a girl he recognised from his visions, and she smiled briefly, holding Hal's blank gaze with no sign of discomfort before turning back to her book. He nodded once, sensing power in her, power worth respecting, then sat in one of the chairs and opened the book Karl passed to him from a shelf on the back wall, one of several dozen thick leather bound tomes that made up a significant part of the Laumpir archive.

"This mainly pertains to the uses of our black gems, but there is a section on Ildraya. I fear you may be wasting your time, the creation process is complex, and as I said before, the power required is...considerable. Even for a Lemirda."

Hal said nothing, unable to articulate his thoughts, feeling only the pressing need to achieve this, the desire to be free of the gnawing void in his spirit. He would sacrifice a great deal to achieve that, and was willing to go to any lengths.

A thought struck him as he took the book, as he realised he no longer felt any reaction to Karl's presence. He still felt the urge to kill, to rage, to unleash sorcery, but no more than usual. It was as if Karl wasn't there, and as he thought that, he felt a touch of pressure from the girl in the armchair, a barely perceptible nudge of power in his head as she glanced up and met his gaze for an instant.

He dismissed her from his mind, turning instead to the book in his hands, knowing he had to find an answer.

* * * * * * * * * *

Harpen was silent, unmoving as he lay in a ditch beside a broad flat field, taking in the scene before him with an expert gaze. The field was uncultivated, surrounded by a line of tall trees and empty except for a single aircraft that lay, partly covered by a camo net, in one corner. Beside it, a pair of police cars and an armoured van were parked, their lights still flashing, illuminating the scene.

He cursed.

His raid, like the others, had gone without a hitch, the target cleared and cleaned in less than half an hour, and they had left the site without incident. Like Mike, Harpen had led a team of Hunters to hit an upmarket apartment, this one taking up the entire top floor of a New York skyscraper, and then had got in and out with no trouble. Unlike Mike, Harpen had opted to go in on foot, unwilling to risk taking an aircraft over New York City, knowing any attempt to gain permission would have brought the attention of the Fratriae, but it seemed he had not entirely avoided that. Either that, or they were suffering an extremely ill-timed run of bad luck.

They had left the aircraft miles from the city, travelling in one of their own vehicles, but had returned to find their plane discovered and the crew being led away to the waiting van by what looked like a larger than necessary number of police officers.

Harpen cursed again. This was too much to be a coincidence, and he knew that if he let his men be taken they would not return, unable to trust in the usual back channel dealings they were capable of. The Fratriae had to be behind this, and that meant there was only one option.

He had seven Hunters with him, and he directed them with a series of gestures, watching them shift slightly, moving towards the one track that led from the field. They pulled hoods over their faces as they went, making themselves almost invisible in the gathering gloom. A moment later, he followed them, sending one final message to them all.

Keep them alive.

They couldn't reply, and he felt the familiar calm descend as he drew his weapon, although it was tinged by the knowledge that the men approaching him were not his enemy, but unwitting pawns in a game they had no knowledge of. He cursed one final time, hating the Fratriae for what they had done.

What they were making him do.

He gave the order with a thought, and the eight of them emerged from hiding, rising from the ditch that ran around the field. Hooded and armed, they were a chilling sight, and the first car slew to a halt, its doors opening. The officers inside had little time, barely on their feet before two Hunters had laid into them, smacking them against their own vehicle with savage body blows and cracking them around the head with pistol butts. Harpen led the rest forward, weapons aimed, surrounding the remaining two vehicles. One door opened, and a man climbed out slowly, his hands raised and a scowl on his face. Harpen saw fear and anger in his eyes, and reached into his mind tentatively, unsurprised to find it closed to him, protected by a crude mental barricade, confirming his suspicions.

The subtle route denied to him, Harpen simply ripped into the man's mind, lancing into his nerves and watching as his eyes rolled back in his head. He felt his heart pound suddenly, felt the rush of power course through him, and fought it down with the ease of long experience. None of the other officers seemed willing to act as their leader dropped to the floor, frothing at the mouth, and Harpen ignored them, leaving them under the watchful eyes of his men as he walked to the back of the van and tapped three times, sending a mental impulse to the men inside. A second later, the rear door crashed open, ripped partly off its hinges by a savage kick from inside, and an Obur Vampire emerged, leading two Hunters out through the dismantled cage door. Inside, Harpen saw a pair of men, unconscious and slumped against the walls.

Harpen directed the pilot to head for the plane, ordering him to get ready to go, then turned to the rest of the officers. The Hunters had bundled them from the vehicles, forcing them to lie face down beside the lead car, and had removed the weapons from each of them. Harpen sent his men running for the aircraft with a gesture, then addressed the prone men.

"You have no idea what you are tangling with. I have a great deal of patience, and I bitterly regret the chain of events that has made us enemies. I will leave you unharmed, free to live your lives, as a gesture of goodwill, but be aware."

He stopped speaking and spoke straight into their minds, feeling the dull pressure of the defences there.

If you cross us now, if you make any attempt to prevent our departure, I will burn out your minds and leave you empty.

With that, he turned and ran, desperately hoping they would do nothing that would force him to keep his word.

* * * * * * * * * *

Hal had barely moved for three days, absorbing every scrap of information he could on Ildrayas, digging through Karl's archives for even the briefest reference, and it seemed he was nearing the end of the archive's worth. Ildraya were a curiosity, a minor trinket in the eyes of Vampires, and so were mostly beneath the notice of the Families. Very few had ever been made, mostly as gifts for promising humans, and none had been developed for the Brothers of the Order. There was no reference to his Ildraya, not that he expected there to be given its recent creation, but Hal had found enough to go on.

The door opened as he rose to his feet, and Karl appeared. He had dropped in briefly each night, helping Hal to sort through the archive but otherwise keeping to his own business. He stopped when he saw Hal had left his chair, and...

nodded once before turning away, walking to join a girl whose aura shone with power. She, like Karl, was clad in segmented body armour of clearly ancient design, and the two of them exchanged a few words as they walked away over the ridge.

Hal turned back to his Brothers and led them into the cave, plunging into darkness. The walls were rough and uneven, a network of tunnels that led down into the base of the island. He led his Brothers now to the lowest levels, where the tunnels opened out onto a broad moonlit beach. Above them, a sheer cliff face loomed, *dotted with small openings, Hunters placed in each one, weapons trained on the beach. Above that, on the cliff top, lay the defences Hal had walked minutes before.*

The scene shifted, and he was in combat suddenly, pressed on all sides, fighting with a calm detachment, killing without feeling, each blow landing without rage or hate, until something seemed to strike him, an invisible force that left him shaking, leaning on the wall for support as his Brothers surged into the fray around him. A moment later, he was running, forcing his way through the tunnels, heading for the surface, the moonlight visible ahead of him, and he...

Opened his eyes.

Karl was watching him, one eyebrow raised, but otherwise unconcerned. He knew enough of the Lemirda's ways to know what had just happened.

"What is it?"

Hal blinked, a strange feeling in his throat.

"A battle. Hunters and Vampires, you, the girl, the Order."

Karl just laughed.

"I have no plan for a battle."

"I know what I saw," Hal replied evenly, his tone calm. Karl didn't seem concerned, merely nodding.

"Time will prove you right, I'm sure. I thank you for the warning."

Hal made no reply as he walked from the study, turning his head to see the girl...

Running, frantic, rage in her eyes, a pair of ornate daggers in her hands, vaulting the stone defences and making for the very edge of the cliff, where a horde of figures were locked in combat. Screaming a war cry, she...

Walked down the stairs, her arms by her sides. Hal ignored her and turned back to Karl.

"Your help has been invaluable."

Karl nodded, knowing that was the closest he would get to thanks.

"As I said, I doubt it will get you anywhere. The skill to create or even modify an Ildraya is beyond all but the most powerful Strigoi. This one was almost certainly created by the Family Head, and the energy needed to alter it would be enormous, far more than you or the Brothers possess. I am glad to have served, but I fear my help will be limited."

Hal nodded and made his goodbyes, walking from the mansion without a backward glance. Karl was an immensely powerful being, with the vision and scope to oversee this war and his allies for hundreds of years, but in this matter, Hal knew better. Battle was coming, and it would test them all. How, why, Hal didn't know or care.

Hal felt his heart rate increase again the further he got from the house, and he realised now what he had suspected since he got here, something in there had kept his impulses in check, dulling them to the point where he could stand to be around a Vampire for any length of time without ripping him apart. This alone told him that something could be done, something Karl had chosen to keep to himself, but Hal didn't care about that either.

He didn't care because he had greater things on his mind. He was close now to correcting the damage the Fratriae had done to his mind, banishing the addiction. He had the information he needed, the knowledge to remake the Ildraya. There was only one thing still standing in his way.

Karl had been correct in one particular. The task Hal had in mind, the one that would free him from this all-consuming, destructive hunger, would require a massive amount of power. Fortunately, Karl had already told him where to find it, and Hal had learned a great deal recently by leaching power from the dead.

The greatest source of sorcerous power was required, and that meant Hal would have to undertake a task no Hunter had completed, a challenge finally worthy of him.

Soon, a Family Head would die.

* * * * * * * * * *

Harpen was fuming as walked through the halls of the HQ, leaving his quarters behind. He stretched as he walked, easing out the muscles of his shoulders, running his mind over the events of the last few days. The journey back from America had been tense, expecting any moment to be shot out of the sky, but the Obur technologies had kept them hidden, bringing them safely home.

Not all the Hunters had been so lucky. Two bands, one of them of them Kym's, had joined together, boarding a civilian passenger plane for part of the journey. That plane was now wreckage floating in the South Atlantic, all of its passengers killed after an explosion had torn through the hold. Of the Hunters, only Kym had survived, his enhanced physique keeping him safe through the explosion and the crash, and Harpen had already despatched help, unwilling to trust any coast guard or navy or civilian company, instead counting on their own shipping to recover him, and an Obur cell had already made contact.

Mike was waiting for him in his quarters, Cal in his arms, and Harpen accepted the drink that was offered.

"So it didn't work," Mike began, his voice heavy.

"It got their attention at least," Harpen replied.

"Didn't we have that already?"

Harpen didn't reply at first, idly picking a handgun from Mike's armoury and holding it up to his eye.

"You know, I always thought that if it all ended, it would be in combat. One Family ascendant, hordes of Vampires sweeping down on us, some sort of glorious last stand...I never thought we could just be picked apart like this."

"We aren't done yet."

"And neither are they. We've seen nothing of them, and we've done nothing that's stopped them."

"Then we need to try something else. Or at least buy us some more time."

Harpen nodded, but only one idea occurred to him, and he recalled what he had so recently said to Kym.

He was going to have to do something he would almost certainly regret.

* * * * * * * * * *

"Can I help you sir?"

Hal twitched and glanced up, meeting the eyes of the steward for a second.

"No."

The man wavered for a moment, then turned away, clearly resolving to keep well away from the overly tense, angry figure of Hal. Hal, for his part, stared straight ahead, fixing his gaze on the back of the seat on front of him, ignoring the people around him and the strange looks they were sending his way.

He had contacted no one after leaving Karl's mansion, unwilling to make his plans known to any of his Brothers. He wasn't sure how they would react, but knew they had enough to concern themselves with. He considered Harpen for a moment, knowing he at least would condemn this course of action, but he had no choice, feeling himself lose control. The Ildraya was in his pocket, and he could feel its influence upon him, seeping into his mind.

His whole body was tense, his hands gripping the arm rests tight enough to leave indentations, and he had to blink several times to clear his vision. He had teetered on the brink of a fit for hours, only forcing it down by strength of will. Boarding the plane had made it easier once he had been sure there were no Vampires on board, but he couldn't escape fully.

Time was short.

The door in front of him was plain and unadorned, just one in a long row of ordinary looking homes on an ordinary looking estate. Inside, the illusion carried on, a coat rack and a hall table holding a handful of everyday items – keys, a phone, a pile of letters.

Hal ignored them all, pushing forward into the front room, pulling aside a hearth rug and raising the floorboards beneath. A metal rung was set into the side of the gaping hole that he had uncovered, and he lowered himself into the blackness.

His vision cleared, and he glanced to his left and right. No one paid him any heed. This was the third time this vision had assailed him, guiding him to the hunt ahead, and he had seen enough to know where to go. It was reassuring to know that his gift had not left him, despite what the Fratriae had done.

He didn't move until the flight had landed, rising to his feet at the first opportunity and shouldering his way to the front of the plane, ignoring the muttered curses and foul looks. His bag was under his shoulder, a handgun and his knife strapped inside. He was as prepared as he could be for the task ahead, but his vision had not yet gone far enough to know if this would succeed.

He walked through passport control and customs undisturbed, the enchantments on his weapons still holding despite the work of the Fratriae, and climbed into the nearest taxi, pointing curtly to a tourist map and sitting back to concentrate.

He had landed in Norway, in the airport of Alesund, and as he watched the city pass by, he cast his mind out, searching for a hint of Vampire, but there was nothing. To his knowledge, the last hunt here had been over a decade before and had cleared out a cell of Strigoi. The follow up had found nothing, and Hal could see why – the power of a Family Head was clearly enough to throw a veil over the presence of a significant number of Vampires. He wondered what else they could conceal.

The road took them into a long tunnel, and as the light dimmed Hal took the chance to stretch out his hand, allowing a spark to run over his skin, earthing some of the energy coursing through his being. The driver didn't notice, and Hal repeated the process with the other hand, feeling the pressure on the back of his skull ease a little. As the car emerged into the sunlight, he felt a little better, and began to focus his mind, strengthening his defences for the coming conflict.

The taxi drove through the city centre and on, crossing a bridge and heading on through a harbour district. A short while later, it pulled to a halt at his direction, in the middle of the residential district on the island of Heissa. As it drove away, Hal glanced around, recognising the area instantly. Just a few steps away, set back a little way from the road, a plain, unadorned door was set into the side a wood panelled house, one of a row of modern, glass fronted homes in an unassuming estate. Behind the house, a mountain rose, and he knew his target lay beneath it.

He didn't hesitate, hopping the wall without even looking around, noticing with detachment that there was still no scent of Vampire. This lair had probably been here, undetected, for centuries if not longer, and he was about to remove it forever.

He didn't waste time with the door, simply ripping the lock free with three fingers and stepping inside, casting his eyes over the convincing illusion of normal life. Only his enhanced senses would ever pick up the fact that no human had entered this room in years.

He pulled the rug aside and raised the floor boards, revealing the tunnel entrance from his vision and lowering himself inside. The hole went straight down, a rough metal ladder set into the wall taking him to a rocky floor almost a hundred metres below the house. The tunnel was almost circular, a smooth walled passage that ran, straight and unlit, in the direction of the Sukkertoppen Mountain, and the lair of the Strigoi Family Head.

Hal drew his weapons and headed into the darkness.

* * * * * * * * * *

Several dozen figures had occupied one of the larger training halls in the Hunter HQ, and Harpen took a moment to glance around, meeting the gaze of those few who were looking his way with gratitude on his face.

It was not returned, but he wasn't put out. The men were Obur Vampires, of the cell that had recovered Kym from the South Atlantic, and they had arrived suddenly, unannounced and unnoticed until the resident Oburs had opened a hanger for them. Harpen had headed straight for them as soon as he had been told. Kym had already returned to his quarters, unharmed by his ordeal and unbowed by the losses.

One Vampire detached himself from the group and headed for Harpen, bowing slightly as he did so. Harpen raised an eyebrow as he realised it was Joseph Obur, the most senior surviving member of the Oburs after the death of the Family Head, and leader of the strongest and largest cell. The men here were just a fraction of the Vampires that served him directly, and represented the very best of the Family.

Harpen wondered just what the hell had brought them here, and asked as much.

"My Lord Laumpir requested that I place my men at your disposal."

Harpen took a moment to look around before he replied, not quite understanding.

"Why?"

"His plans are nearing fruition, and he will have need of you and your men for an undertaking soon. He requires that your struggles with the Fratriae are brought to a close soon, and my men and I will help you to that end."

Harpen paused, glancing around again. This band was exceptionally powerful, with thousands of years of experience between them, but still...

"What aid can you offer against this enemy?"

"I have served alongside the Fratriae, and I know their ways. They have no weakness, no mortality, nothing that you could use to attack them, but there are possibilities, chances to hold against them. At the very least, they could buy you time until a more permanent solution could be found."

Harpen didn't hesitate.

"Tell us what to do."

Joseph bowed his head, lowering himself to the floor and directing Harpen to do likewise.

"The Fratriae care for two things. The first is their prey. Every deal they enter into is designed to gain them information on the Vampiri, and a bargain can be struck if you can offer them such."

"We can't. Only Hal could, and that seems to have ended."

Joseph lowered his head again in acknowledgement.

"Then the second. Each other."

Harpen raised an eyebrow.

"They don't strike me as the caring type," he said drily.

"They operate alone, and always have done. They hold anyone outside of their group with supreme distrust, only interacting when it is necessary to gain access to knowledge. This has made them insular to the point of xenophobic, but has created a certain pack mentality. They may not care for one another, but they would be affected if one of their number was taken away, and could no longer hunt with them."

"They cannot be killed..." Harpen said tentatively, guessing there was more to this.

"They do not have to be. Remove one from the pack, and you would have something to bargain with. Enough to buy time, perhaps enough to reach an accord."

Harpen nodded.

They had nothing to lose.

* * * * * * * * * *

Hal ducked back suddenly, pressing his back against the wall and sliding slowly around the corner he had just turned, his movements silent. Nothing happened for a moment, and he began to think he had jumped at nothing when he felt it again, a gentle pulse in his temples, a dull pressure in his head that had nothing to do with the power coursing through him.

Instinct took over, and he pressed himself closer to the wall, moulding his form against the smooth rock, noting with detachment that it was warm to the touch. There was something ahead, a sorcerous barrier or void, but he couldn't fathom its purpose, couldn't even work out where in the tunnel it lay. The darkness was total, forcing him to rely on sound and his preternatural instincts to guide him, but they wouldn't guide him through whatever lay ahead.

A moment later, he realised they wouldn't have to.

"Hello."

Hal froze, his pistol aimed straight ahead, but there was no one there. He concentrated, hearing breathing a short way away, but unable to pinpoint the location.

This made no sense. He would have sensed a Vampire, but no human could be that silent. The voice had been that of a girl, curious but unafraid, wholly out of place in the entrance tunnel to a Vampire's lair, but then no human girl should have been able to see him coming.

And no human girl should be speaking the Strigoi dialect.

"I know you're there. You may as well talk to me."

Still Hal didn't move, his knife hand inching higher, poised to strike.

"Please don't try to kill me. I'm not your enemy, and my masters would be cross."

Hal lowered the blade and finally stepped out, moving away from the rock wall and walking forward slowly, his enhanced senses suddenly picking out an alcove to one side, barely large enough to fit a single person. As he approached, he felt a shift in the air current, realising there was a room hidden beyond the cleft. He could make out little, still seeing no clear sign of the occupant beyond the sound of shallow breathing, still unwilling to lower his weapons.

"Hello," the girl said again, moving into a standing position in front of him. He blinked, uncomprehending. She was human, barely older than seventeen, wearing plain baggy grey overalls and a faint air of curiosity, but that didn't explain why he couldn't sense her, why she had been able to appear like a shadow brought to life.

Moreover, it didn't explain how she was looking straight at him through eye sockets that were completely empty.

"Who are you?" Hal asked in the Vampire language.

"You're thinking about killing me."

"Who are you?" Hal repeated, not lowering his knife.

"Please don't."

Hal paused, finally lowering his weapons but not sheathing them.

"Tell me who you are."

"Lyra."

"Who taught you this language?"

"My masters."

"The Strigoi?"

"Yes."

"Did they take your eyes?"

"Yes."

"Why?"

"So that I could see better."

Hal paused again, unsure of what to do or say. He felt the urge to kill her, but it was dampened by her sheer lack of presence, not even a hint of power emanating from her form, and he understood what she was.

"You're a thrall. A servant."

"A servant? No, not me."

"Then what?"

"An apprentice."

"To who?"

"My masters."

The truth dawned as Hal remembered where he had seen this before.

"You are to be a seer."

The girl smiled wanly.

"When I am old enough for the blood kiss."

"Is that what you want?"

"That hardly matters now."

"Why are you out here?"

"To guard them and warn them against intruders in the daytime."

"You don't seem to be doing a good job."

"Why do you say that?"

"Because I'm..." Hal trailed off, realising just how perfectly she had trapped him. In an instant, he had turned, his weapons raised again, crouched into a fighting stance in the cleft. Behind him, the girl laughed nervously.

"What are you doing?"

Hal didn't answer, casting his mind out into the tunnel, finding nothing, but still not reacting as she spoke again.

"I said intruders, not you. You're welcome here."

* * * * * * * * * *

"Are we sure about this?

Harpen laughed curtly and shook his head, glancing once at the silent, motionless figure of Joseph Obur. The Vampire was lying prone on the couch in Harpen's quarters, wrapped in a thick blanket, locked in a deep sleep. Down the hall, the rest of his cell were likewise unconscious, laid out in a training room, waiting for sunset. Harpen realised suddenly that he had no idea just how much Vampires could perceive when they slept. Joseph had simply lain down shortly before dawn, leaving Harpen and the Hunters to carry out the scheme they had devised together.

Joseph had seemed quietly confident, outlining a plan that had seemed audacious to say the least, but Harpen hadn't questioned a word, knowing he had to trust in Joseph's experience.

Now, with Joseph and the Oburs asleep, he wasn't so sure.

Kym appeared in the doorway, a grim smile on his face. Unlike Harpen and Mike, he was armed and armoured, one of the Hunters designated to act as back up if the next few hours went badly. In truth, that probably just meant he would be the first to die.

"They're here."

Harpen nodded and pulled on his jacket, removing the blade from the sleeve and placing it on the low table. Mike did the same, disarming and then picking up Cal. The two of them would be moving to a deep vault with the rest of the younger generation of the Order. In the event things didn't work out, they would escape while Kym and the others bought them some time, and attempt to rebuild the Hunters.

Harpen wasn't sure who had the worse deal.

The two men shook hands without a word, and Harpen waited a few minutes after Mike had left, glancing once more at Joseph before leaving the room.

The halls of the HQ were practically empty, every Hunter holding pre-prepared positions throughout the complex, manning hastily thrown up barricades or sealing off sections of the compound, stockpiling ammunition at choke points and locking away anything they couldn't afford to lose. Harpen passed a few of these groups, nodding in greeting as he went, seeing men and women he had known for years, had trained and overseen and led, and who might all be dead in a few hours.

He left them behind and walked on, stepping into a large room, one of the spaces used as a secondary hanger for routine deliveries or smaller aircraft. It had been selected for its position, well away from the crucial areas of the HQ, and raised to the surface by Joseph's men before dawn, allowing a single doorway to break through the surface. A rough staircase had been added, running around the walls, allowing access to the woods above.

Harpen stopped at its base, looking upwards with a neutral expression at the three figures descending the stairs. They were here by his invitation, had responded almost immediately through the channels Joseph had opened.

Smiling, walking with an easy gait and a confident air, Simeon of the Fratriae entered the Hunter HQ.

* * * * * * * * * *

Lyra had refused to explain, ignoring or deflecting his questions, simply insisting over and over that he was welcome in the Strigoi lair. He had given up, and allowed her to lead him deeper into the tunnels, passing through the barrier he had detected without concern. She had led him confidently, surefooted despite her blindness, to a point where the tunnel widened slightly but was otherwise indistinguishable from any other point.

"Now we wait," she had said quietly, sliding down the wall into a sitting position and resting her feet on the opposite side. Hal had remained standing.

"For what?"

"Sunset."

She had said nothing more, and Hal hadn't been interested in conversation once it was clear she wouldn't explain what was going on. Instead, he paced back and forth, flexing his mind and fighting down the killing urge, building up his mental defences in preparation for the conflict that would inevitably come. Every time he passed Lyra, he felt a twitch in his head, but she didn't seem to notice or react, sitting motionless with her hands in her lap.

He checked his watch periodically, noting the passing time. This was not ideal, but he had no choice until Lyra chose to reveal what was going on. He had been hoping to enter the lair during the day, to hunt unopposed, but it seemed that option had been taken away.

He paused midstep, suddenly realising that something was very wrong, and simultaneously realising what the barrier they had passed through had been designed to do. He raised his hands, trying without success to summon energy to his fingertips.

Lyra stirred suddenly, and he lowered his hands, thinking she had noticed something. She didn't react, instead rolling to her feet and turning to face the wall. Hal looked on, seeing nothing until a section of the wall suddenly shimmered and disappeared, revealing another passage. It was wider and taller than the ones he had moved through, but unlike those, this one was lit by a dull green glow that emanated from the walls. He saw Lyra properly for the first time, noting the deathly pale skin and hair cropped close to the head, seeing clearly the empty sockets that somehow still locked on him. She was smiling vacantly as she gestured for him to lead on, and he resisted the urge to draw his weapons again. The whole situation was baffling, even to his uncaring mind.

The tunnel grew lighter as they progressed, and Hal noted each passage and room they passed, committing to memory the layout of the warren as he went. He caught a glimpse inside some of the rooms as they went, seeing a curious array. Some were brightly lit modern laboratories, all stainless steel and gleaming white surfaces, decked out with bottles and instruments and chemical paraphernalia, while others were little more than caves, low roofed and dark, only the occasional growl or moan denoting any occupation. The Strigoi were sorcerers, capable of employing a range of dark magicks, and this was clearly a research facility of sorts, but Hal could feel nothing from any of these rooms through the block that had now unquestionably been imposed on him. The implications of that were concerning, particularly as that block obviously couldn't affect the Strigoi themselves.

Not that Hal had seen any yet. The rooms so far had been deserted, but he got the sense that they had been abandoned suddenly, leaving their work unattended to clear the way for his passage. He knew that was probably for the best given these strange circumstances. He had intended to simply slaughter his way through the lair, siphoning their life force from them as he went, but the mental preparations he had made to do so had dissipated, shunted aside in his head to ensure that all his focus was on reinforcing his mental defences, ensuring he could be ready for whatever might be thrown at him. He had no idea what was going on, and if this was a trap, it was elaborately convoluted to the point of nonsensical, but he still wouldn't let himself relax.

Lyra led him around him a corner, and Hal felt his body tense, his pulse suddenly elevated. A wide double door lay in front of him, a heavy metal hatch that wouldn't have looked out of place on a ship if it wasn't for the glowing rock where the lock would be. In front of it, Hal saw the first Strigoi.

He was standing casually, his hands clasped behind his back, dressed in form fitting black overalls that had been reinforced with metal plates. He had a pistol on one hip, a misshapen lump of rock that oozed power on the other, and he regarded Hal with a cool wariness, his eyes free of the hostility that might have been expected. He made no move as Hal approached, merely inclining his head in greeting, and Hal shuddered as the killing urge washed through him, repressing it savagely, determined to get to the bottom of what was going on here, unwilling to show his hand just yet.

The Vampire turned, taking the rock from his belt and passing it over the larger one in the door. There was a shrill note in the air, and the door opened inwards to reveal what was obviously the inner sanctum of the lair, and the home of the Strigoi Family Head.

Hal stepped inside as he was gestured to, looking around slowly. The room was roughly circular, twenty metres from side to side, well lit by stark white lamps that were mounted high on the walls around the edge. Beyond the lights, Hal could just make out the room above, seeing a vast deep well lined with cages and cabinets with no discernible way to reach them. On the ground level, the walls were obscured by more cabinets, and in the centre of the room a metal gantry rose above the floor, filling the space with a wide circular stage. Across this space, a number of tables were laid out, covered with a baffling range of items. In amongst them, a single figure was working, leaning over one of the tables with a magnifying lens clamped over one eye. As Hal walked up the short flight of stairs onto the podium, the man looked up, and Hal saw the power in his eyes, an ageless depth that was curiously at odds with the youthful features.

He appeared little older than his mid-twenties, a lean young man dressed in a wide collared shirt and a short waistcoat, smiling a curious half smile as he approached Hal and held out his hand. Hal made no attempt to take it, regarding the Vampire coldly. There was nothing particularly special about him, nothing to suggest this was one of the most powerful Vampires in the world, but as they stood there, the veil seemed to slip for a second, revealing the torrent of energy contained within his flesh. The smile on his face told Hal this was almost certainly deliberate.

"Hello Lemirda. I'm Tor Strigoi."

Hal didn't reply, swallowing several times and forcing down his rage for a moment, his fingers hovering over his handgun.

"I see your masters changed their minds again," the Vampire said casually, ignoring the threat implied in Hal's posture, if he noticed it at all. Hal didn't react except to move his hand away, not understanding. The Vampire leaned back on a table and continued, his tone conversational.

"The last I heard they were offering a Fortaca child."

At last, Hal understood. The pieces fell into place, a dozen separate occurrences suddenly making sense, and Hal saw the true scale of what the Fratriae had been doing since before he had even known they existed. The depth of their malice had been laid bare once again, and the enormity of it was staggering.

"Things changed," Hal said carefully, readying himself for combat. The Strigoi had got this badly wrong, and this misunderstanding would kill one of them in the next few minutes.

"Of course. But I am afraid that I do not consider your presence here enough to square the debt I am owed."

Hal made no reply, opting for a neutral gaze that disguised the rising urge in his mind, the urge to rend and kill, an urge only held in check by the outrageous scheme being revealed to him.

"I put a great deal of time and effort into the creation of that Ildraya," the Strigoi went on, gesturing towards Hal's pocket. "Your presence here suggests that it served its purpose, and in exchange, your masters promised me the blood from a Brother of the Order. They let me down, but I forgave them when they promised me a Fortaca child. Then they let me down again, and only their continued promises of something greater than a Brother of the Order has stayed my hand. And now you arrive."

Hal didn't react as the Vampire fixed him with a baleful glare.

"My generosity and my patience have been insulted by mongrel creations who think it acceptable to cheat me. You may return to your masters, and tell them that you are not acceptable. I expect payment in full, as we agreed the last time we met. If they fail, they can expect me and my men to fall upon them with fire and rage."

Hal shuddered, knowing he wouldn't last much longer.

"I'm not sure they would consider that a threat," he said through gritted teeth.

The Vampire's eyes flashed an angry red.

"You should learn your place, Lemirda. You are nothing more than a pawn in the game of greater beings. You serve the Fratriae, and they serve me. Go to them, and tell them that if I am not paid in full, I will end them."

Hal paused one last time, not quite believing what he was hearing.

"They cannot be killed."

The Strigoi fixed him with a withering glare.

"Please. They are creations. They can be unmade."

Hal had heard enough. The hunger in his head was a raging torrent, forced into a tumult by being forced to stand next to a living Vampire for this long. In his mind, a swirling vortex of power was held captive by pure force of will, and now, at last, he released it, sending it flooding into his body. His offensive powers curtailed by whatever defences protected this lair, Hal instead channelled every ounce of his mental strength into his limbs, shoring up his already formidable defences.

His handgun was drawn in the blink of an eye, shots fired quicker than a human could register. In the same moment, he drew his knife and leapt, but his opponent was so far from human, far outstripping anyone or anything Hal had faced. His weapons were barely drawn when the Strigoi had moved, impossibly quick as he ran and vaulted the gallery rail onto the stone floor below. Hal followed, hitting the floor in time for the Vampire to parry his knife with a curved blade taken from a shelf set into the wall. They duelled, Vampire and superhuman, filling the air with the sound of ringing metal, bringing every power at their disposal into play. As they fought, Hal's mind was battered by waves of power pouring from the Vampire, deflected by Hal's defences, but each time he felt himself weaken, his own formidable powers already cracking under the ancient, unstoppable force of a Family Head. He could feel himself give way, physically pushed back by the energy, and as he did so, he felt the hunger in his mind strain to be unleashed, the urge to kill this creature and feast on his life force finally overwhelming him, and at last, he did nothing to restrain it. Raw energy coursed through his limbs, filling him with a vitality beyond anything he had felt. He could feel the Ildraya pulse in his pocket, whispering into his thoughts, and he let it take over, giving himself utterly to its addictive hold.

He moved like lightening, smashing aside the Family Head's block and drawing blood, thick and bright in the dim light. He felt rather than saw the glimmer of panic, the momentary lapse in confidence of a creature that had had the playing field suddenly and unexpectedly levelled. Hal swung again, a killing blow, but the Vampire had gone, disappearing in a shower of black droplets, leaving a dark cloud and a foul odour behind.

Hal staggered suddenly, dimly aware of a blade protruding from his collar bone, but he simply shrugged, reaching behind him and grabbing the Strigoi, one of several who had entered the room with a flash and cloud of black smoke. They had come to protect their master, but Hal just laughed, lashing out savagely, catching the Vampire squarely in the chest, seeing the surprise on his face as he surged to his feet, ignoring the rending wound in his shoulder. He felt the Vampire die, felt the life force drain from him, and he harnessed it, dragging it into his mind and allowing it to fuel his rage, feeling the power run through his flesh and heal the wound he had sustained. Around him, almost a dozen Vampires were approaching, armed and armoured, some of the oldest and strongest of their kind, the bodyguard of a Family Head who had chosen to flee and leave Hal to his men.

Hal laughed aloud as they moved to attack, ducking the first blow with ease, feeling the stolen life force of the dead Vampire mingle with his own, empowering him beyond his own limits. He tried to harness as much as he could, to store it ready for later use, but allowed a measure of it to run through his limbs, revitalising him and driving him forward. The first and second died easily, too easily for Hal to even notice, their bodies hitting the floor and their life essences drained in the blink of an eye and a blur of movement. Hal registered a brief feeling of disappointment, but that was dispelled as he was sent flying, an invisible wall of force hurling him across the room to smash into the rock wall. He was on his feet in seconds, the wounds healing, but he could feel that old feeling, enhanced by the Ildraya to a screaming urge.

At last, he had found a challenge worthy of his abilities.

* * * * * * * * * *

"I would like to thank you for this opportunity to negotiate," Harpen said carefully, leaning forward in his chair. Across the table, the three Fratriae were regarding him coldly, and he looked Simeon in the eye, matching his steely gaze with little effort.

"This is not a negotiation. You have nothing to offer us."

Harpen smiled slightly, although the pronouncement puzzled him. He had risked a great deal to bring this meeting about, hoping something could be gained from it, and already it seemed he had wasted the effort.

"With respect, why would you be here if that were true?"

Simeon smiled a chilling smile that didn't seem to reach his eyes.

"We could wipe you all out if we chose. Your continued existence is only allowed, only tolerated, because we have not yet decided to do so."

Harpen leaned back, his confidence growing by the minute. This was bluster, nothing more, and he decided to call their bluff. If they wanted him dead, he could do nothing about it now.

"Then what would you like to discuss?"

"This is not a discussion. We are here to dictate terms."

"Then by all means, dictate," Harpen shrugged.

"We will tolerate your survival as a body, in exchange for certain provisions and agreements on your part."

"And supposing I agree, what would guarantee your continued tolerance?"

"Nothing. As I stated, this is not a negotiation. You have nothing with which to bargain."

Harpen nodded, seeing again the false bravado behind Simeon's confidence.

"What provisions do you demand?"

"You will furnish us with a selection of weapons from your armoury, a continued supply of ammunition, free use of any and all safe houses you operate, a regular supply of blood samples from a selection of operatives, detailed information on any Vampiri you are aware of and a continued promise of the same, and a body from each of the bloodlines of the Brothers of the Order."

Harpen said nothing for a long time, considering the offer carefully.

"Providing I agree, we will be allowed to live and continue to operate under our own direction."

"We have no interest in your organisation, provided you do not oppose us again."

"May I be permitted to consult with my men?"

To his surprise, Simeon just shrugged, and he rose to his feet, expecting the Fratriae to reach out for him as he walked for the door. Instead, they simply watched him, disinterested, knowing they held all the cards here.

And yet...

He closed the door behind him and headed for a console in the wall, waving his hand over it and calling up an image of Mike, safely sequestered elsewhere in the base. The relief was clear on his face as he saw Harpen appear.

"So you're not dead."

Harpen shook his head, speaking quietly.

"No, and I think there's something going on here."

In a few words, he relayed the nature of the demands, watching as Mike raised an eyebrow.

"Well most of that is crap. They don't need weapons, or safe houses, or blood."

"That's what I thought. And it's nothing they couldn't take without killing us all."

"Maybe they're being nice. Or can't be bothered."

"Maybe," Harpen mused. "This is clearly about the Order. But there's something they're not telling us."

"Does it change things?"

Harpen smiled.

"I guess not."

"Well then."

Harpen cut the link with a wave, composing himself before walking back into the room. The Fratriae had not moved, and he ignored them as he took his seat, only making eye contact once he was settled again.

"We accept."

Simeon inclined his head, before rising to his feet.

"Then let us go now."

Harpen nodded, but remained seated.

"I can have my men arrange delivery of weapons now, and a vehicle if you wish. We also have blood samples immediately available. However, access to the Order Tombs cannot be achieved without an Obur to unseal the vault. We'll have to wait until sunset."

There it was. Just for an instant, there was a barely perceptible tic in Simeon's face, a glimmer of disapproval that told Harpen what he needed to know, what the Fratriae were really after. The other demands were just a distraction, a front to cover up what they really wanted, what they were clearly willing to wait for.

Harpen smiled to himself, and settled in to wait.

* * * * * * * * * *

A single kick smashed open the metal doors, sending one of them spinning to the floor as Hal emerged from the central lab, wild eyed and raging, his chest heaving and his shoulders hunched. Blood was running down his arm, dripping from the point of his knife, but most of it belonged to the bodies that lay behind him. The Strigoi were dead, dismembered and drained and left to rot, and their life force was now contained - barely - within Hal's mind, mixing with the newly resurgent addiction to killing that had plagued him for so long, now unfettered and driving him to ever greater depths of destruction.

He was sated a little by the fight he had just left, the hardest fight and the greatest challenge he could remember facing, but already it was wearing off with the Ildraya pulling on him. The energy of the dead pulsed beneath his skin, and he convulsed, dropping to his knees as a burst of force washed out from him, cracking the rock walls. He had little time remaining, and less control, the last of it fading away as a Vampire appeared in front of him, an ordinary Strigoi, looking for his master or the bodyguard. He barely had time to notice Hal before he was dead, his heart carved out by a downward stab, and then Hal was running, casting out with his mind, seeking the last beacon of power in the lair and hunting it down.

He pounded through the tunnels, hardly registering the few Strigoi that rose up to stop him, his soul empty and his urge to kill taking over with a vengeance, the satisfaction of the last fight already stolen by the Ildraya. He had his sights set on one target, and he smiled as he hurtled round a corner, seeing his quarry further down the tunnel.

Lyra was with him, but Hal ignored her, seeing the Family Head turn to face him, raising his hands. Hal saw into his eyes, seeing through the rage and fear there, and beyond that, the power that he had come all this way to claim, the power he had suffered and killed for.

The Strigoi shifted, extending his fingers with a cry, casting a jet of darkness from the palm of his hand. Hal deflected it with a flick of his head, but the edge of it caught him, blackening and blistering his arm from the shoulder down. His knife dropped from his now useless hand, but that was all the Strigoi had time for before Hal's good hand was clamped around his throat. The two of them faced each other for what felt like an age, their eyes fixed on each other, their minds locked together. The Strigoi was frighteningly strong, but Hal was coursing with power, stronger than he had ever been, fuelled by the dead and his own desire to kill, but more than that, deeper in his head, the desire to be free of that urge. He had lived with this for too long, had nearly been driven mad and taken from his Brothers, devolved by the Fratriae and left as a damaged shell. A moment of humanity broke through his resolve, the hatred of what they had fashioned him into, and he screamed as his fingers clamped shut, crushing the Vampire's neck. The body slumped to the floor, still alive and grasping, but the fight had left him, and he couldn't prevent Hal lashing out, driving a boot into his head and chest over and over again. The bones gave way eventually, snapping under the hammering force, his ribs grinding together, his skull caving in, and Hal dropped to his knees, breathing in deeply. He held his good hand over the dying Vampire, feeling the energy inside him, seeing the dying light in his eyes.

Hal paused for a moment, savouring the anticipation. He had been working toward this moment for so long, was at last about to be free, and his mouth twisted into a grim smile as he struck for the last time, punching his fingers into the Vampire's chest and piercing his heart. He felt the beat against his fingertips, felt it grow erratic at his touch, and he flexed once, ripping through the muscle and drenching his arm with thick, warm blood. The power he had drained so far from the dead was swirling in his head, a whirlwind of pure thought, but it was nothing compared with what he was now taking from the Family Head, an intoxicating cocktail of dark energy that would have overwhelmed him in seconds if he hadn't prepared for this moment, if his defences hadn't already been shored up by the dead. Instead of drawing it in, he channelled the energy, harnessing it beneath his flesh but keeping it from his mind. There was one more thing he needed to do, one more step to freeing his mind forever, a step he could at last take.

He surged to his feet, hearing footsteps receding through the tunnels as Lyra fled, but he had no urge to hunt her down. She was nothing in his mind, so far beneath his notice now that she barely registered.

He stumbled back through the tunnels, shuddering, gagging with the effort of controlling himself, random bursts of flame rippling over his body, scorching his flesh and searing his clothing to the wounds. With no target to occupy his mind, it began to unravel, and the remaining rational part of his mind recognised how little time he had left. With dimming eyes, he scoured the tunnels, wincing as he registered real pain for the first time in his life. His right arm was dead and blistered, the skin across his body riddled with wounds, some raw and bleeding from the fight, others blackened by flame.

The main lab lay before him at last, blood running over the cluster of devices gathered on the gantry, and he made his way through the room, dismissing each machine in turn until he found what he was looking for, tucked away in a side tunnel. There wasn't much to it, most of the device being made up of a thick column of rock seemingly grown down from the ceiling, meeting an identical column growing up from the floor, thick at the base and tapering toward the centre. A narrow opening separated the two, laid with a light stone surface that was warm to the touch. A series of stones were set in the surface, humming with a dull power, connected by channels of liquid that flowed between them, changing course without any visible reason. In the centre was a shallow depression, and it was here Hal placed the Ildraya, shaking as he released it from his grasp and placed his hands flat on the stone column, one each below and above. He shut his eyes, casting his mind back, dragging up every detail he had gathered from Karl's archive and focussing all his efforts on making this work. At last, he could release the energy pent up in his mind, sending it channelling into the device, running over the surface of the rock into the liquid now pooling around the Ildraya. The life force of over a dozen Vampires and a Family Head poured into the stones adorning the gap in the column, directed by Hal's own power, running through the liquid and causing it to bubble and glow. His brow furrowed as he went to work, burrowing with his mind into the Ildraya, unpicking its design and remaking it, forging the stone again with a new and potent fuel, placing his own sorcery into the stone and guiding the creation of a fresh Ildraya.

His flesh began to burn where he was touching the column, blood leaking from his eyes as the effort overtook him, but he gritted his teeth against the pain, determined to complete his task. With a last effort, he cast out the last of the negative power from the Ildraya, sealing it again with his own crafted spell inside, locking the energy within the surface of the stone and at last breaking free from the device, his skin smoking. As he slumped to the floor, he plucked the Ildraya from its resting place, clutching it to himself with a sigh. For so long he had felt rage and hunger and addiction, been overwhelmed by it, driven to ever increasing heights of excess, but now, as he slipped into unconsciousness, his face was blank and his mind likewise.

At last, at long last, Hal Lemirda felt nothing at all.

* * * * * * * * *

Harpen's eyes flickered as the door opened and an Obur stepped inside, nodding respectfully to the Hunter and ignoring the Fratriae. Simeon rose to his feet without a word, gesturing to his companions to remain seated and walking for the door, forcing Harpen to catch up.

Harpen had only left the room once all day, spending the rest of the time sitting motionless, watching the Fratriae through hooded eyes. They hadn't moved once, apparently uncaring of the wait after their first reaction, although Simeon's reaction now told Harpen everything he needed to know, his agitation betrayed by his eagerness.

They moved at pace through a series of passages, descending into the bowels of the base, and Harpen could see the occasional flash in Simeon's eyes as they went, a smile briefly appearing as they stopped outside a wide set of double doors, emblazoned with a series of runes.

The Obur paused for a moment, casting a questioning glance toward Harpen, who simply nodded. The Obur went to work without ceremony, manipulating the runes with a few deft movements of his hands, standing back as the doors opened inward, revealing a wide circular room on the other side, a second door set into the far wall, identical to the first.

Harpen led Simeon into the room, feeling his heart begin to race. This was the most crucial moment of this entire scheme, one of the most dangerous moments of his career, and he knew there were so many ways this could go wrong. As the doors closed behind him, sealing him and Simeon in the room, he breathed out slowly, then met Simeon's gaze.

"It will just be a moment. The vault is kept as secure as possible. Not even the Oburs are allowed down there."

Simeon's expression didn't change, but his eyes darkened for a moment. Harpen leaned back against the wall beside the door and went on, his tone conversational, hiding the tension in his body.

"It is quite an ability you possess, to be immune to sorcery. A great advantage in a war between sorcerous beings."

Simeon finally reacted, his mouth twisting into a contemptuous sneer.

"You have wasted enough of my time. Unseal this..."

"Of course," Harpen interrupted, uncaring. "Have you never considered the disadvantages?"

The sneer remained, but Harpen could sense the unease at last, see the flicker of doubt in the creature's eyes, and he smiled as he continued. This was the riskiest moment of this whole plan, and it seemed to have paid off.

"Because you can't even sense sorcery, can you?"

"We have no need to fear it."

Harpen chuckled.

"Of course not."

Simeon must have noticed something was amiss at last, and his face twisted into a mask of rage, his fists clenched, his muscles coiling to launch him forward...

Harpen didn't move except to stretch his fingertips towards the floor.

The stone under Simeon's feet was suddenly liquid, rising up and closing around his legs. Where it made contact with his skin, his immunity drained the power, and the rock reverted to its natural state, sealing tight against his legs. Immediately, Simeon lashed out furiously, smashing the stone with his fists, loosening his legs enough to start kicking out, but it was too late, layer after layer of liquid rock pouring up and over his limbs, encasing and immobilising him.

Harpen took a step forward, a smile on his face. Simeon was still fighting, but his movements were weakening, his body weighed down. The fight finally went from him as he noticed the rock that was growing out of the walls, flowing across the room and dividing it in half, leaving a narrow window between the two men, through which Harpen was now smiling coldly.

"If you could, you'd have sensed the power saturating this room. Did you really think we would just let you take our Brothers from us? Did you think we would just allow you to walk through our base unguarded? You have lived for so long without considering yourselves to have any weakness, and at last, that arrogance has brought you down."

The rock encasing Simeon shattered around him and he hurled himself forward, clawing at the wall between him and Harpen, but the floor simply rose up again, seizing him in a cocoon of liquid stone, and his face was composed suddenly.

"You have killed all your men with this action. You cannot hold me forever in this room, and you certainly cannot hold my men from tearing you all limb from limb. They will not stop until I am free and you and all your men are dead."

"Maybe," Harpen shrugged as the window closed, sealing the Fratriae in his cell. "But your world is a lot less certain now."

Harpen was still for a long time, breathing out a sigh, watching as the walls around him flowed into the floor, opening up a vast chamber, filled with Oburs. They were silent, some standing, some kneeling, all of them channelling their unique power into the walls and the floor, causing runnels of liquid rock to flow through the room, closing around the vast and growing cell at its centre. Harpen could feel the energy in the room, the heaviness in the air, and his head was beginning to pound. The power had been assailing him since before he had entered, and he shook his head, concentrating for a moment to strengthen his defences.

Joseph was standing at the centre of the Oburs, and he raised a hand in greeting as Harpen approached him.

"He is fighting us still."

Harpen glanced back at the cell, seeing nothing, but Joseph could feel much more than he could.

"Can you hold him?"

"His rage gives him strength to tear apart rock with his bare hands, but it is nothing that we cannot contain. He will not tire, but he may give up. Eventually."

Harpen nodded then left the room, making his way up through the base. There was one more thing left to be done.

Simeon's two companions were where he had left them, and they rose to their feet as he stepped inside, their eyes narrowed. They must have known something was wrong, a fact made more obvious by the armed Hunters crowded into the passage behind him, but he gave them no time or chance to act. His voice was low, his tone hard.

"We have Simeon held captive, and you have a choice. Kill me, and this room will be sealed around you and the Oburs will bury you under miles of solid rock. They will make you disappear where your brothers will never find you, and you will live out eternity, starving and alone."

He leaned forward, his eyes cold.

"Or you can leave, and tell your kind that we are willing to negotiate."

* * * * * * * * * *

The first thing Hal noticed when he regained consciousness was the void in his mind, the utter absence of any hunger to kill or unleash his powers. The second thing was the damage his body had sustained, the weakness and pain in his limbs that was wholly alien to him.

The third was the figure crouched beside him.

He turned his head and lashed out with his good arm, but the figure dodged easily, and he fell back against the wall. He felt no panic or fear, nothing but a detached calm as the figure took hold of his damaged arm and lifted it up slowly, and he raised his head to look her in the eye, only then realising that wasn't possible.

"What are you doing?"

Lyra ignored him, her empty eyes fixed on his arm.

"You are hurt."

Hal didn't reply. The logical part of his mind was casting out, analysing his predicament. The base was empty, every Strigoi lying dead in the tunnels. The newly crafted Ildraya was clasped in his left hand, its influence subtle but clear by the flat calm in his mind. The girl beside him was equally calm, and he could sense no threat in her posture or her mind.

Curious.

"I can't help you," she said quietly. "And you need help."

"Why?" Hal said, his voice low.

"Because you're hurt."

"No, why are you..."

"I'll come back with help."

He watched as she disappeared into the tunnels, unsure of what to do. He had no idea what she was doing, and truthfully didn't care. His mind was clear, analysing each aspect of his situation carefully, all trace of rage and desire finally banished. He noticed that he couldn't even be pleased at the change, which meant the Ildraya was already surpassing his expectations.

His arm was the most severe injury, every inch of flesh blackened and charred and the muscles unresponsive. Beyond that, he had a series of major wounds that he had no recollection of receiving, including a deep cut across his abdomen and a series of small punctures in his chest and shoulder that his body had barely begun to heal. He considered that for a moment, unsure if it was the severity of the injuries or the power he had expended in the course of the fight.

The point was academic, and the fact was that he had no movement in his upper body beyond a slight shift in his left arm. It wasn't enough to raise him to his feet, and he slumped back after just one effort, settling in to wait for his injuries to heal, accepting his situation calmly.

He wasn't sure how long he had waited, the passage of time marked only by the state of his injuries, and the deepest cuts had barely scabbed over when Lyra reappeared, moving silently towards him. His senses screamed out a warning suddenly, his mind reacting as a second presence revealed itself behind her, the unmistakable aura of a Vampire suddenly visible.

There was still no panic, and he didn't move as the Vampire leaned down beside him, his hands reaching out, concern on his face...

"This is nothing I can't fix," Karl Laumpir said quietly. "You just need to hold still."

Hal watched him work, seeing a light purple mist flow from his hands and seep into the wounds in his chest. They closed in seconds, then Karl turned to Hal's arm, clamping his hands down. Hal winced, unaccustomed to feeling any pain at all, but it receded almost immediately, the blackened skin sloughing off under Karl's touch, the flesh beneath forming in moments, and he flexed his fingers as life returned to them.

Hal glanced up, seeing Karl's companion lurking in the shadows, her mind a beacon of power despite her humanity, then turned his attention to Lyra, standing to one side with her shoulders hunched.

"They were in the tunnels," she said quietly.

"We followed you here. Fortunately for you," Karl said, a hard edge to his voice. Hal sat up, curling his arm to his chest, his face blank as he cocked his head.

"What is it?"

Karl stood back as Hal got to his feet, his face a mask of barely restrained fury.

"I was here to negotiate."

Hal nodded, unapologetic.

"For what?"

Karl paused, and Hal didn't miss the look he shared with the girl.

"That hardly matters now. Please tell James that I will contact him shortly. I may need his help. And yours."

With that, he turned away, although his companion remained for a moment, watching Hal with narrowed eyes. Hal looked into her eyes, seeing them...

Looking out to sea, watching the sunset with a blank look. She was armoured in scaled body armour, a pair of daggers sheathed on her hips. She seemed troubled, but unafraid.

Hal turned away from her, seeing his Brothers around him, all of them armoured and armed and yet sitting relaxed, unconcerned by what was to come.

They waited until dark before they moved, heading out to look over the half built defences. As they went, Oburs emerged from a series of shelters along the cliff top, immediately going to work, reinforcing, shoring up, and digging out a series of pits in the solid rock.

Hal walked the line, seeing men manning the defences. Many of them were Hunters, heavily armed and armoured, taking up position alongside the Obur Vampires who were spread among the line, still constructing the defences even as the enemy ships bore down on the island. Others were armed, standing motionless and staring out to sea, their faces unfathomable.

Hal walked on, finding his Brothers waiting for him at the mouth of a cave, each of them greeting him warmly, smiling in anticipation of what was to come. Mike clapped him on the shoulder, a gesture that was meant to be reassuring but was lost on Hal.

He paused suddenly, glancing upward to the cliff top, raising his blade in salute. Karl Laumpir stood there, clad in segmented body armour of clearly ancient design, his sword held loosely in his hands, and he nodded once to Hal, before turning away, walking to join the girl who stood nearby, her eyes cold.

Hal turned back to his Brothers and led them into the cave, plunging into darkness. The walls were rough and uneven, a natural cave network twisted in places by Obur artifice into a warren of tunnels that led down into the base of the island. He had walked them before, committing every inch of them to memory, and he led his Brothers now to the lowest levels, where the tunnels opened out onto a broad moonlit beach. Above them, a sheer cliff face loomed, dotted with small openings, Hunters placed in each one, weapons trained on the beach. Above that, on the cliff top, lay the defences Hal had walked minutes before.

He and the Brothers were to be the first line of defence, luring the attackers into the tunnels and holding them there. It would be tight and brutal, close quarter killing in the confines of the tunnel network.

The scene shifted, and Hal was suddenly in combat, locked in a death struggle in the darkness, his mind clear, blank, composed. He killed without feeling, each blow landing without rage or hate, until something seemed to strike him, an invisible force that left him shaking, leaning on the wall for support as his Brothers surged into the fray around him. Hal was still, stricken by some unseen malady. There was a moment of panic in his eyes, an all too human look that shouldn't, couldn't be there, then he was gone, forcing his way through the tunnels, heading for the surface, the moonlight visible ahead of him, and he...

Blinked.

"Wait."

Karl turned, his rage already subsiding, one eyebrow raised.

"There will be a battle. Soon."

Karl paused thoughtfully.

"We have had this conversation before. As I have said, I have no plans for a battle. I have no means to bring one about, and even with the setback you have caused me, I have no need to do so."

Hal said nothing, watching as the girl stepped forward and rested a hand on Karl's arm. Karl's expression didn't change, but Hal picked up the inkling of power that suggested the two of them were communicating. A moment later, Karl nodded grudgingly.

"I do not doubt your visions. I simply do not know why this would be so."

"When you call, we will be there."

Karl nodded, then shrugged.

"Very well."

He turned away and disappeared, his companion in tow, leaving Hal in the tunnel. Lyra had not moved throughout the exchange, and even now stood motionless, watching Hal with her empty gaze.

"You are better," she said, her voice soft.

Hal nodded, unsure of what to make of her, knowing she was no threat. He made no reply, merely glancing at his arm, now whole and healthy, but she shook her head.

"Not that. Your mind."

Hal held the Ildraya up, regarding it for a moment before tucking it away into his pocket.

"Was it worth it?" she asked, glancing back into the lair to where the dead were piled.

"Yes."

"Then I am glad for you."

"You could have killed me," he said, his voice blank,

"Why?"

"Vengeance."

"You have not wronged me."

"I killed your masters."

"Then they are no longer my masters."

Hal saw the earnest look in her face, the blank naiveté, a twisted mirror of his own newfound mental state. He considered the options, knowing in the past he would have simply killed her. Now, his ordered mind could weigh up the options, consider the possibilities as cold hard facts, unclouded by rage or desire, and he saw no benefit from her death. She was a puppet, a tool, a single playing piece in a much bigger game, bound to play her part just as he was.

Until now. He saw the possibilities unfold, the options laid out before them both.

"I can help you if you do one last thing for me."

She raised an eyebrow, and Hal considered the options, the possible deals. In a moment he weighed up the two sides, considered what each could offer the other, then settled on a deal that would benefit them both. Mike had always seemed so troubled by these choices, and Hal didn't – couldn't – understand why when the balance of decisions seemed so obvious.

"Tor was building something to fight the Fratriae. A weapon of some sort, a way to kill them. If you help me retrieve it, I will give you a new life."

Lyra pondered this for a moment, then nodded.

* * * * * * * * * *

Part Six – Lemirda Returned

Harpen stood with his hands clasped behind his back, his face expressionless but for a slight smile. Truth be told, he had had little time to spare a thought for Hal, receiving only the occasional curt message from him since he had left, but he shuddered now as he recalled the haunted look in Hal's eyes, the turmoil in his mind. He had left them to find a solution or die trying, and if he was returning now, it could only be in triumph.

Despite everything, Harpen's smile broadened.

The hanger was cleared, but to his surprise, there were several dozen Hunters gathered around. Word of Hal's return had spread, and while he was very much an outsider, he had garnered the respect of the organisation. While most of them were unaware of the details, it had been clear Hal had been away on some great venture, although just how great, none of them, not even Harpen, were yet aware.

Mike entered the hanger with Kym, Cal in his arms as always, and Harpen nodded in greeting.

"Any word?"

"Nothing from the Fratriae yet. Given how they travel, it's possible they haven't even reached the others."

"And Simeon?"

"No change."

"He's tough," Kym said, his voice carrying a hint of grudging respect. Simeon had been sealed without light or air for days now, and was still tearing at the living rock of his cell without respite.

"Do we have a plan?"

Harpen shrugged.

"Not really. We have a bargaining chip, that's all. We'll just have to see what comes of this."

"The moment we release him, they'll slaughter us all."

"I know. But if we don't release him, they'll slaughter us all. To be honest, I'm amazed we've got this far."

Mike grinned, but it was hollow.

"So do we know where Hal has been?"

Harpen shook his head, unwilling to share what little he knew just yet, wanting to see Hal in the flesh first.

He didn't have long to wait.

The roof began to rise, the stone peeling back as the hanger was opened, allowing a single aircraft access. It was small, capable of holding just a handful of men, and Harpen had ordered it to Hal's location the moment he had received word that the Hunter was still alive, a typically laconic statement that had given them no information.

The aircraft touched down lightly, the engines winding down as a side hatch swung open and Hal stepped down.

His face was as blank as ever, his movements controlled and precise, but Harpen could sense the difference. Gone was the darkness in his aura, gone was the air of repressed rage, replaced by the cool calm that Harpen had seen in him the first time they had met in a cliff top garden in South Africa. Whatever Hal had done, it had worked, and as Harpen stepped forward to greet him, he realised just how much of the old Hal had been taken by the Fratriae, and was now back with them.

The welcome was subdued, no cheers or applause, just a few greetings as Hal strode through the assembled Hunters, but it was clear from their reactions that Hal was making a welcome return, body and mind.

"Welcome back," Harpen nodded, seeing Hal glance around with a blank gaze before settling on him. He paused, unsure of what to say now Hal was before him.

"I trust all is well."

Hal nodded, and Harpen suspected that he wouldn't have chosen to discuss what had happened even if he had the inclination.

"It's good to have you back with us."

Hal nodded again.

"You have a Fratriae prisoner," he said evenly, a statement rather than a question. It was as if he had only been gone a few hours.

"We do," Harpen replied, knowing he would get nothing more from Hal. "We're hoping they'll be willing to negotiate reasonably."

"They won't," Hal interrupted, unconcerned.

"Have you seen it?"

"No. But I know enough of them."

"Then what do you suggest?"

Hal seemed to ignore the question, pushing through the Hunters.

"I'm going to see Simeon."

Harpen stepped back to allow Hal passed, sensing for a moment the power emanating from his form, the taste of the cursed Ildraya lingering for a moment, but different now, bonded with Hal's aura. It was gone in an instant, and Harpen hurried to catch up as Hal strode purposefully from the Hanger, leaving the subdued Hunters in his wake. Only Mike and Kym followed them, winding their way down to the cavern where Simeon's cell was placed.

The Oburs were back in their positions, feeding new rock into the cell to make up for the space Simeon had carved for himself during the daylight hours. According to Joseph, they had sealed him completely in an all enclosing cavity, but bit by bit he had created a hollow that gave him the room to attack the walls of his cell. From the outside, nothing was visibly changing, but they could hear the dim noise from within the cell, enraged screaming and the scrape of clawed hands against stone.

Hal walked up to the outside of the cell, a vast sphere of constantly shifting rock, his gaze fixed on one point for a minute or two before he turned to Harpen.

"I will deal with him."

"Hal, I..."

"I have seen this. Open the cell."

Harpen was torn, his faith in Hal warring with the obvious danger. He had no idea where Hal had been, what he had undergone, what deals he had made to return him to his natural state. The idea that he would release Simeon passed through Harpen's mind for an instant, but he dismissed it immediately. For all his faults, Hal was a Hunter through and through, unable to even consider any other life.

"Are you sure?"

"I have seen this," Hal repeated, and Harpen simply nodded, gesturing to Joseph. The Vampire made no argument, but Harpen noticed that he drew his sword as he stepped toward the cell, gesturing for a handful of his men to do the same. The rest moved back, pulling walls of rock up in front of themselves, creating a shield between them and the cell. After a moment's deliberation, Mike joined them. Kym and Harpen stood their ground.

Hal stood alone in front of the cell, waiting as Joseph approached, resting a hand on the surface for a moment. The rock crumbled at his touch, leaving an opening just big enough for a man as he stepped away.

There was a moment of silence, followed by a howl of triumph.

* * * * * * * * * *

Hal watched as Simeon launched himself from the darkness, his mind calm and detached. He looked into the face of the Fratriae for an instant, seeing the rage and hate and malice of the man that had enslaved and nearly destroyed him, but he felt nothing. Simeon was an enemy like any other, a target to be fought and bested, nothing more. Hal didn't even feel satisfaction as he attacked, pulling a blade from beneath his jacket. It was a curious design, liberated with Lyra's help from the Family Head's inner sanctum, split in two halfway up its length to form a two pronged point, with a flat gemstone set into the base of the blade. The power that had gone into its creation was nothing next to the power Tor could wield, but it was enough.

Before Simeon could even reach him, Hal had sidestepped, thrusting the blade with all the power he could put behind it.

* * * * * * * * * *

Harpen faltered in his dash forward, lowering his weapons slowly. He could barely believe his eyes, not trusting his own senses as he looked on the scene before him. It had been over in an instant, one blow from Hal sending the Fratriae to the floor, gasping and clutching at the blade protruding from his chest. Harpen saw the disbelief in Simeon's eyes, the shock and panic and fear in a creature that had never felt anything of the sort, the dull, defeated air of a man whose spirit had been suddenly and irrecoverably broken.

Harpen kept his distance as Hal leaned in close, his blank eyes regarding the dying Fratriae without any sense of triumph.

"You shouldn't have crossed me," Hal said simply, before wrenching the blade free, not even glancing down as Simeon died.

There was silence for a long time, broken only by the rumble as the Oburs began to dismantle their defences, reforming the room as it had been before. They seemed as moved by events as Hal, although Harpen noticed that Joseph was regarding Hal with something akin to respect, something he had rarely seen from an Obur. Hal seemed not to notice, unperturbed as he picked up the body and made to leave.

"What just happened?" Harpen asked quietly, still not quite comprehending, staring at the weapon in Hal's hands, the key to the problem that had nearly undone everything he had spent his life working for.

Hal paused, turning to fix him with a calm look.

"I know how to stop the Fratriae."

* * * * * * * * * *

Hal was in combat, locked in a death struggle in the darkness, his mind clear, blank, composed, each blow landing without rage or hate. Suddenly, something seemed to strike him, an invisible force that left him shaking, leaning on the wall for support as his Brothers surged into the fray around him. He was still, stricken by some unseen malady, a moment of panic in his eyes, an all too human look that shouldn't, couldn't be there. A moment later he was gone, forcing his way through the tunnels, heading for the surface, the moonlight visible ahead of him, and he...

Opened his eyes, returning to his work immediately. The contents of his armoury were laid out before him, the floor of his room covered with guns and ammunition and armour. Piece by piece, he worked through it, checking each item, placing some into the kit bag that lay beside him and rejecting the rest. His carbine was already there, along with a handful of pistols and a selection of long blades, most of them chosen by his vision.

He was unconcerned, feeling only a mild curiosity over the content of the vision. He knew, rationally, that there was nothing that should be able to affect him like that beyond a serious injury or sorcerous attack, but the vision didn't indicate any of that.

He shrugged, dismissing the detail calmly and rising to his feet. The bag was full, and he began to pull on his body armour, a full suit of reinforced plate, crafted from a tough material that was warm to the touch. He finished by hooking his visored helmet to his belt, then sat down to wait.

He knew what was coming, and knew now that it was coming soon. The frequency and intensity of the visions had increased, and whatever Karl Laumpir was planning was going to be derailed in the next few days. Hal breathed in, seeing...

The girl, a stoic look on her face as she pulled a bundle of scrolls from a shelf, placing them out of sight in a dark cleft in the stone wall. Karl appeared suddenly, a smile on his face as he saw the shelf, a smile which faded as he searched in vain.

Hal's face remained blank. He didn't care. Whatever great venture the girl had ruined was inconsequential to him, the reality of what was to come all that mattered to his cold and calculating mind.

He glanced up as the door opened, and James Harpen entered the room, his armoured jacket half open, securing a pair of bulky shoulder pads in place.

Harpen was standing in the same stone room as Karl and the girl, a long bookshelf on the wall behind him. Karl was shaking his head, a defeated look on his face.

"There is another way," he was saying, his voice firm. Behind him, the girl was impassive, her features carefully composed. "We can use the artefacts here to summon them to one place, and destroy them once and for all."

"A battle," the girl said pointedly.

Karl just nodded, and turned to face Harpen.

"Will your men support me in this?"

James Harpen...

Smiled.

"Going somewhere?" he asked, glancing over the weapons Hal had secured around his person, noting the bag full of spares beside him.

"Yes," Hal nodded. "But not with you. Not yet."

"Karl has just made contact. He's asked for our help."

"Did he say why?"

"No. But Joseph tells me he has been planning this for centuries. Some grand attack on..."

"It won't work."

Harpen raised an eyebrow.

"The girl will prevent it, in secret, and he will be forced to bring about a battle."

Harpen didn't reply for a moment, his features composed. He had no idea what Hal was talking about, knowing only a little about Karl's companion, but enough to know that this seemed unlikely at best. He dismissed the issue, unsure of what to think, and instead focussed on the latter point.

"Karl said he had no plan for a battle."

"He doesn't. Not yet."

Harpen nodded calmly, willing, at least, to accept this without question.

"Where will you be?"

Hal rose at last, pulling a long black trench coat over his body armour.

"I'm going to finish the Fratriae."

"By the sounds of it, we're going to need you with us."

Hal shook his head, his eyes glazing over as a vision came to him.

"Not yet. I'll be there when you need me. A battlefield. An island with a cliff. You, me, the Order. Karl Laumpir and the girl. The Ultor Family. A reckoning. Karl Laumpir's final greatest act."

He shook his head as he came away from the vision, his posture relaxing.

"But that is not yet. Soon, but not yet."

Harpen stepped aside to let him leave, nodding thoughtfully.

"Good luck."

Hal looked back for a second, but made no other reaction as he walked from the room.

* * * * * * * * * *

Harpen stepped from the room once Hal had gone, making for one of the briefing rooms in the base, where the available Order were waiting for him. Mike, Kym and his son Senna, and Ralph and Jason Tyler were armoured and armed, and Harpen nodded as he entered. It was not many, the remaining Brothers either elsewhere or too young to accompany them, but even so, whatever Karl was planning, he would have the support of some of the very best the Order could muster.

After his conversation with Hal, Harpen knew this was only the first step, and he was content to walk the path that had been laid out for him. He had spent his life serving and leading the Hunters, and if Joseph and Karl and Hal were to be believed, what was coming would overshadow all of that.

None of this was reflected when he spoke, his voice as relaxed as ever.

"Karl has asked for our support on a hunt. He hasn't shared any details with us, but it looks like this is going to be something big."

"Define big?"

"It could rewrite the war and dwarf everything we've ever achieved."

Mike nodded, and there was no need to say anything else.

As the Order rose and made ready for combat, James Harpen smiled.

* * * * * * * * * *

Unlike his Brothers, Hal had no appreciation of the gravity of the events he was living through. He knew better than any of them what was coming, and yet he felt nothing; no pride, no elation, nothing to indicate that anything out of the ordinary was coming. Even now, Karl Laumpir was taking steps that would change everything, that would set in motion a vast chain of events that would turn the tide of a secret war, and Hal simply didn't care. There would be a hunt, and a battle, and that was the limit of his interest. The causes and consequences he left to people who cared.

This was how it should be, he knew, how it would have been all along without the Fratriae to bring him down. The Lemirda line had always had a place, a purpose, and no interest beyond that.

He glanced to his left and right, seeing nothing among the trees. The forest where he had first met the Fratriae was silent and dark, but he knew they were out there. They couldn't ignore the challenge he had issued, left written in blood among the bodies of a Vampiri coven, nor would they have delayed in answering.

Too much was at stake.

He was calm as he became aware of something, an absence of movement that suddenly betrayed the presence of the Fratriae all around him. Hal's fingers closed around the blade strapped across his chest, the twin prongs gleaming dully in the moonlight.

His instincts screamed a warning and he rolled to his feet, but the blade remained sheathed. Instead, as the full force of the Fratriae appeared around him, he pulled something from his kitbag, a small parcel wrapped in dark cloth, and with a single flick, ripped it apart, throwing its contents into the air.

To a man, the Fratriae froze as Simeon's head hit the floor.

Hal walked forward slowly, looking each of them in the eye. The effect was immediate and total, each of them looking at him in horror, faces that had never known fear suddenly twisted in terror. With one action, Hal had broken them, smashed a millennia long lifetime of arrogant self-belief and brought them lower than anyone had thought possible.

Yet even now, he felt no triumph.

"Your immortality is ended," he said quietly, still looking around at each of them. They remained frozen, none of them knowing what to do. Their existence had been thrown into question, everything they believed about themselves damaged beyond repair by this one act.

Hal paused. He had spent little time considering his options, and the decision had been an easy one.

"You may go from here and continue your lives, such as they are. Continue in your work, hunt the Vampiri and hide yourselves away for the rest of your lives. I have no interest in killing you, no need to do so, but be aware: If you cross me, if you undertake any action beyond the wishes of my Brothers or any of our descendants, we will not even need to take action against you. We will simply provide the Vampiri with the weapons they need, then stand back and watch you destroy each other. From now on, you serve my purposes, and as long as you continue to do so, I will let you continue to do so."

There was silence for a long time, before, as one, the Fratriae skulked away into the darkness.

Hal watched them go, turning the events over in his head. He was finally free of their influence, satisfied he had ended the threat they posed. Their will was shattered, their minds broken by fear of their own new found mortality, and their existence ripped asunder.

And still Hal felt nothing.

He lingered for a while, seating himself once more, the vision of battle in his mind for a moment, before a low buzzing brought him back to his senses. Already knowing what was coming, he held his radio to his ear.

"Hello James. How was the hunt?"

The voice on the other end was low, but Hal could hear the tension and anticipation clearly.

"Challenging. Ralph is dead, and Mike took a hit. But it was a success, of sorts. Karl has sent out a summons to the Ultor Family, and they will answer it in force. I'm going to order the Hunters in to support him and the Oburs."

"A battle," Hal said drily.

Harpen chuckled.

"You were right."

* * * * * * * * * *

Part Seven – Lemirda Found

The island was small, a long narrow strip of land surrounded by broad beaches and topped by tall cliffs on every side. As he had flown in, Hal had spotted the dark opening of a cave on the south side of the island, and above that, the wide expanse of flat rock that was just beginning to be shaped by the Oburs.

He had arrived with Harpen and the others, having met with them at Karl's mansion for a final briefing. He had barely listened, already knowing his place in the battle, uninterested in anything else, and now, as he stood on the cliff top in the sunlight, as he had for three days now, his vision was flashing before his eyes, overlaid with the scene before him, although each time, his vision ended with him running, inexplicably stricken, from the tunnels.

He turned as Mike approached, passing him a whole pineapple with a grin. Harpen was behind him, dressed like the rest of the Order in just a shirt and combats, their armour removed in the daylight hours. Only Kym and Senna were armed, neither of them ever comfortable without weapons, but on the whole, the Brothers were enjoying the rare opportunity of being forced to relax. All of those old enough were there – James and Yuri, Mike, and Jason Tyler, unaffected by the loss of his father only a few days before. Only the Forjay line was missing, Joe's son still too young, remaining behind in the HQ along with the other children of Order. With them, Harpen had left a skeleton crew, mostly Bloodhounds and a few veteran Hunters who would be responsible for the Hunters in the event the coming battle went badly. The bulk of the organisation, thousands of Hunters, armed and armoured for the fight of their lives, had arrived at the island over the course of the last few days, and even now were readying themselves, scattered across the length and breadth of the defences. Only the Order felt no need to prepare.

"Funny, isn't it," Mike began conversationally. "We just survived near total destruction at the hands of the Fratriae, and yet here we are risking it all again."

That got a muted reaction from the Brothers, although Harpen was grim faced as he replied.

"If we pull this off, we wipe out the Ultors. Worth it?"

"I guess," Mike conceded with a nod.

"Although," Harpen continued, "this battle will apparently not be confined to the Ultors."

He said it casually, but they took notice. By the best reckoning, the Ultor Family numbered less than fifteen thousand Vampires across the world, and despite the fact that they were thought to be the smallest of the Families that the Hunters had devoted themselves to destroying, they still greatly outnumbered the Hunters when gathered all in one place like this. A number of Obur cells had rallied to Karl's banner, but it would still be a tough fight. If their numbers were bolstered...

"Mostly Strigoi, some Kappa," Harpen went on. "Nothing like the numbers of the Ultors, but enough to bear in mind."

"Strigoi?" Mike asked, glancing sidelong at Hal.

"They're angry. And they're scared."

"Of us?"

"Of him," Harpen nodded at Hal, who didn't even turn to face them. The news that he had killed a Family Head had been greeted with a mixture of awe and genuine concern by many of the Hunters. In all their history, the Hunters had never achieved such a thing, and it had seemed likely that the Strigoi would react, keen to redress the balance of power or simply seek revenge.

"It hardly matters now," Hal said quietly.

They followed his gaze, rising to their feet as they looked out to sea. The sun was beginning to dip, and in the distance, a trio of ships were visible. Their enhanced senses began to pick out details, and a short way away, the assembled Hunters fell silent. One by one, the Brothers turned to face Hal, still seated with his eyes riveted on the horizon, their faces asking a question they already knew the answer to.

He nodded.

* * * * * * * * * *

Each of them passed the last few hours in their own way. Kym and Senna sparred in full armour, a ringing clash of arms that ran up and down the length of the cliff top, both of them already brimming with focussed rage. James wandered among the Hunters, exchanging a few words here and there, guiding, supporting and bolstering the men and women of the Vampire

Hunters. Jason went off alone and perched on the cliff top with his rifle, training it on the ships now lying at anchor a few miles away, scanning for targets but finding none. Yuri had spent his time ritualistically preparing his kit, loading and unloading his weapons and drawing his knives with methodical and obsessive precision.

Mike, for his part, had spent some time inside the only building on the island, a fortified house at the highest point, chatting with the handful of friends Karl appeared to have brought with him, a curious band of human teenagers, but then had come down to find Hal, sitting alone on a gentle slope. He was wearing his body armour, only his helmet on the floor nearby, and his expression didn't change as Mike sat down beside him.

"You ok?"

Hal cocked his head, as if puzzled by the question.

"I can only see so much."

"Do we win?" Mike grinned.

"I don't know."

They sat in silence for some time.

"I just wanted to say," Mike began, his voice uncharacteristically serious. "I'm glad we found you."

Hal didn't reply, and Mike sighed to himself.

One by one, the Brothers gathered together, each of them energised by the anticipation. Hal watched them, feeling the energy in their auras, the adrenaline, the sheer power of their unnatural abilities, but more than that, the thrill of what was coming, a turning point that they could witness and be a part of, the end of a great many years of struggling.

One way or another.

Hal shook his head slowly. He felt nothing of that. He knew his place, and that was all that mattered.

"Brothers," Harpen began, his voice light, a smile on his face. "Do what you do. Do it well. Do us proud."

He drew his knife and rose to his feet, surveying the forces arrayed around them before glancing back at the Brothers with a grin.

"Good hunting."

Hal raised his head, seeing Karl's companion appear on the small cliff above them, clad in a suit of scale armour, a pair of daggers worn on her hips. He saw the look on her face, troubled yet unafraid, and he saw the brilliant power in her mind. She looked at him for a moment, meeting his gaze with a nod, then fixing her eyes on the sun as it slid beneath the horizon.

The Brothers waited a little longer for darkness, then rose to their feet, moving along the defences that ran across the entire length of the cliff top. Hunters were everywhere, calm, resolved, each of them nodding respectfully as the Order passed, Harpen at their head.

They reached a point in the line where the defences drew back, leaving a broad space, undefended and flat, along the edge of the cliff. It was here that Harpen halted, sending the Brothers onward to their positions. Harpen would be at the centre of the line, visible to the Hunters on each side, all at once a rallying point, a calming voice, and an immovable force.

Hal paused as the Brothers walked on, meeting Harpen's gaze evenly. He knew what Harpen thought of him, of his sudden change, and he struggled to articulate the thoughts in his head. Harpen watched him for a moment, an amused half smile on his lips.

"Something on your mind, Hal?"

Hal faltered inexplicably, his mind not just blank but empty of anything at all, until a thought came to him, a rare moment of reflection clouded by a series of memories that clashed with the visions in his mind.

"You've led us well," he said simply, his voice blank. "You've led me well."

Harpen didn't reply, his smile broadening, and Hal simply nodded and turned away.

Oburs were appearing as he walked, emerging from a series of shelters buried within the defences, going to work immediately, shaping whole sections of trench with a series of deft gestures, moulding rock with their bare hands. Others, most of them members of Joseph's own cell, were armed and armoured, ready to commit themselves to the battle, their faces unfathomable.

Hal looked back one last time, seeing the ships beginning to move, to bear down on the island with a slow inevitability, before striding up to the mouth of the cave where the Order were waiting. Each of them were smiling as they greeted him, fitting visored helmets into place, and Hal looked up, seeing Karl Laumpir standing there in segmented body armour of a clearly ancient design, his sword held in his hand. His aura was glowing with power, his eyes alight, and Hal recognised the bloodlust there from all too personal experience. With a nod, Hal raised his blade in salute, and Karl returned the gesture before turning away and walking towards the girl.

She was running, frantic, rage in her eyes, her ornate daggers in her hands, vaulting the stone defences and making for the open area on the very edge of the cliff, where a horde of figures were locked in combat...

Hal shook his head, banishing the vision, and led his Brothers into the cave.

The tunnels were twisted and interlocked, weaved by the Oburs into a complex series of connected passageways, designed to waylay any attacker but favour the Hunters who had spent time committing them to memory. Hal led them easily in the darkness, winding down to where the tunnel opened out on the beach, taking a moment to glance upward at the defences riddling the cliff face before fanning out with his Brothers, hunkering down behind pre-prepared positions near the mouth of the cave.

A single ship was visible from his position, looming over them as it approached the beach, and he raised his carbine, counting down the minutes. After a while, he sent a message to his Brothers.

Battle was joined.

The oncoming ship struck something beneath the water, the air suddenly rent by the sound of metal twisting against rock, the hull listing to one side as the rear of the ship swung round at speed, turning side on to the island. Hal lost interest in it a moment later as he saw figures appearing, some jumping over the side, more emerging from the holes torn in the ship's hull. Dozens became hundreds, pouring over the broad beach towards the cliff, firing upwards as they went.

They were met by a storm of gunfire, Hunters firing down into the ranks, crippling hundreds in the opening salvo. As Hal watched, thick wooden bolts began to rain down as well, fired by Oburs armed with oversized crossbows, launching stakes directly into the horde.

It was not enough to stop them, and as they reached the cliff, the Ultors began to climb, hauling themselves effortlessly up the sheer rock face.

Time to go, Hal sent, before raising himself from concealment and opening fire, emptying his carbine in a few short bursts. That was enough to get the attention of those closest, but that wasn't enough.

But then, it wasn't meant to be.

Hal brushed his fingers over his throat briefly, feeling the Ildraya held there by a thin metal chain. He composed himself for a moment, banishing the memories that assailed him, summoning the power locked in his form and striding boldly to meet the Vampires that were bearing down on him.

He breathed in deeply, then unleashed the fury of his mind.

The front rank was gone instantly, slammed back into their fellows by a wall of force. Hal drew his hand back over his shoulder, tearing a rent in the floor beneath the charge, sending dozens to their knees, giving them no time to recover as he swept his other hand round, ripping a solid wall of force through the stumbling figures. Unlike the Fratriae, the enemy facing him had no immunity, no defence that could withstand his unfettered mind, and dozens were torn apart by the blast, smashing a hole in the advancing line.

Hal stood his ground, feeling the power in his hands, controlling it effortlessly. He could feel no pull from it, no urge to push himself, nothing but the cold reality of his abilities, all at once given free reign but held in check by the pulse of the Ildraya, beating in time with his heart. He paused as his Brothers moved up to his side, unleashing their own abilities, sending spark and flame washing into the Vampires, burning and killing indiscriminately, but he could feel their restraint, the focus they were clinging to, unwilling to unleash their minds as he did for fear of losing control, constrained by the lure of excess.

Unbound by emotion, unrestricted by a fear of discovery, Hal had no such limits.

* * * * * * * * * *

Harpen laughed as he heard the conflagration below and felt the sheer power being unleashed. Every moment of doubt in Hal was gone, his faith in his young Brother rewarded in the most gratifying way, and even as Vampires began to appear over the lip of the cliff, even as he launched himself forward, James Harpen laughed, fearless and proud.

* * * * * * * * * *

In a matter of minutes, they had piled up corpses three and four high across the beach, but more importantly, they had the attention of their enemy. Hal paused in his assault as he felt rather than saw the first Strigoi to appear in the midst of the Ultors. Immediately he directed a blunt force in that direction, watching without expression as the creature met his gaze across the battlefield, moments before his chest was struck by the centre of the blast, his ribs splintering and driving into his own heart. Before his body had hit the floor, Hal had moved on, meeting each target as he identified it, killing and moving on, methodical, cold, unfeeling.

Even with all their power, the Order could never hope to hold this line, hordes of Vampires still pouring from the stricken ship, more arriving from further around the beach in response to the presence of the Order, and Hal knew they had served their purpose. Down here, unsupported and alone, the Order were too tempting a target, even for Ultors, and they had drawn whole waves away from the cliff top. Now they could close the jaws of their trap, and with a gesture, the Order broke suddenly, fleeing for the darkness of the cave mouth, an army at their heels.

Hal passed the first corner and turned, drawing a pair of knives. His breathing was shallow, level despite what he had gone through, and he noted that around him, his Brothers were panting, the exertion of using and controlling their powers more than they were used to.

The first Vampire hurled himself round the corner, launching himself down from the tunnel wall, and Hal moved first, sending a back hand strike into the creature's chest, the downward turned blade meeting no resistance as it punched through the Vampire's heart. Then they were committed, a handful of men holding a narrow tunnel against an unnumbered horde, tying down many times their number by the simple nature of who they were and what they represented. More and more Strigoi were appearing, drawn to Hal himself, vengeful and raging as they assaulted him with bolts and waves of solid darkness, but they were feeble attempts compared with the Family Head and Hal batted them aside, duelling three or four at once, planting himself in the centre of the tunnel to take on all comers. Behind him, his Brothers swiped at the edge of the attacking line, felling those who tried to flank Hal, occasionally firing into the mass of bodies. Only Jason stayed back, firing his rifle around Hal, each shot striking a throat or head or heart, crippling a Vampire and leaving them easy prey for his Brothers.

As Hal fought, he half expected the tide to slacken, his enemy to see sense or try a different tact, but it seemed they were hell bent on hurling themselves forward en-masse. They were no more trained for open warfare than the Hunters, but in that situation, as they had intended, the terrain favoured the defenders.

Hal saw his opportunity, a momentary gap in the forces pressing him in, and he sent a simple impulse to the Order. In an instant, they had scattered, vanishing into tunnels on all sides. The horde faltered, then surged forward, splintering as the tunnels diverged, rendering them easy prey to the Brothers who could appear at will, utilising their knowledge of the network, striking from the darkness then vanishing. Hal killed in quick succession, feeling the power around him as his Brothers did likewise, then with a thought called them back together, each of them converging perfectly to cut the head from the advancing column as they reunited. Hal directed them calmly, analysing every move of the fight, seeing the moments ahead before they came, guiding and aiding even as he fought ferociously himself. Deep in his head, he began to feel something akin to satisfaction, as much as he could feel anything anymore, and he saw clearly his place, his purpose...

A vision flashed across his head, Jason falling in a spray of blood, and he let him know, feeling no remorse or sympathy. Jason barely reacted, nodding once and dropping his rifle, drawing his knife with a cry, killing one, two, three before an Ultor swept in, pinning him in place long enough for a second to deliver the killing blow, a sweeping slice that cut through the armour over his throat and bit deep into his neck, sending his body spinning to the floor to be trampled. Hal ignored him, dispatching his own opponent before turning, dropping the two Ultors as they became the next most logical target. He could feel the tinge to his Brothers' auras, the restrained rage at the loss, but it was carefully controlled, harnessed to push them to ever greater feats of combat. Only Hal was completely unaffected, cold and silent.

He had lost track of time, lost track of the number of bodies they had left through the tunnels, the blood they had spilled. All that mattered was the fight, the next few seconds and then the seconds after that, step by step, killing, killing, killing...

Then the visions changed, and Hal Lemirda understood the only thing left that could stop him, even if only for an instant.

He staggered as if struck, although he was as yet unwounded, shaking and leaning on the wall for support. Uncomprehending but unable to help him, his Brothers surged into the fray around him, surrounding him with a ring of fire and blade, not seeing the moment of panic in his eyes, the all too human look that shouldn't be there. He was as affected by what he saw as by the fact that he could be affected at all, a flow of uncomfortable memories assailing him suddenly, along with the image of one man. Without explanation, without even understanding himself or his actions, knowing he never would, never could understand, Hal ran, forcing his way through the tunnels, heading for the surface, the moonlight visible ahead of him, his weapons held tightly in his hands...

And rage in his eyes.

* * * * * * * * * *

There were bodies everywhere, battered and torn, lying where they had fallen right across the island. Thousands were dead on both sides, but as the sun rose, it became clear that the Vampire Hunters had had the best of it, their defences and the work of the Order cutting a swathe through the Vampires. The fighting had gone on into the early hours of the morning, but there had come a point where the Hunters had been simply holding out for dawn. The Ultors had failed to take a real foothold, and as a result, they had had nowhere to run to when the sunrise came, and though they had fought to the end, they had ultimately lost everything. There had been a few that had apparently escaped somehow, but to all intents and purposes, the Ultor Family was defeated. It had been a victory worth celebrating.

For most.

Hal Lemirda's armour was removed, a series of rents scoring its surface. One particularly vicious blow had ripped open the front and cut deep into his chest, but the wound had already healed by the time Mike had laid down his weapons and gone to work on the wounded. There had been little for him to do. Most of the injuries sustained through the night had been fatal, the open and brutal nature of the fight ensuring that no quarter was given, and only a mere handful of the wounded had survived long enough for Mike to treat them. There was no clear idea of the losses yet, but it was obvious that the Hunters would take years, if not decades, to recover from this fight.

Some losses were more damaging than others. After Jason had fallen and Hal had left the tunnels, Senna Malum had been killed. Kym's rage took time to subside after the battle was done, and for a moment it had appeared he would vent his anger on Hal, whose absence from the tunnels had ultimately led to the loss. Mike had seen him coming and placed himself between the two men, a warding hand held up to stop Kym in his tracks.

"My son is dead," Kym had spat, and Mike had just looked him calmly in the eyes.

"Your son was always going to die," he had said, simply, and Kym had turned away, his rage dissipated, replaced in a moment by calm acceptance. As he walked away, Mike turned to face Hal, who hadn't moved through the exchange.

"And we've all lost something."

When Hal didn't respond, Mike turned and walked away, his face grim and his shoulders slumped, to continue his work.

Hal looked at the body in front of him blankly, his mind running through what had happened. He still couldn't explain the impulse that had sent him running from the caves, his total lack of emotion rendering him unable to grasp the reasoning. As he had emerged on the cliff top, ferocious and raging, he had been forced to fight his way through the vast horde that had begun to overrun the first line of defences. Ahead of him, he had seen the clearing where Harpen had placed himself, the heart of the Hunter line and the most brutally contested place on the island. As Hal had foreseen while fighting in the tunnels, James Harpen was standing alone, a dozen Ultors ranged around him, a carpet of bodies beneath them. He fought with passion and fury, killing the first and second to approach him with a dizzying display of martial skill, fuelled by rage and decades of experience, but then, just as Hal had foreseen, Harpen had been cut down, a single blow punching through his back, the tip of the blade emerging from his chest just beneath his throat.

There had been a roar from the Hunter lines, a scream of rage and hate, and in their midst, Hal had led the charge that had finally broken the Vampire line, but inevitably, they had been too late.

Hal breathed in slowly. There was a void in his mind, a missing piece, a realisation that he should be feeling something. The Hunters had lost their leader of decades, one of the longest lived Brothers of the Order, who had used that experience to guide and shape the Vampire Hunters to ever greater works. His loss would be felt as they began to rebuild, but there was more to it than that. He had been instrumental in Hal's training, showing him what they were capable of, protecting him, training him, and ultimately risking his life to bring Hal back to the Hunters when the Fratriae had taken him. No one, not even Mike, had done as much to make Hal who he was, but even now, he felt nothing except the vague realisation of the loss, and a tiny, alien voice in his head that told him that wasn't right.

Hal reached up to his throat suddenly, taking the Ildraya in his hand and pulling it up and over his head. He contemplated it for a moment, then threw it away with a flick, watching it land on the rough stone floor. He breathed in again, feeling his mind adjust slightly as the Ildraya's influence was removed, something akin to sadness brushing over his thoughts. He considered that feeling, but still he felt no real connection to it. He was an outsider, an impassive observer of whatever passed for grief in his head, and as he rose to his feet, his mind reasserted itself almost immediately. By the time he had picked up his Ildraya and returned it to his neck, he had already moved on, issuing a string of orders to those Hunters within earshot, strapping on his damaged armour, his mind devoid of any feeling.

He paused as he saw Karl's companion in the distance, her armour shredded and her eyes drained and weary. He was about to turn away, when…

He saw her, older, tougher, her body and mind honed and enhanced by years of experience. She was standing in the window of a ruined house, gazing out over the ruins of a city in darkness. It was a warzone, rent by fire and combat, hordes of figures clashing among the ruins. Hal saw people he recognised, Hunters and Brothers, and then he saw himself, little different to how he looked now, the same empty gaze as he fought, the same cool detachment, the same methodical precision as he cut down anyone who approached him…

Hal shook his head as the vision faded, looking over the battlefield. It seemed that the carnage and death around him was just a precursor to something greater, a skirmish before a battle, and he simply accepted it. This battle had been just one event in his life, no greater than any other, and it seemed there would be a great many more before his inevitable death.

This was the life he had been born to, the life he had chosen, and the life he had suffered and fought to hold onto. Everything he had experienced since joining the Vampire Hunters, every hunt, every kill, his struggle with the Fratriae, everything up to this battle and the loss of James Harpen, made his life very simple. The path of his life was clear to him, unaffected by any emotional entanglement. He was a Hunter, designed and created to kill without fear and without once questioning that purpose. He would fight and kill until the day he met someone or something strong enough to bring him down, and none of that gave him the slightest pause or concern.

He was already considering the future, the events of this battle a memory and Harpen's death behind him.

As Hal walked from the battlefield, his face and mind were blank and cold.

But at least, at last, he was content.

Made in the USA
Charleston, SC
14 November 2015